A PARISH MURDER

MARY GRAND

Boldwood

First published in 2024 as *Death at St Jude's*. This edition published in Great Britain in 2025 by Boldwood Books Ltd.

Copyright © Mary Grand, 2024

Cover Design: Head Design Ltd.

Cover Images: iStock

A CIP catalogue record for this book is available from the British Library.

Paperback ISBN 978-1-80426-911-4

Large Print ISBN 978-1-80426-912-1

Hardback ISBN 978-1-80426-913-8

Ebook ISBN 978-1-80426-909-1

Kindle ISBN 978-1-80426-910-7

Audio CD ISBN 978-1-80426-916-9

MP3 CD ISBN 978-1-80426-918-3

Digital audio download ISBN 978-1-80426-915-2

This book is printed on certified sustainable paper. Boldwood Books is dedicated to putting sustainability at the heart of our business. For more information please visit https://www.boldwoodbooks.com/about-us/sustainability/

Boldwood Books Ltd, 23 Bowerdean Street, London, SW6 3TN

www.boldwoodbooks.com

To my lovely mum and dad. This book is dedicated to them. I was fortunate to have such wonderful parents. They gave me the priceless gift of knowing I was always loved, and also shared with me their passion for books and reading.

PROLOGUE
LATE FRIDAY EVENING

Leaving the warm summer's evening, I enter this dark, silent place. I reach out and touch the cold, damp wall. As I climb up the ancient stone spiral steps of the bell tower, I know ghosts are watching me.

I am strangely calm; I feel no guilt: this is about you, not me. If you were different, then we could have resolved this. But you will never see any other way than your own. This is on you; you leave me no choice.

This tower is hundreds of years old, but until tonight, it's never been a place of execution. Tonight, I shall add a page to its history. Unfortunately, my name will not be mentioned; no one will know I was here. But your name will be in that book; 'On Friday, 6 May 2016, Lawrence Stone, local head teacher, died in a tragic accident.' I've made you immortal.

I am nearly at the top. Thin, cold fingers of night air touch my face. I see glimpses of the night sky, a sprinkling of stars. You love it up here, high above the world. It's the right time, the right place for you to die.

1

EARLY FRIDAY EVENING

Susan settled the dogs, left her new cottage and strolled down through the close.

She'd only moved over to the village of Bishopstone about a month before, after living in Ventnor on the other side of the Isle of Wight for nearly forty years. Susan had loved her life there, bringing up her daughter and foster children, teaching, and walking her dog with friends on the beach. However, following her divorce, Susan had decided to return to the west side of the island, and for the first time in her life had bought a home on her own. It had been daunting; friends talked about a fresh start, but to be honest, she felt a little lost.

Bishopstone wasn't completely unfamiliar. She had grown up over here on West Wight and her grandparents had actually lived in Bishopstone. Although she didn't know anyone living here now, the thatched cottages, church, school and shops were all familiar.

Leaving the close brought her into the heart of the village. To her right the road led out of the village to the nursing home and manor house, passing the hairdresser and vet. Opposite her close was the village shop. To her left, the road led to the pub and St Jude's Church.

As she crossed the road, Susan was greeted by Tracy, the owner of the

village shop, who was busy restacking fruit and veg in the wooden crates in
an area in front of the shop.

'Wonderful evening, Susan,' said Tracy.

Tracy's small black dog, Lottie, greeted Susan, wagging her tail. She was
a friendly cocker spaniel like Susan's dogs, Rocco and Libs, and they often
played together over at the local park.

Susan leant down and stroked Lottie. 'It certainly is.'

'I went up the downs this morning,' continued Tracy, 'there was a bit of
a fog up there, but it cleared even as we walked.' Glancing down at files
peeping out of the bag Susan was carrying, she added, 'Off to choir then? I
hear you've already been co-opted onto the choir committee.'

Susan laughed. 'That's right. I offered to help sort out the sheet music
and the next I knew, I was on the committee.'

'I hope you can raise a decent amount at the harvest fundraiser. That
old church hall is desperate for a facelift,' continued Tracy. 'I hear it may be
extended to the whole weekend; Ross has some friends from London
coming down, apparently?'

Susan grinned. She'd been told in confidence that this was on the cards,
but she was learning that news flew around the village on some kind of
invisible telegraph. 'It will be interesting to find out,' she replied tactfully.
'Nice to chat, but I'd better get on. Don't want to be late.'

A car with a weary young couple and sleepy toddlers drove past. They
were part of the early wave of holidaymakers coming to the island. May was
a great time for people with young children to come for a cheaper break
outside school holidays.

Susan could still feel the sun, warm on her back; the gardens were full
of colourful early bedding plants. A thrush sang from the top of a tall, waxy
green-leafed bay, while swallows swooped low, feeding off insects.

She noticed the pub was already busy as she crossed the road to St
Jude's. The road to the east eventually took you all the way to the main
town, Newport. Westwards it led past the school and the park on one side,
the vicarage and doctors' surgery on the other and, after about a mile,
meandered down to the sea.

Susan walked down the path that led to the old stone church. Inside,
she saw her neighbour, Hazel, tidying hymn books. Hazel had wispy,

pointed features, and peeped out at the world from behind a thick fringe of straight brown hair.

'Good evening, Hazel,' said Susan.

Hazel saw the files Susan was holding. 'Thank you so much for sorting all those out.'

Susan grinned. 'I'd rather be doing this than emptying boxes. Heaven knows when I'll get the house straight.'

'There's always so much to do when you move house.'

'I've unpacked the essentials, but not much else. My daughter doesn't approve.'

Hazel raised her chin and briefly made eye contact. 'I, um, met a friend of yours on Wednesday.'

'Really? Who was that?'

'An elderly lady called Alice. I'm her chiropodist.'

Susan knew that Hazel worked at the doctors' surgery but hadn't realised she went into the local nursing home.

'Fancy you meeting her. I'm so pleased she moved to the nursing home over here to be closer to her daughter. Alice and I became good friends over in Ventnor.'

Hazel leant forward, her head slightly to one side. 'She was telling me that you solved a murder case over there. Is that true?'

Susan grinned. 'I was involved in one, yes, and I have to say that without Alice, I'm not sure if I'd ever have got to the bottom of it.'

'Goodness, so it really happened?'

'It did, but I hope life here will be a lot more peaceful.'

'I'm sure it will be,' replied Hazel, adding, 'by the way, I do hope my husband hasn't been badgering you too much to go and help at the school.'

Susan smiled. 'I've agreed with Lawrence to go in one day a week. I've even completed the DBS form. But I'm happy to; it will be a good way of getting to know people.'

'That's okay then.' Hazel looked towards the choir. 'I think we'd better go and join them all.'

Susan and Hazel walked down the nave to join the rest of the huddle of about twenty choir members. A group of young children were chattering excitedly; a few teenagers stood slightly apart, staring down at their phones;

the adults talked in measured tones. There was an understated but genuine sense of family, one that comes from a group of people who mostly know each other well.

Susan took the music files over to Ross, who stood at the piano. Ross was the inspiring and gifted musical director, who had been employed by the school and St Jude's to set up this choir. He thanked Susan briskly, but then paused and smiled, his eyes mahogany-brown and gentle.

In his mid-thirties, Ross was different to any other musical director Susan had worked with. He had scruffy brown hair and a beard. Whatever the weather, he wore an old, overlarge woollen coat. Despite the appearance of a man who had been up all night, he had a charm which you warmed to. This and his engaging musicality had attracted both adults and children to the choir and it was thriving under his leadership.

The rehearsals were held in the choir pews: altos and basses on one side, the sopranos and tenors facing them.

Susan sat next to one of her fellow altos, Jessie. She was the vicar's wife, in her late twenties. She was as unlike the stereotypical vicar's wife as you could imagine. She wore skinny jeans, a tight white T-shirt, large hooped earrings, and pin-like black stiletto heels. At that moment she was busy texting on her phone while chatting in a loud voice to Fiona, the deputy head of the local school.

Fiona was in her early fifties, tall, slim, with cropped white hair, and always seemed to dress in tracksuit and trainers. This, with the running belt and whistle around her neck, made her look more ready to umpire a game than attend a choir rehearsal. Fiona was also Ross's stepmother. Hazel was sitting at the end of the pew, turned slightly away from them, and appeared to be studying her music intently.

'Right then, let's get started,' said Ross in a slightly raised voice. It was spoken with just enough of a hint of authority to make everyone stop chatting and listen. He lowered his voice. 'Firstly, thank you, Susan, for sorting all the sheet music. Everyone now has a complete set of music for the harvest fundraiser. Please keep it that way. So, let's get started with some warm-up exercises.'

In a slightly self-conscious way, they stood up, but slowly everyone relaxed and joined in.

'Good, right, let's start on the first piece in your folder,' said Ross.

As they sang, Susan was impressed. Ross had really got them working as a whole, no one voice standing out.

'Good, that's coming on nicely,' Ross said. 'Now, we'll sing the piece that opens with Hazel's solo.'

Hazel blushed and stood up self-consciously. The air suddenly stilled, everyone holding their breath, waiting.

Ross played a simple introduction for Hazel to begin. When she'd first heard that Hazel was to sing a solo, Susan had expected a gentle, understated voice, but when Hazel had started it had been incredible. There was depth, emotion and purity of tone that was utterly mesmerising. It was as if Hazel became the song. The experience of listening to her was not only something that you could hear, but one you could feel too. Again, this evening, Susan sat transfixed, lost in the moment.

When the song ended, there was a hush.

Ross smiled. 'Well done, excellent. Hazel, we'll go over that together on Monday evening. It's coming on very well.'

They practised the third piece before Ross told them that the vicar, Daniel, would like a word.

Daniel stood up. He coughed nervously. Although of similar age to his wife Jessie, he appeared more conservative in every way. Every time Susan had met him, in or out of St Jude's, he had been dressed in sober black, with a white clerical collar. At services he wore a plain cassock and white surplice and black preaching scarf; not for him anything embroidered with spiritual flames or bright crosses.

There was, however, something attractive about Daniel's sincerity, and everyone listened to him respectfully.

'Um, right, thank you.' He spoke with a slightly hesitant public-school voice, and focused his eyes just above the heads of those he was addressing. 'As you know, we have the fundraiser coming up and lots of new ideas for it. Maybe, Jessie, you could talk about it?'

Jessie smiled and jumped to her feet. Her eyes shone, her excitement and passion palpable. 'It's going to be brilliant. We can now announce that the event will be spread across the whole of the last weekend of September. Ross has persuaded friends who play in orchestras in Birmingham to come and perform on the Saturday night, alongside, of course, us. The concert that evening will be the main event. Ross knows a sound engineer who can come and record the whole event. We'll have a CD to sell, and it may be featured on a BBC Radio 3 programme. Again, that will be through Ross's contacts. It's an amazing opportunity for our choir. I have started working out the practicalities but please offer any help you can, and feel free to share this news with the village.'

Susan smiled. As so often, the village was ahead of them.

Jessie flicked back her long hair, her hooped earrings catching the sunlight coming through the stained-glass window. 'This is so important for us. For once we'll be able to raise a decent amount of cash, and it's not for patching up a damp wall or a leaking roof. Our aim is to convert St Jude's church hall into a fantastic facility for the whole community. We're so grateful for all the support Ross is giving us.'

Ross quietly stood up and nodded in Jessie's direction. 'It's an exciting project. I'm only too pleased to support you. Right, let's get back to rehearsals. Cerys and Jessie, let's start with your duet.'

Cerys was the young teacher from the primary school, in her early twenties, with sparkling blue eyes and wearing a flowered smock dress with short puff sleeves. Her long honey-blonde hair was tied up in a ponytail, adorned with a long chiffon scarf that matched the pink of her dress. When Susan had first heard her speak, she'd been surprised at how high and childlike her voice was, but it was softened by a Welsh lilt. She stood very upright, smiling broadly and confidently.

Jessie, in her heels, towered above Cerys, but gave her a friendly grin as they waited for the introduction from Ross.

The song was undemanding, but their voices blended well, and Susan was enjoying listening to them. However, suddenly Cerys's voice began to shake, and she crumpled her music and covered her face with her hands. Ross stopped playing.

'I'm so sorry,' she sobbed. 'Today is the anniversary of when I lost my mam. It's been three years.'

Jessie put her arm on Cerys's shoulder. 'Hey, come on, let's get you back to your seat.'

Ross cast a concerned look at Cerys, but moved on to the next piece.

Suddenly, the church door was flung open. Lawrence, Hazel's husband, came rushing down the aisle. He mouthed, 'Sorry,' to Ross and rushed to join Daniel, the vicar, and the other tenors, where a file lay on the chair ready for him. Lawrence was the head of the Bishopstone village school, where Fiona and Cerys also taught. He was short, with fair hair, a thin face and piercing blue eyes.

At the end of the rehearsal, Ross congratulated everyone on their hard work. With a slightly smug air, they all began to pack up.

Lawrence interrupted, in a quiet but commanding way. 'I apologise for the short notice, but I need to see all members of the choir committee for a brief meeting. I won't keep you any longer than I can help, but I do need everyone to stay. This is important, and, I'm afraid, difficult news. I suggest that once we have tidied up, we walk over to our house, where we can at least sit on comfortable seats.' Glancing around, Susan picked up a strong feeling of apprehension and concern. An invisible web of foreboding wrapped itself around her: what was about to happen?

2

As the rest of the choir members headed off, the remaining committee members helped tidy up. Once this was done, they all left the church. Hazel locked up behind them.

Fiona walked briskly in her trainers, her whistle swinging around her neck, giving the vicar, Daniel, instructions for an assembly he was due to be taking in the school the following week.

Susan walked beside Lawrence and Hazel. It soon became clear that Hazel had been away the night before and the couple were catching up.

'So, what time did you get back on the island this morning?' Lawrence asked Hazel.

'I did text you; it was about eleven. I wanted to be around for the workmen this afternoon,' replied Hazel. She turned to Susan. 'I went to see *Mary Poppins* at the Mayflower, and then stayed with a friend. It was part of my birthday treat.'

Hazel and Lawrence continued chatting. Ross and Cerys were walking close by. Susan could hear snippets of their conversation. After asking how she was, Ross began reassuring Cerys about her performance that evening.

'You're not to worry about the duet. I'll go through it again with you and Jessie tomorrow. By the way, did you find your purse yesterday?'

'Oh, yes. Sorry, I should have let you know. The receptionist found it at lunchtime and gave it to Lawrence, who returned it to me after school.'

Cerys turned back to glance at Lawrence, blushed slightly, and then beamed at him.

'That's good,' Ross replied. 'I had a brief look in the caravan, but you know what it's like in there. How was school today?'

They passed the shop, crossed the road, and entered the close where Susan and Hazel lived. This short 'unadopted' close consisted of only the two cottages, with more recently built garages, one of which belonged to Susan and the other to Hazel and Lawrence.

They were just arriving at the house when Hazel received a face-to-face WhatsApp call, and she held the phone in front of her. Susan could see the screen. She saw a man standing outside Reading station.

'Hi, Hazel, God, I'm so sorry. I've just come here to pick up my son and realised I've come away with the vicar's keys.' The man held up the bunch of keys.

'Oh, thanks for letting me know,' replied Hazel.

'I'm up here for the night, but I'll be back on the island tomorrow. Is that okay?'

'Of course. I have spares. See you tomorrow.'

The call ended. Hazel sighed, and they entered the cottage.

Hazel and Lawrence's home had a similar layout to Susan's own but was far tidier. The living room had white sofas and a pale brown carpet. On the walls were neatly framed photographs of groups of teachers and the names of their schools underneath.

Susan wandered over to a wooden cabinet that contained various awards. On the top shelf was a trophy in the shape of a book, engraved with Lawrence's name. Below were framed photographs of Hazel performing.

Hazel sidled up to Susan and smiled. 'That's me and my friend Blodwen; we were singing in an opera in Cardiff. It was exciting, we were all in medieval dress. I remember we had this idea of buying each other some kind of reproduction jewellery associated with our names – she gave me a bracelet of kind of copper hazel leaves. It was a wonderful time.'

On top of the desk and cabinet, Susan noticed a neat arrangement of birthday cards.

'Lawrence and I are both fifty-five this year,' said Hazel, and lifted her wrist towards Susan. 'Smell this, my gift from Lawrence; it's a gorgeous perfume.'

Glasses and bottles were arranged on the side table. Lawrence offered everyone a glass of port or a soft drink.

Once they were all seated, Lawrence began, 'Thank you for staying.'

He paused, clearly choosing his words carefully before he spoke. 'There is no easy way to put this, and I'm sorry I've not had time to see people individually, particularly Ross, but I need to share some rather difficult news.'

Glancing around at the looks of confusion on the faces of the choir committee members, Susan realised that no one, including Hazel, had been prewarned of this announcement.

'The reason I was late to choir was that I have just agreed an exciting new project for the school. However, there is a downside, and that is that I'm afraid the school can no longer contribute towards the funding of our musical director.' Lawrence spoke firmly, shooting a quick glance in Ross's direction. 'To be frank, it has always been a stretch for us. Since we took on Ross two years ago, our school budget has been cut and, at the same time, we have been under pressure to upgrade our IT provision, which is badly out of date. Earlier this evening, I spoke to the county IT advisor, who told me of a computer consultant who was prepared to come and work with us in the coming school year. It will be fantastic for the school but of course it will cost us, and something has to give.' He sat back, arms crossed, ready for any reaction that would come his way.

Daniel, pulling at his clerical collar, was first to respond. His stammer was more pronounced as he looked in Lawrence's direction, although still avoiding eye contact. 'I say, you, um, you can't do this. The funding of the choirmaster was always a joint venture between St Jude's and the school. We simply cannot afford to do this alone. You know that.'

'You say it's a joint venture, but the school has borne the lion's share of the financial burden and I'm afraid we can no longer afford to do it. The choir only benefits a small portion of our pupils, whereas updating our IT provision will be of huge benefit for them all.'

Fiona grabbed the whistle around her neck and tapped it irritably against her chest. Glaring at Lawrence in her most teacher-like manner, that would make any child and many adults shrink, she demanded, 'I canna understand this, Lawrence. Why the urgency? Ye've not discussed this with me.' Unlike Ross, Fiona had retained a strong Scottish accent, and that evening it seemed sharper, more pronounced than ever.

Lawrence appeared undaunted. 'You knew that we were looking at our IT provision, but I'd never envisaged we would be offered someone of this calibre to support us. I had to make the decision on the spot or we'd have lost her to another school.'

'And so how much longer are you able or willing to support Ross?' asked Jessie. Her voice was steady, but hard. There was an air of threat about it.

Lawrence appeared undaunted. 'Ross's contract provides a month's notice. We will comply with that, which would mean our last contribution will be for the month of July.'

A shocked hush descended on the group, until Cerys whispered, 'July this year?'

'Yes, July this year.'

'If we can't afford to pay you, Ross, would you have to leave the village?' asked Daniel.

Susan could see Ross's clenched fists, the fire in his eyes. 'Of course. I'll have to return to the mainland.'

'And what about the fundraiser?' asked Cerys quietly.

'I'm afraid if you want to go ahead it will have to be without me,' said Ross, adding, 'I'm afraid the Saturday evening concert will not take place. The musicians and sound engineer are coming as a favour to me. It won't happen if I'm not here.'

'This is a travesty; you can't do this,' Jessie said to Lawrence.

'Look, I'm very sorry about the fundraiser. I would suggest we have enough talent and experience to arrange something else, obviously on a smaller scale.'

'It was possible that we could have raised thousands with this weekend. Nothing we do on our own will raise anything like that. You are in effect killing off our plans for a new community centre,' said Jessie.

'The rest of the choir will be so disappointed,' said Cerys. 'It's such a special opportunity to perform with professional musicians and to be on the radio. I admit I was excited to be singing my duet with Jessie, and we have Hazel's solo – it's so sad not to make the recording as well.'

'I'm sorry, but the decision is made,' said Lawrence.

'Have ye consulted with the governors?' asked Fiona.

'I've not had time, but I know they will agree with me. I will be telling them and the PCC on Monday.'

'I am completely at a loss,' said Daniel. He shook his head, looking down at the floor in despair.

'Maybe if you handled your affairs better you wouldn't be so dependent on the school and would be able to afford to pay for Ross out of your own funds,' suggested Lawrence.

Daniel looked up. He was very pale. His hands were tightly clenched as he spoke, for the first time making eye contact with Lawrence. 'How dare you—'

The words, though few, were white-hot. Susan caught her breath.

Jessie interrupted. 'Leave Daniel alone,' she blurted out, jabbing her black-painted fingernail. 'St Jude's costs a packet to run. It's falling apart. The fundraiser was the first opportunity to do more than just pay the bills.' Her voice shook with emotion. 'You're not going to get away with this, Lawrence. I will fight you all the way.'

'You have nothing to fight me with. The decision is final,' responded Lawrence firmly.

Fiona turned to Ross. 'I canna apologise enough. I had no idea this was on the cards.'

'I'm appalled and hurt, both by the decision and the way it is being handled,' replied Ross. 'But you don't need to apologise, Fiona. You would never have made this decision, and not simply because I'm your stepson. We all know Lawrence only cares about his own career. He wants his school to become one of those beacon schools. Nothing will be allowed to stop that.'

Lawrence sat forward and glared at Ross, his blue eyes screwed up and brows furrowed. It was the first time Susan had seen him appear anything other than amiable.

'I have always put the needs of the children and the school before anything else.' He scanned the group. 'I promised to keep this meeting brief, and I would like to close now.'

'No way,' said Jessie. 'You can't just drop this bombshell and walk away. Fiona, you have to stop this.'

Fiona shook her head. 'I have to back Lawrence. He's the head teacher.'

'But you wouldn't do it, we all know that,' shouted Jessie. She turned to Lawrence. 'You are so full of yourself, always telling people how they should live, pretending to care. But when it comes down to it, you don't give a damn about anyone but yourself.'

Lawrence coughed, and spoke firmly. 'As I said, I don't want to prolong the discussion now; you all need time to assimilate what I've told you. Ross, I apologise for springing this on you, and I suggest you, Daniel and I have a meeting on Monday lunchtime. Everyone else, we can have further discussions after choir next week. Meanwhile, you can of course come and talk to me at any time about this decision, but I can assure you nothing is going to change my mind.'

Too stunned to speak, even Jessie now sat in silence.

Taking advantage of this, Lawrence continued. 'Right, I am sure we all have other places to be.' Turning to Hazel, he said, 'It all looked very tidy around the tower door. Have the workmen actually finished?'

Hazel blinked, her mind clearly elsewhere. 'Um, the workmen, yes, they told me this afternoon. It's a few weeks ahead of schedule. The steps up the bell tower are now safe. I've not had a chance to tell anyone yet. I will have to let the bell-ringers know tomorrow.'

'Brilliant,' Lawrence replied. He was grinning now, apparently oblivious to the upset in the room. 'That means I can go up the tower this evening. I was told that some long-eared bats have been sighted around here and I am dying to go and see if I can spot them.' He leapt up. 'Anyone else fancy coming up?'

No one looked his way, apart from Susan.

Catching her eye, he asked, 'Oh, you'd like to come? Do come, it's very exciting. Are you interested in bats?'

'I don't know anything about them,' she replied. 'I do love to see them in my garden in the evenings, though.'

'You're in for a treat then. You'll need a coat. It's chilly up there.'

Susan glanced around the group. Only Jessie met her eye, and she shot Susan a look as if she was betraying the choir. It was an awkward moment. She felt she'd been manoeuvred into taking sides. However, the atmosphere in the room was dark; she would be glad to get out of there.

3

Susan picked up her bag and joined Lawrence, who was already on his feet. Hazel said she would walk over to St Jude's with them as she wanted to check the workmen had cleared up properly. Lawrence turned to the others, who had remained sitting on their chairs, still all looking stunned.

'Do stay and talk if you want to. Have another drink; the bottle is on the side.'

No one looked at him, although Jessie grabbed the bottle and poured herself a drink. Daniel continued to sit very still and stare at the floor. Ross had his hands thrust in his pockets, and was glowering at the table. Next to him, Cerys had taken out her phone and was texting. Fiona drank from her water bottle. Nobody spoke.

Susan followed Hazel to the door. Hazel picked up a bunch of keys hanging on a hook and put them in her pocket, but then hesitated and said, 'Sorry, I just need a word with Daniel.'

Hazel went over to Daniel, who still appeared dazed and stunned.

'Daniel,' Hazel said, raising her voice to get his attention. 'I had a call from one of the workmen who went off to the mainland with your bunch of church keys. He'll bring them back tomorrow. Do you need one off my bunch?'

Daniel blinked and turned to her. 'Oh, um, no, thanks. I don't need to go in the church until Sunday. I know where you are if anything crops up.'

'Okay, just checking,' Hazel replied. She then went to the sideboard, opened the top drawer and took out a small packet of tissues. Before she closed the drawer, she called over to Susan, 'Come and see these old church keys. Aren't they interesting?'

Susan walked over and saw a large assorted collection of old keys, some of which were very ornate.

'Those are very fancy,' she said.

'Yes, most of them are redundant church keys. I found them in a drawer in the vestry and asked Daniel about them. He has no idea what any of them are for, but I asked one of the older parishioners. She recognised this one. Apparently, the flower ladies used to use the side door. I love the intricate Celtic cross some of them have on the top. I don't suppose this one's been used for years, but I couldn't just throw it away.' She touched it lovingly.

Cerys joined them. 'I would love to show some of these old keys to the children.'

'I'll give them a clean and then you are welcome to borrow them. It was a good idea having keys this huge, wasn't it? Much harder to lose.' Hazel put them away.

'By the way, will you be in later?' asked Cerys. 'I could return those books about the history of the village.'

'I've a work Zoom meeting about half nine—'

'I'll come before that.'

'Okay, then yes, I'll be here.' Hazel turned to the others. 'If you leave before I get back, just pull the front door behind you.'

Lawrence was still getting his things together. Susan watched him put on a strappy chest harness over his jumper. At the front of this was a pouch. From this he took out an expensive-looking pair of binoculars, the cords of which were securely attached to clips in the pouch.

'These have to remain attached at all times,' he said, laughing. 'Hazel took out a second mortgage to buy me thermal imaging binoculars. Wait till you get to look through them.'

'You've got your pen and journal?' Hazel asked him.

He smiled and patted the rucksack he was tucking a thermos into.

'You must show it to Susan once you are up the bell tower. That journal is amazing, a full record of your sightings.'

Lawrence grinned. 'Right, it's time we were off.'

They left the house, but Susan said she needed to check on Rocco and Libs as well as to find a coat so would catch them up. Hazel then remembered a message she needed to give to Cerys, and Lawrence waited impatiently for them.

As Susan entered her house, both Rocco and Libs ran to greet her. She let them out into the garden for a quick run and then settled them down.

She set off, then saw that Hazel was also coming back out, and they walked down through the close together.

'I'm sorry, that was a bit heavy for your first meeting,' said Lawrence. 'Things will settle down.'

'It was a shock for us all, particularly Ross. People were bound to be upset,' said Hazel.

'Ross will get a new job easily enough. He's massively overqualified for this work,' said Lawrence.

'Well, I'll miss him,' said Hazel. 'He's been so encouraging and taught me a lot.'

'We'll find you a new teacher.'

'Of course. Cerys was terribly upset, though. Those two are together now.'

'She can do better than him.'

'I'm not sure she would agree with that. I wonder how Fiona feels. After all, Ross is her stepson, even if they are not that close.' She turned to Susan to explain. 'Fiona was only with Ross's father a few years and, even then, Ross was off at university, but she invited him here when she knew he was looking for work.'

'Fiona knows this is the right decision. She will always put the school first,' said Lawrence.

'Well, you've a fair way to go in persuading Jessie, she is absolutely gutted. Also, Cerys was right, a lot of the choir are going to be very upset. This isn't over, Lawrence.'

He shrugged. 'It'll be okay.'

They were close to St Jude's now, but before they went in Lawrence received a notification on his phone. He glanced at the message and frowned. 'I'm so sorry, Susan. I just need to go over to the school and check something. I won't be long.'

He ran across the road, and over to the school.

Hazel shrugged apologetically to Susan. 'He never stops, never takes a holiday. He's promised me that he will retire at sixty and we can use all our hard-earned savings to travel to all the places we've missed out on.'

'That'll be so exciting. His job must be so stressful. This decision about Ross can't have been easy. Do you think Lawrence is right and it'll all blow over? He seems certain it will.'

'Lawrence is very certain about everything.'

Susan saw the lines of consternation on Hazel's face. 'Is something worrying you?'

'Well, he has all this confidence and self-belief, which is great and probably why he achieves so much. However, he underestimates how strongly people feel, assumes because they go along with what he says, they agree and back him. He can miss the resentment and frustration that people feel.'

'Do you think he's made a mistake with this decision?'

'I suppose he knows what is best for the school. I just worry that Lawrence doesn't appreciate how strongly people feel about it.' Hazel suddenly gave an indulgent smile. 'Never mind, I'm sure I am overthinking this. Lawrence will win them round, he always does. Let's go on into the church.'

Before they were through the door, Susan caught a glimpse of Fiona striding towards the school. 'Is Fiona going back to work?' she asked.

'She practically lives in the school,' was Hazel's brisk reply.

Hazel switched on the lights and walked quickly down the nave to a small wooden door Susan had never noticed before.

'This is the bell tower. It leads to the roof.' Hazel looked around. 'I would never go up to the top of the tower, but I love the building.'

'Do you enjoy being a church warden?'

Hazel blushed. 'I am only church warden by default. No one else wanted to do it when the last person retired. I'm on my own, and I fill in for all kinds of people, doing flowers, even cleaning sometimes as well as all my other duties.'

'You don't mind? That's a big commitment.'

'Lawrence is always so busy; and it's nice to feel you're doing something useful. With the surgery where I'm based so close by, it's very handy. I like St Jude's to be open for prayer every morning or for Ross to practise, although, of course, he won't be doing that much longer.' Hazel picked up a small screwdriver from the bottom step. 'They always leave something. Still, it's pretty tidy.'

'You have an exceptional voice. I'm guessing that as you sang in opera you went to music college?' asked Susan.

'No, I wanted to have a steady career, so I went to Cardiff to study chiropody and worked there. I joined a choir, met Blodwen who you saw in the photo, and she talked me into auditioning for the opera there.'

'How wonderful.'

'It was the best time of my life. Blodwen was a schoolteacher and working with Lawrence. In fact, they were dating when I first met her. When they split, Lawrence asked me out; it was a real whirlwind romance. We started going out in the January, married in February. In May, Lawrence was approached by a Bristol school who were in urgent need of a new head teacher. This was a massive opportunity for him, and we both agreed he had to go for it. He asked for permission to leave his Cardiff teaching post mid-term and fortunately it was given. The head of chiropody at my practice was also great and allowed me to simply work two weeks' notice. Suddenly we were off. It was all so quick.'

'What happened to your singing?'

'Oh, that fell by the board, I'm afraid. I joined choirs but I was never able to get into anything like the opera in Cardiff.'

'So, did you come to the island from Bristol?'

'Yes, after twenty years there Lawrence was ready for a change.' Hazel smiled. 'I'm so pleased we came here. It's a beautiful island and, of course, we've had the choir with Ross.'

Susan was pleased to see Hazel start to relax and chat.

At that moment, the front door burst open, and Lawrence came rushing in. He was very red-faced, and he stumbled over a flagstone on the way down the aisle. He was blinking fast; that confidence, for a moment, seemed to have faded.

'What's happened?' asked Hazel.

'It's nothing. Fiona and I will sort it out.' He frowned. Susan was unable to tell if it was with stress or anger.

'Is this about Ross?' Hazel asked, touching his arm.

He shook his head. 'No. Fiona knows I'm right about that. It's a few other things.' He glanced over at the wooden door. 'So, is everything okay for us to go up?'

'Yes, it's fine.'

Suddenly it was as if he had changed the mask, and he was all smiles. 'Great, I can't deny Susan the opportunity of a lifetime, can I?' he laughed, and the sound bounced off the stone walls.

'Be careful, Susan,' warned Hazel. 'I've never had the nerve to go up there.'

'I keep telling you, you don't know what you're missing.'

Hazel flashed him a smile and handed over her bunch of keys. 'Remember to lock the front door before you go up the tower, you don't want all sorts wandering in here and, most importantly, lock up when you leave.'

'Will do.'

'And make sure you put the keys in the rucksack... they are the only keys we have at the moment.'

'Of course. Now, I need to get up the bell tower... I'll see you later.'

Hazel left and Lawrence locked the door behind her, putting the bunch of keys into the small rucksack, laughing.

'You're my witness, I've put them in here. Hazel has bought me this. There's zippy bits inside and it's very handy.'

With the front door closed, the church was suddenly deathly quiet and cut off from the outside world. Susan followed Lawrence to the entrance to the tower.

'Come on then,' said Lawrence, his voice echoing. 'Let's go up.'

Susan stared up into the darkness, unable to see the light at the top. She could smell the damp, musty stone. Lawrence walked in front of her with his torch on, but she felt a fearful deep clench in her stomach as she began to climb the steps.

4

Climbing up the spiral steps was unnerving. There was no handrail and so Susan had to steady herself, touching the cold, wet walls, all the time trying to stay on the wider part of the steps. They passed a dark room where the bell-ringers would meet but carried on.

It was a huge relief when she finally saw the moonlight. She felt like she was leaving a spaceship and stepping out onto the surface of the moon. The darkening night sky surrounded them: she felt she could reach and touch the stars.

'Amazing, isn't it?' whispered Lawrence. His face was glowing with excitement, with dimples in his cheeks. When a wide smile reached his eyes, he looked like a young boy. 'I've so missed coming up here over the past months. It's my favourite place on earth.' He laughed nervously. 'You wouldn't believe it, but I'm terrible with heights. I stay away from the edges, always sit in the centre, with my torch.'

He took a small blanket out of his rucksack.

'Sit on this, it soon gets cold otherwise.'

Susan sat next to him, and she noticed the racing of her heart slow down. She heard someone call to a friend, a car drive past. The slightest sounds seemed to travel up from the pavement and street below.

'You okay?' asked Lawrence.

'I'm feeling a bit less stressed now.'

'Good. It's worth remembering that no one has fallen from here, even though the bell tower has been here for hundreds of years. I'm going to switch off the torch now, let our eyes adjust to the light.'

They sat immersed in the semi-darkness. Susan was always amazed at the way it was so easy to ignore the sky during the day, and yet at night, in places where there was little artificial light, it dominated.

'I feel very small and insignificant up here, but it's wonderful,' she whispered.

'It pays to try and overcome your fears, doesn't it? I try to find time every weekend to get out into nature and at this time of year I am always on the lookout for bats.'

'Where have you been while the bell tower has been closed?'

'Sometimes the woods, sometimes on the downs. Last Friday I was over at Castleford. There's a pub garden there with a huge pond and you can see Daubenton's bats zooming low over the water, catching insects with their feet. It's incredible.'

'Have you always loved bats then?'

'Yes. Coming to the island has been amazing. There are fourteen of the sixteen British species of bats here. That's extraordinary.'

'I hadn't realised. To be honest, although I can understand the fascination, I'm also a bit scared of bats.'

'So many people are,' said Lawrence. 'There are myths, for example that they go for your hair, which is rubbish. I read somewhere that it comes from the time when they believed you would be sent to eternal damnation if a bat got caught in your hair.'

'But there is something ghostly about them.'

'That's what I love. Did you know they are the only truly flying mammal in the world and that on their wings there is a thin layer of skin between the four long fingers, not that different to your hand?' He paused and laughed. 'I could go on. Ross is like it with owls. He goes on and on about the different calls.'

'Isn't it just too-wit too-woo?'

'Don't say that to him, he'll have a fit,' Lawrence laughed.

'So, tell me more about these long-eared bats?'

'They're quite rare but beautiful. Their ears are nearly as long as their bodies – hence the name.'

As her eyes became accustomed to the light, Susan could make out the wall at the perimeter of the tower. The highest parts of the tooth-like crenellations were at about shoulder height, the lower parts just below her waist.

Lawrence pushed back his shoulders, raised his head, relishing the space. 'The air up here's so good.' He pointed to the walls. 'On the other side, apparently, there is the most amazing lichen growing, a witness to how good the quality of the air is.'

He took a device out of his rucksack, a kind of small black radio.

'This is my digital bat recorder. A lot of the sounds bats make are ultra-sonic, so we can't hear them. This device transforms those noises into a range audible to the human ear, and allows us to identify which species of bats are around.'

'That's very clever.'

Lawrence sat up, the needle on the recorder was moving. 'Hang on, listen – they are on their way.'

They sat waiting patiently. Suddenly Susan was able to hear a rapid clicking sound and she looked up. She couldn't see much, just the move-ment of small black shapes, but she felt totally surrounded by them.

Lawrence opened the pouch holding the binoculars and was able to use them while they were still attached to the cords. 'That's wonderful. There must be seven or eight up there. You must look. Hang on, I'll unclip the cords from the pouch on the harness. It's got clever clasps, very secure and well designed.'

He handed her the binoculars, and she looked up. The bodies of the bats shone white, and she could make out the limbs, even the eyes.

'Wow!' she gasped. 'This is incredible. I can't believe it; I can make out their faces. How on earth do the binoculars work?'

'I don't understand all the technology, but they use a kind of infrared sensor to detect the heat given off by an object. They work even in total darkness.'

'Oh, of course. I've seen that technique used on *Springwatch*. I love it when they show you hares and deer in the fields. Being here, though, wow, it's fantastic.'

She looked down and saw Lawrence had taken out a notebook and a different torch.

He switched it on, and she saw it had a red beam. Lawrence explained that he always used a red beam at night because people's eyes adjust far more quickly to the red than white light and wildlife is less likely to see or be disturbed by it.

'That's a brilliant idea.'

'It is. Now, I need to record my sightings.' He opened his rucksack, took out a silver pen and clicked it on. Susan watched him run his fingers gently along the barrel of the pen, which had a small heart engraved on it. As if suddenly catching her eye, he said, 'It was a gift, um, from a school where I worked. Anyway, look at this, my pride and joy – my journal. I've been keeping it for the past two years.'

The journal was a large spiral-bound book with a waterproof cover. Lawrence opened it, proudly turning the pages. Each page was a neat recording of the date, location and time of a sighting, but there were also line drawings and photographs.

'It's a work of art,' said Susan.

He smiled. 'It's nothing compared to some I've seen. I have friends who record the phase of the moon, cloud cover, type of cloud, time of sunset, the list goes on. I do basic illustrations occasionally, but some people are real experts at watercolour.'

'I love it,' said Susan. 'Have you shown it to the children at school?'

'I have, some of the older children keep them now.'

He turned to a clean page and started to write, and she noticed he held his pen with that slightly awkward way left-handed people can. The red beam picked out the pen, his wedding ring but also a black leather bracelet with a plaque inset bearing the engraving of a complex design.

Susan leaned back, looked up at the sky. 'It's like another world, isn't it, working in darkness.'

'That's it exactly. The darkness is what frightens some people but for me, it makes it so much more intriguing and exciting.' He continued writing. 'I'll send the results in to the bat-watching society. It's important we keep track.'

The bats started to drift away, and the silence enveloped them again. Susan handed the binoculars to Lawrence, and he clipped them back into the pouch on the binocular harness.

He closed his journal, clicked off the pen and put them away. As he did so, he brought out a thermos. 'Coffee?'

'No, thanks.'

'So, how are you finding things here in the village?' asked Lawrence, sipping his coffee.

'I'm settling in well, thanks. You've been here three years now, haven't you? How are you finding the island?'

'It took me a while to really believe I couldn't just drive off the island. I know it's stupid, but it's hard to get used to the idea of always getting on a ferry to leave. It also took me a while to realise how close so many of the people who live here are. Many of the parents went to the school and are related to each other by family or marriage. And my life is under a microscope. For example, I popped in the shop for paracetamol at lunchtime the other day, and, at the end of the school day, I had three parents ask how I was as they'd heard I was unwell!'

A cold breeze suddenly cut across the tower and Susan pulled her coat around herself. 'The problem is that by knowing the minutiae of people's lives, we start believing we know everything about them, which of course we don't. Even in a village people keep secrets.'

Lawrence put his head to one side. 'You're right. As a head teacher I occasionally find out what happens behind closed doors and I'm shocked. However, this is generally a supportive community.' He paused and then looked at her sideways. 'It's why having this anonymous complaint hurts.'

'Sorry?' said Susan, confused. She saw deep lines of concern on his face and suddenly realised that Lawrence might be more sensitive to criticism than he'd initially appeared. 'Is this something to do with Ross?'

'Oh, no. Sorry, I should explain. A complaint was sent to the local authority about two weeks ago, but I've only just heard about it. Usually, if a parent is upset or frustrated by something, they come and see me or a member of staff, and we can sort it out. Why did someone feel the need to do this?' He flicked his hand in the air. 'Never mind, it will get sorted. Just as this business with Ross will.' Lawrence paused before saying, 'I know the way I told everyone appeared rather brutal, but this way everyone was told in one fell swoop, no time for gossip and rumour to spread. This is a better way.' He refilled his cup of coffee. 'And, of course, Jessie is resourceful. She'll find new ways of raising money.'

'She's very committed to the work, isn't she? Daniel and her seem like chalk and cheese and yet they work well as a team.'

'Do you think so?'

Susan was surprised at Lawrence's response and replied, 'In the short time I've known them, I would say Jessie seems pretty devoted to Daniel.'

'Their relationship is complicated. Jessie and I got off to a bad start. She was angry with me for asking her to go through a DBS check to work in the school. Then there was the business at Christmas. I was very upset with her. I'd always assumed Daniel was the steady one of them. But in the last week I've found out things about Daniel that have shocked me. I tried reasoning with him, but he became incensed, I'd never seen him react like that. I told Jessie they needed to talk but was ignored. I don't know quite what to do next, but they can't go on like they are. The positions they hold in the community are too important.'

'Oh dear. So, um, what have they done?' Susan asked, curious and hoping Lawrence would tell her more.

However, he simply replied, 'I shouldn't be gossiping about it. Hazel is always telling me not to interfere. She had a real go at me for talking to Ross about his relationship with Cerys—'

'Oh, what happened?'

'I was concerned that Cerys was getting far more serious about the relationship than him, and I told Ross to back off. He got very upset about that.'

'Do you think she will go with Ross if he leaves the village?' asked Susan.

'No way. They've only been together for a month or so. I'm not sure he'd even want her following him. No, I will make sure she stays. She will be going into her second year of teaching and needs to build on that experience. She has the makings of a first-class teacher, and I can give her the support she needs to climb the ladder.' His face broke into a warm smile. 'I am sure she will stay with us for a long time.'

He took a deep breath, looked up at the stars.

'Enough of all the problems down there. We can escape all that up here.'

Susan started to get up. 'Thank you. It's been wonderful, but I'd better get going now. My dogs will wonder where I am.'

'You must come again.' Lawrence picked up his rucksack. 'I'll let you out. Follow me down the steps.'

He switched off his red torch and they used the white-beamed torch to descend the spiral staircase.

Going down was even harder than going up and Susan was tense with concentration.

They walked to the front door, their feet echoing on the stone floor, the windows black, closed, unseeing. It struck Susan that churches at night seemed to lose their warmth and comfort and were full of shadows and whispers instead.

They'd reached the door. Lawrence gave her a weary smile, suddenly looking much older. Susan saw the exhaustion in his eyes.

'Maybe you should go home too,' she suggested.

'No. I'll relax better up there with my bats and the stars than in front of the TV.' He placed the rucksack on a chair close to the door, opened it and, leaving it flapped open, took out the bunch of keys, and unlocked the door.

Susan looked over at the primary school opposite. 'The lights are on over at the school – do they leave them on overnight?'

'No, that will be Fiona. She hates taking work home. She would rather stay in school as late as it takes. Still, I've never worked with such a good deputy. I'll miss her.'

'She's leaving?'

He cringed. 'I shouldn't have let that slip. Keep it to yourself.' He looked up at the sky. 'Feels like rain could be on its way. I'd better go and make the most of my time. I'll see you around, Susan.' He held up the keys. 'If you see Hazel, tell her I haven't lost them yet. I'm keeping them safe. Right, see you around, and thanks for being brave enough to come up the bell tower.'

She smiled. 'Thank you, Lawrence. That was quite an experience.'

She saw him disappear back into St Jude's, heard him turn the key in the lock. There was a brief pause and then she heard footsteps as he made his way back into the heart of the church.

Susan walked down the path. The security light went out and she was in darkness. This was the oldest part of the graveyard. The gravestones were pale silhouettes, leaning, abandoned. No one visited them now. No one laid flowers, cleaned them lovingly. The inscriptions were mostly worn away, and yet they remained and, in the night, felt strangely alive.

She heard rustling in the long grass – a mouse or vole rummaging around. She felt herself breathing hard. The breeze felt like ghosts tapping her on the shoulder. The church clock struck nine, the measured tones deep and dark.

Susan looked at the bell tower. Lawrence was up there alone, and the thought frightened her. She wanted to shout to him, tell him to come down, but the fear of looking foolish stopped her. Instead, she turned quickly and walked home.

5

As Susan approached her house, she saw a light over her neighbour's front door. Hazel was taking some books from her visitor, the young teacher Cerys. Susan heard her high-pitched laugh, saw her high blonde ponytail shining in the light.

Cerys waved over to her. 'Hiya, you survived the bell tower then?'

'It was interesting, but pretty scary.' Susan walked over to them. 'I left Lawrence up there. He said to tell you that he hasn't lost the keys yet.'

Hazel smiled. 'Good to hear. I hope he comes home soon; it looks like rain.'

Cerys pulled her pink cardigan around her. 'It's getting chilly now. I saw you walking with your dogs this morning, Susan. They're so sweet but I don't know how you cope walking two dogs. I'd get pulled over. Are they sisters or something?'

'No. I adopted Libs after her young owner who was living with me died.'

'Oh, God, is that the girl Alice told me about? The one whose death you investigated?' asked Hazel.

'You were in the police?' asked Cerys.

'Oh, no, nothing like that. Colette was my lodger. She died tragically last year. The police thought it was an accident, but I wasn't so sure.'

'And it turned out you were right,' said Hazel.

'Anyway,' said Susan, eager to move on, 'I took on Colette's dog, Libs, and she lives with me and Rocco now. They get on so well, it's lovely.'

'So have you lived all your life on the island?'

'Yes, I grew up over here on the west side.'

'It's so sweet the way you islanders talk about different sides of the island, and yet it's tiny. Do you know, I've children in my class who look wide-eyed at the idea of going over to Shanklin, let alone the mainland. Mind you, I've friends back in Swansea who would never dream of going to Cardiff, let alone "over the bridge to England". We all like to stay where it's familiar, I guess.'

'And yet you came all the way here,' said Susan.

'I know it sounds daft, but I saw the island featured on *Countryfile* one evening and I'd always wondered what it would be like to live on an island,' said Cerys. 'The children are lovely and there is a real sense of community. I do hope you can get Lawrence to change his mind about Ross.'

'I don't have any influence over school matters, that's his department. He will assume everyone will come round. You know how he is,' replied Hazel, giving Cerys a knowing look.

'I suppose so. Oh, could I just use your loo?'

'Of course, you know where it is.' Once Cerys had disappeared into the house, Hazel said, 'She's such a sweet girl and is such an asset to the school; Lawrence speaks very highly of her.'

'It can't be easy for a young girl coming all this way to the island, not knowing anyone.'

'I agree. We're lucky she came. I've tried to be friendly, and I'm so glad she's joined the choir.'

'I hope the choir carries on in some form; it's helped me settle in.'

'You mentioned you were divorced?' asked Hazel gently.

'Yes, I've been separated from my husband for nearly three years now. We were married for forty years before he left.' Susan was amazed at how easily the words slipped out, giving no hint of the heartbreak involved.

'My God, I would fall apart if Lawrence did that to me. How did you cope? I mean, you seem very together.'

Susan smiled; she was glad she at least appeared to be holding things together. 'I've always been quite independent and resilient. I have a feeling that was why my ex, Steve, felt he could just up and leave. I wasn't quite as shellproof as he thought, but I've survived and picked up the pieces. It's not all bad news, you know. I like having my own space, and I never have to plan meals. I was always more sociable than Steve. I have good friends.'

'That would worry me. I've always been dependent on Lawrence socially. I hide behind him.' Hazel's face relaxed. 'We have a good life: look at this beautiful home we have.'

At that point Cerys returned, slightly out of breath and pink-cheeked.

'Everything okay?' Hazel asked.

'Um, yes, fine. My phone dropped out of my bag, and I was a bit worried I'd broken it, but it's okay.' Cerys smiled at Hazel. 'Did you say you have a meeting now?'

'Yes, a Zoom meeting for work at half nine. Why?'

'Oh, nothing. It would be good to chat sometime, that's all.'

'Why don't you come for lunch on Sunday? Unless you have plans, that is—'

'I've nothing on. Thanks, it's lovely to come round here and have proper home cooking.' She turned to Susan. 'I usually cater for myself at the vicarage, so I live on pasta and sauce. Right, I'll be off, thanks so much for the books. They've been a lot of help with our project.'

'I'll see you on Sunday.'

With a brief wave, Cerys walked away.

'Um, I have this meeting soon, or I'd ask you in,' said Hazel awkwardly to Susan.

'That's okay. I need to see to the dogs.'

Suddenly they both heard a cry from Cerys. Susan turned. Through the darkness she could see Cerys sprawled on the ground. She ran over to help her up.

'Are you okay?'

'It's my ankle. *Duw*, God, that hurts.'

'Let me look at it,' shouted Hazel and came running over. She gently felt Cerys's ankle. 'I'm guessing it's just a sprain. Did you fall on your wrist?'

'No, thanks, that's fine,' Cerys cringed. 'I reckon this is going to swell up as soon as I take my shoe off.'

'Does it need a trip to A & E? I could drive you there,' offered Susan.

'No, thanks. I'll put a cold compress on it.' She grimaced.

'Let me drive you home then. Didn't I hear you're in digs at the vicarage? My car's just over there.'

'You can come in if you'd like?' said Hazel.

'No, thanks. I'll get on home.'

'Take care then,' said Hazel. 'Ring me if you need anything.'

Susan helped Cerys into the front passenger seat, moving the seat back so that Cerys's injured foot wasn't too close to the gearstick.

Susan drove the short distance to the vicarage. Daniel and Jessie still lived in the original vicarage, a rambling Gothic building which, while being very atmospheric, Susan assumed must be a nightmare to keep warm and clean. As she pulled up, she saw Ross walking past, hands in his pockets. Seeing them, he paused.

Getting out of the car, Susan explained. 'Cerys has hurt her foot; I was bringing her back. I'll just help her to the front door.'

Ross opened the passenger door and gently helped Cerys out of the car. 'What happened?'

'It's nothing, just me being stupid,' said Cerys. 'I hurt my ankle.'

'Oh, no. You poor thing, come here, I'll help you.'

Susan supported Cerys on the right but immediately regretted her choice as this was the side Cerys was leaning on heavily, avoiding putting any weight on her foot. Ross, however, did his best to support on the other side, and together they helped her down the drive, which was lit by individual small solar lights, forming a runway to the front door.

Ross held Cerys's bag while she found her door key. 'Daniel and Jessie are out; both their cars have gone.'

'I'll look after the invalid,' said Ross, clearly signalling for Susan to leave.

'At least it's Saturday tomorrow, no school,' said Cerys.

'I'll be off then, take care,' said Susan and returned to the car. She could see lights still on in the school. Checking her watch, she saw it was half past nine, and guessed Fiona must still be in there. She was guessing, as he'd not returned yet, Lawrence was still up the bell tower. The crenellations at the top of the tower were silhouetted against the night sky, it looked forbidding up there. She hoped he'd return home soon.

Susan drove back to the close, parked and approached her new house. The old stone cottage was very different to her large Victorian terrace over at Ventnor but as soon as Susan had seen it, she knew it would be her new home. It was solid, at peace with itself, it had lived and breathed here for hundreds of years. It was built of local chalky limestone rock, clinch stone, and had the quirky appearance of a house that had been extended many times over the years.

Susan hesitated at her front door, dreading facing the mess and boxes inside. However, as soon as she opened the door, her two cocker spaniels, Rocco and Libs, came running to meet her. Their greeting immediately warmed her heart. Rocco was a gentle sable roan, with a black nose and paws, Libs's coat was a soft velvet black. Susan leant down to fuss them and glanced around the living room.

It was untidy, full of packed boxes and books piled on the floor. She may have been rather flippant when she talked about the boxes earlier to Hazel, but the truth was, she found facing them completely overwhelming. They contained a lot of Steve's and Zoe's things, and she had no idea where she was going to put them. Trying to ignore them, she looked around the rest of the room.

She loved the low beams, inglenook fireplace and, of course, against one wall was Susan's piano. She also had her familiar old sofa and chairs, and other bits of furniture she'd brought with her from Ventnor.

On the mantlepiece she had arranged her favourite photographs. One of the celebration of her daughter Zoe and her wife Fay's original civil partnership, and of course a beautifully framed photograph of her baby granddaughter, Jamari.

She picked up the photograph and touched it gently with her fingertips. She had been over to stay with Zoe and Fay for a week after Jamari had been born and it had been incredibly special. Nothing had prepared her for the deep attachment she felt towards this little one, and tears had fallen down her cheeks the first time she held her. She had, however, forgotten how tiring and all-consuming a new baby was, and she returned to the island exhausted.

Susan replaced the photograph and glanced around the room.

She was on her own now: this was meant to be her fresh start, but the optimism of the words was lost on her. In fact, she wondered if such a thing was even possible. Starting her life again wasn't like starting a piece of music she'd badly messed up. It wasn't a clean slate. She had all her past, a lot of which she valued, and she didn't want to forget it, to live as if it had never happened.

Susan shook her head. She was overthinking all this. She would sort things out tomorrow. She suddenly realised she'd not eaten since lunchtime, so she chose a supermarket lasagne from the freezer and put it in the microwave. For years she'd cooked proper meals for the family, but one of her reactions to Steve leaving was to stop all that and at the moment she was enjoying not having to plan or cook.

She ate it quickly, while scrolling through her laptop. After this, she pulled the curtains, settled the dogs down and headed up to bed.

Susan heard St Jude's clock strike ten and wondered if Lawrence was still up the tower. She stood looking over the village from her window. All was very still and quiet. Susan still missed the sea, which she could always see and hear from her old home in Ventnor. However, it was only about a mile down the road, and she could smell and feel it in the air.

Susan was climbing into bed when she heard rain crashing against the window. It had started with no warning, as if a hole had been ripped in the sky. Susan glanced at her clock: ten past ten. She listened for the dogs, but there wasn't a sound.

Going back to the window, she saw that as so often happens after a dry spell, the rain was bouncing off the ground, the drains seeming to panic and spit back the water. The noise was deafening.

Closing the curtains, Susan climbed back into bed and switched off the light. The rain calmed to a steady patter about ten minutes later and eventually she fell asleep.

Susan was woken by blue flashing lights piercing her bedroom curtains. She saw that it was still dark out and, checking her clock, she saw it was three o'clock. She went to look out of the window. There were actually two police cars there now. The lights on the one that had just arrived were turned off and she saw an officer go into Hazel's house.

What had happened? Had there been a break-in? She remembered how she had laughed off her daughter's warnings about 'sticking herself down a side street' and how vulnerable her house would be.

Pulling on her dressing gown, Susan raced downstairs. The dogs rushed out of the kitchen, wagging their tails. As she pulled on some shoes, she talked to them. 'Stay here, I'm going to find out what's going on.'

6

Susan opened her front door just as a police officer was emerging from Hazel's.

'Has something happened? Can I help?' she called.

'Are you Hazel's neighbour?'

'Yes, Susan Flynn.'

'I see.' He paused. 'Um, could you just wait there a moment?'

He went back into Hazel's house and quickly returned.

'I've spoken to Hazel. She'd be grateful if you could go in to be with her. Do you want a moment to put on something a bit warmer?'

'Thank you.' Susan ran inside, changed and gave the dogs quick treats. 'I won't be long.'

By the time she was back, one of the police cars had left. Susan walked along her wet path and then to Hazel's door, where a different police officer let her in.

Hazel sat huddled in the corner of a white velvet sofa, red-eyed. She looked at Susan with such distress and heartache that Susan ran over and sat next to her. 'Whatever has happened?'

'It's Lawrence,' Hazel gulped. She held her arms around herself tightly, rocked slightly, and silently sobbed.

The police officer interjected, speaking gently. 'My name is Detective

Constable Ian Price. I'm sorry to have to tell you that Hazel's husband, Lawrence, was found an hour ago in the churchyard. He appeared to have had a fall. It was fatal.'

Susan gasped. 'Lawrence fell? How?'

'We understand he was up the bell tower. It appears he fell from there.'

'Oh, God.' Susan covered her mouth and stared at the officer. She couldn't believe it; only hours before, she'd been speaking to Lawrence. She turned to Hazel. 'I'm so sorry.' The words were not enough, but then words never would be.

Hazel stared at her blankly. She now sat very still, her breathing light, as if frightened to even blink. Her hands were clenched together in her lap.

'Is there someone in the family I can phone?' asked Susan.

Hazel raised her head slowly. 'The police officer has phoned my sister, but she won't be able to come until the morning – there are no ferries.'

Detective Price sat forward, speaking gently but firmly. 'We would like to get into St Jude's, and gain access to the bell tower.'

'You can take my keys – oh, no – I gave them to Lawrence, and the only other set are over on the mainland. A workman took them—'

'There are no other keys to the church front door anywhere?'

'There's the old one to the side door...' Hazel stood up slowly, walked over to the sideboard and opened the drawer. She rummaged around and then stared over at Susan. 'I can't find it.'

Susan joined her. 'Let me look.'

'Remember, it was one with a cross on the top, that one where the cross was enclosed in a circle of twisted metal.'

'Yes, of course.' Susan looked among the old keys, but she couldn't find it either. She checked in the other drawers: no, it definitely wasn't there.

'I'm sorry, I can't find it either.'

'Don't worry. Now, the main door. Are you sure no one else has a copy of that key?'

'Yes. When we had new locks fitted recently Daniel wanted to keep it to four keys, which I have to say is very inconvenient, but he insists we always know where every key is. He has two on his key ring. I have two on mine. Apparently, he's worked in places where there were hundreds of copies and he hated it. I'm sorry.'

'No problem. We'll have to use the keys we found with Lawrence if needs be. Now, I'd just like to ask you a few questions.' Hazel stared at him, unseeing, but he continued. 'You said Lawrence liked to go up the bell tower at night, but he'd not been for a while. Was there a reason he went up tonight?'

'The tower steps had been out of action so no one has been up recently, not even the bell-ringers.'

'I see, thank you. Susan, is it right you'd been up there with Lawrence earlier?'

'Yes, I went to see bats with him.'

'What time did you leave him?'

'About nine, I heard the church clock.'

'He let you out?'

'Yes, and I heard him lock the door behind me.'

'Good. We'll come and have a longer chat with you later, Susan, but I wonder if you could just briefly tell me how Lawrence seemed to you, both when you were talking and when you left him.'

The inference was clear, and Susan glanced at Hazel. However, she was just staring again at her hands, so it was difficult to know if she was even hearing them.

'To begin with he seemed quite stressed. We'd had a difficult committee meeting earlier, but once the bats arrived, he was completely taken up with them. I did think he looked tired when I was leaving him, and even suggested he call it a night, but he was keen to go back and carry on looking out for bats.'

'You say he was stressed by events that happened earlier. Did he seem depressed or down about what had happened?'

Susan paused and screwed up her eyes. 'He'd found it a difficult day, but Lawrence seemed to me to be a pretty optimistic kind of person. He told me he believed problems usually got resolved. Being up the tower definitely relaxed him and, like I say, he was very excited about seeing the bats.'

'Thank you, that's helpful.'

Suddenly, Hazel looked up. 'It was so cold. Who did you say found him?'

Susan guessed Hazel had already been told these things, but Detective Price explained again slowly.

'Some young people had been dropped off at about two in the morning and were walking though the graveyard when they found him. It was one of the sides of the bell tower not facing the road, where there are concrete slabs laid. They called an ambulance and the paramedics, we understand, were able to confirm your husband had been dead for some time.'

'Had he been lying there in pain, on his own there in the dark?'

'We will know a lot more soon. Try not to imagine things. It won't help.'

Susan could feel Hazel starting to shake and she shot a concerned look at Detective Price, who gave a brief understanding nod.

'That will do now,' he said. 'I will stay, and we can wait for any more news. Susan, if you need to go home that's fine. It is the middle of the night. You must be tired.'

'It's all right, I'll stay.'

They sat together quietly until there was a loud ring at the door.

The detective opened it and Susan saw Jessie standing on the doorstep. She was wearing her usual skinny jeans, her hooped earrings shone under the porch light.

'I'm Jessie Green, the vicar's wife.'

The detective glanced over at Hazel, who gave a nod of permission for Jessie to be allowed in.

Jessie rushed over to Hazel. 'I'm so sorry.' Susan stood up so that Jessie could sit down, and Jessie put her arm around Hazel. 'Daniel is over at Shiloh, the prayer centre, but I've sent him a text.'

Jessie brought with her a reassuring air of concern but someone in control of themselves, a person who could be leaned on.

'How did you know?' Hazel asked quietly.

'I saw the police at St Jude's when I came back from the hospital.'

'Hospital?'

'I had to take Cerys. She hurt her foot. We've been up there for ages.'

'I didn't realise she'd hurt herself that badly,' said Hazel.

'Yeah, she was in a right state when I got back from the gym. I told her she should have called me sooner. Anyway, I found her a dry coat, bundled her in the car and took her up to A & E. Apparently she's crushed some of those tiny bones in her foot and she's in one of those boots. There's no plaster fortunately. Anyway, she'll be all right. You're the one that matters now.' She turned to Susan and smiled. 'You look shattered. Why don't you go and have a rest?'

Susan was aware Jessie had not even been to bed yet but could see she was happy to stay.

'Thanks.' Susan looked down at Hazel. 'I'll be on my way, but I'm only next door, okay?'

Hazel didn't respond, but Jessie flashed her a smile and Susan left. She returned to the house. It was half past four, but she couldn't face going back to bed, not after all that had happened.

She sat on the sofa and the dogs joined her as she closed her eyes and dozed for an hour. Soon, slivers of light were streaking the darkness and so she decided to take the dogs out. She made a flask of coffee, packed some biscuits, took the dogs to the car, and drove to the end of her road. Glancing back towards St Jude's, she could just make out the yellow tape across the gate that led to the front door. She shivered, indicated right, and drove out of the village, up to the downs.

Although Susan still missed being able to walk out of the house down to the beach at Ventnor, she didn't miss the steep climb back home. Now she could drive down to Brook or Compton easily, or up to Mottistone Down. They differed to the downs at Ventnor and to Susan they felt gentler, and, being that bit further from the sea, were more sheltered and less exposed.

She parked in the Jubilee car park, looked over the gates, checked she couldn't make out any cows and let the dogs run off.

Up here, the air was cool, cleaned by the rain. She walked with the dogs up a damp chalk path to the head of the downs and looked over at the sea. The sun slowly set the sky on fire and, as she sat on the seat and poured coffee, the dogs ran around, sniffing the fresh day.

Susan found comfort in being alone as the darkness slowly receded to be replaced by sunlight. The air was full of birdsong.

Her mind went back to being up the bell tower with Lawrence, hours before he must have died. His excitement at seeing the bats, his love of being up there, his favourite place on earth.

He had talked about escaping into nature, and it was tragic he would never see another morning like this. Above her a lark was trilling. A kestrel hovered above its prey, waiting to swoop down. Way in the distance, the sea sparkled in that special way it has on a summer's morning.

After she'd finished her coffee, Susan reluctantly walked back with the dogs to the car and drove home.

Back in the house, she remembered that Robert, a retired policeman she'd become friends with while dog walking over in Ventnor, would be coming after lunch. He'd helped her move in and was coming over to put up shelves.

They had been out together a few times. Outings, she called them, definitely not dates. Robert couldn't have been less like her ex, Steve, who was serious, academic, loved classical music and reading. Socially, he was quite shy and retiring. Robert was gregarious. He loved sport, was athletic in build, had tattoos on his upper arms, and was very practical, down to earth. Despite all the differences, or maybe because of them, Susan found herself attracted to him. She was fairly sure he was looking for something more serious. Although it was six years since Robert had lost his wife, Susan was not certain at all it was the right time for her.

Susan wandered down to the village shop to buy croissants and some cheese for lunch. Tracy served her and was eager to chat. 'Everyone is so shocked. A good head teacher. Got that school on its feet. Some said he was using the school to make his mark, that he would have been moving on, but fair play, in the three years he's been here he's seemed very committed to the school and the village. Have you spoken to Hazel? She must be distraught.'

'I was with her briefly and, yes, she is devastated.'

'Our paperboy was one of the boys who found Lawrence. He had been into town, was dropped off in the early hours, and walked through the churchyard. What a shock it was for such a young lad, and yet he was still here to do his round.'

Susan smiled, imagined the boy rushing in, full of news.

Tracy continued. 'Poor Hazel. What a thing to happen. If you see her, tell her I can deliver anything she needs, she just needs to give me a ring.'

'That's really kind of you.'

'That's the beauty of living in a village. We'll all rally round. I know Hazel's not one to chat a lot but she's joined the choir and is even standing in for the church warden. She's getting involved. Still, she'll be lost without Lawrence. He was the one to get along with people. Do you suppose the school will be closed on Monday? People have been asking me.'

Susan could see how people might assume Tracy, as a kind of sorting office of village news, might be able to answer this. Susan was tempted to speculate but simply answered, 'Sorry, I've no idea.'

'I'm sure Fiona will let everyone know,' replied Tracy. 'She's probably at the school now, sorting things out. Poor thing, she'll be in shock too, I'm sure, but she'll keep it together.' Tracy moved closer to Susan, lowering her voice. 'Did I hear there'd been a row at the choir committee meeting after the practice last night?'

'Um, there was a discussion. I shouldn't say too much.'

Tracy tutted. 'Well, we'll all know soon enough.'

Susan left the shop and returned home. As she was opening her front door, she saw a taxi draw up in front of Hazel's house and a harassed-looking woman emerged. She didn't notice Susan, but grabbed a large holdall, paid the taxi driver and rushed to the front door.

Susan guessed this was Hazel's sister and she was glad that Hazel had family with her.

The dogs were dozing in their beds. Susan opened the back door. Her garden was bathed in sunshine, and the slabs of stone on the patio were warming up. A blackbird was rummaging under a bush, a magpie shouted down from one of the tall ash trees in the field behind her garden and she saw a robin with a beak full of worms diving into a hedge, where she guessed there was a nest with babies. There were no houses behind hers, which looked across fields and then up to the downs.

The previous owners had left a small wooden bench. Susan took her coffee and croissant and sat down, breathing in the still, fresh air. She could hear someone talking, and guessed Hazel's patio doors were open.

It didn't sound like Hazel: the voice was too loud and harsh. She assumed it was Hazel's sister. The words were hard to distinguish. The person was speaking fast without taking a breath and, as Susan heard the opening and shutting of cupboards and crashing of plates, she was clearly moving around as she talked. The one thing Susan couldn't hear among all the activity was Hazel, and she wondered how she was coping with the whirlwind going on around her.

At the sound of the vacuum cleaner next door, accompanied by the never-ending chatter, Susan heard her own doorbell ring. She guessed Robert had arrived early.

However, when she answered the door, it was a police officer on the doorstep.

Her visitor was DC Kent, who went through her time with Lawrence up the bell tower. Susan gave as much detail as she could but had little to add to what she'd said the night before.

After she left, Susan began to clear up and soon heard her doorbell ring. Her heart raced a little and she felt flustered as she answered the door.

_____

7

'Susan, it's good to see you,' said Robert as he gave her a hug. Although she knew it was meant as a friendly gesture (he greeted a lot of people this way), she still found it a bit overwhelming. Partly because he was much taller and broader than her and also because her family, and indeed Steve, were not natural huggers and tended to greet each other with a brief smile and a nod.

He was looking tanned and fit, wearing his usual jeans and T-shirt. Susan was aware in a way she never was with Steve that she had not been to a hairdresser for months now and her curly hair was even more unruly than usual.

Robert had his two dogs. Dougie was a loving, good-natured black cocker spaniel, with a flash of white on his chest. His coat was like crushed velvet and, despite his age, he was still very active. The other was Gem Gem, a stunning liver and white English pointer crossed with a springer spaniel. She had short hair and silky, soft ears, was very gentle, and loved flushing out pheasants and chasing rabbits.

Robert had brought his box of tools and the shelving she'd chosen with him the week before.

'Let the dogs off, they can join mine in the garden,' Susan said.

He grinned when he saw the boxes. 'Honestly, Susan, you've not done anything since I was last here.' Then he paused. 'Sorry, you look a bit done in.'

'I am, but not because of the move.'

Susan started to tell him about Lawrence's accident.

'God, this is terrible. Sit down and tell me all about it properly. I know Fiona, the deputy head; this must be a nightmare for her.'

'I didn't realise you knew her.'

'My wife Carol and I used to be in the same tennis club as Fiona. Carol became quite good friends with her. I suppose the last time I saw Fiona was at Carol's funeral six years ago.' He paused; a flash of pain passed over his face. 'Anyway, I heard Fiona was still at the school. She was always very conscientious.'

'I'll say. She seems to live at the school. Did you ever meet her stepson, Ross? He's been here for the past two years, working with the choir I've joined.'

'You'd not mentioned that. Fiona must have been here about ten years now. I know she'd left an unhappy marriage. Ross must be the very musical stepson, but he was living in London. I'm pretty sure she wasn't that close to him.'

'She wasn't, but she did get him the job here. He's living in a caravan in her garden, and, of course, running the choir here. Well, he was, I don't know what will happen now, whether he'll still lose his job or not.'

'Tell me everything that happened.'

'Okay, I bought some bits for lunch in the village shop. We can eat them as we chat.'

Susan quickly prepared lunch and they took their plates out into the garden. She went through the whole event, including telling Robert about the choir committee meeting.

'It doesn't sound like Lawrence handled the news about withdrawing the funding very well, which surprises me. I only ever heard good things about him on the grapevine. His death must be a shock, and for you as well. He was your neighbour.'

'It was awful. Not what you expect in the first month of moving into your new home.'

Robert gave a gentle smile. 'At least it was an accident.'

'I suppose it must have been. The main door was locked when the police arrived, and Lawrence had Hazel's bunch of church keys. The only other church keys were with a workman on the mainland – long story.'

'I'm sure the police will establish things, and we don't have to worry about you having a new case to solve! Now, down to more practical things. I'll get on with putting shelves up. You can sort out some boxes.'

They went back into the house. As Robert began his work, Susan looked helplessly at the boxes.

'Should I put these away in the loft?' she asked Robert.

'What's in them?'

'Old books of Steve's, and Zoe's school books. I don't know what to do with them. I suppose I need to see if they want any of them.'

'What about putting them in the garage? You don't put your car in there, do you?'

Susan smiled. 'No, I never bother. Of course, yes, good idea.'

Once the boxes had been moved, the room looked a lot better.

'There you are,' said Robert. 'This is your home now. You don't need to fill it up with everyone else's clutter. It's up to you what you do in here now.'

'The trouble is I know what my parents liked, what Steve and Zoe liked in a home, but I've never really thought what I want.'

Robert put his head to one side. 'Well, it's time you did.'

Susan blinked. Robert didn't usually speak in such a sensitive way. 'Okay, I'll do my best.'

He laughed. 'Right, back to the shelves.'

The afternoon passed quickly, and Susan did manage to sort a few things out.

'Fancy going out for dinner this evening?' Robert asked. 'Try out the local?'

Susan appreciated that Robert was tactfully not expecting her to have anything prepared. They walked through the village to the pub, a large whitewashed building.

Susan took the dogs into the garden, while Robert went to order himself the day's roast dinner and 'something veggie' for Susan, before returning with a glass of wine for her and a pint for himself.

He was just sitting down when Susan spotted Fiona and Ross coming out of the pub. They were heading to the side gate but, upon seeing Susan and Robert, they came over.

Fiona walked quickly, her eyes darting around, as if on high alert. Robert stood up and held his arms out and hugged her. 'How wonderful to see you.'

'It's good to see ye as well.' Fiona's voice was harsh and brisk, but Susan saw a slight blush in her otherwise pale cheeks.

'I heard what happened to Lawrence,' said Robert.

'It's completely stunned us all.' Fiona glanced at Susan. 'I rang Hazel first thing. She said her sister was coming over. I'm glad someone is with her.' She added, 'The governors have made me acting head for the time being. My aim will be keeping things as normal as I can for the children.' Her voice steadied as she talked about school. 'There is so much to do. We're holding a special assembly on Monday. I need to send emails out.'

'The school are lucky to have you.'

Fiona shot a look between Susan and Robert. 'Are you two together then?'

'No, no,' said Susan quickly. 'Robert and I got to know each other walking our dogs over in Ventnor.'

Fiona looked at the dogs under the table. 'You've got quite a pack between the two of you.' Turning to Robert, she said, 'You've not been to the tennis club for years.'

'No, I sort of lost interest after Carol died.'

'Well, you should come back. We had some good games.'

Susan could sense something verging on flirting, and found it disturbing. She waited to see Robert's response.

Fiona continued. 'Good. Now I've not introduced you to my stepson, Ross. He runs the choir here.' Fiona turned to Susan. 'The head of governors has decided Ross will stay on for a while now.'

Susan nodded. 'I'm pleased. Oh, Ross, have you heard about Cerys going to A & E?'

'Yes. I didn't realise her foot was that bad. I was with her until Jessie returned but even then, she hadn't told me how much it was hurting.'

'She rang me yesterday evening,' said Fiona. 'It all sounds very painful.' There was a hint of annoyance in Fiona's voice. Susan guessed she was trying to work out the implications for the school. 'Right,' said Fiona. 'We'd better get on. Robert, I'll be in touch. We'll have a game soon.'

When they had left, Susan couldn't help asking Robert, 'Do you think you'll be going to the tennis club?'

'I might do. Do you fancy coming and playing doubles?'

'Oh, no, my exercise is walking the dogs.'

Robert grinned. 'You never were a team player.'

At that moment, their food was brought out. Picking a Brussels sprout from his plate, Robert fed it to Dougie.

'Ideally he likes them lightly steamed but this will do,' Robert said, smiling, and then handed Gem Gem a piece of meat.

Susan tutted. 'Now mine will expect food. Honestly, Robert.' But she said it with a smile, took a few treats out of her pocket and gave them to Rocco and Libs.

It was growing dark by the time they left the pub, and they decided to take the dogs for a final run in the park before heading home.

They were the only ones in the park, and it was quiet as they walked the perimeter of the football field. Robert looked up at the stars. 'You know, I was hearing on the radio the other day that because of the finite speed of light, when you look at the sky, you're looking at the past. Some stars you see are from a few years ago, some even before you were born.'

'That's amazing and a bit mind-blowing, really.'

'I find it comforting to think that the past is always with us. Too many people talk about wanting to forget the past. I don't. I like to remember Carol and my life with her.'

'I'm glad. I have such lovely memories of bringing up Zoe and the foster children, even a lot of the time with Steve. I wouldn't want to forget them either.'

Back at the house, Robert put Dougie and Gem Gem in the car.

'Thanks for all your help today,' said Susan.

'It was lovely to spend time together. I miss our walks on the beach every morning,' said Robert. Their eyes locked.

Susan felt a shiver. 'I had to move—'

'I know. Maybe we could go for a walk soon, though?'

'I'd like that.'

Robert smiled, got into the car and drove away.

Susan went back in the house, took a deep breath. She had been so close to admitting to Robert that she also missed him, but it wouldn't have been right when she couldn't promise anything more. At the same time, she knew she'd been unsettled by Fiona's invite to tennis. Well, she was jealous: she had to admit that. How confusing life was!

8

It was very still and quiet when Susan took the dogs for their early walk the next morning. The churchyard was cordoned off. The service was cancelled. Everywhere seemed quiet.

As she walked down the road to the school, she was surprised to see Fiona approaching the front door. Her tracksuit and her running belt made her look very energetic.

'You're early to work, and on a Sunday as well,' Susan called.

'Aye, there is a lot to do.' Fiona ran her hand through her short hair as Susan approached her. Fiona glanced over at St Jude's and shuddered. 'I canna help but feel guilty. I was in school, so close by, while Lawrence was lying there after his accident.'

'You'd have been home by then—'

'Oh, no. I was here until about one in the morning. When I left, of course, I had no idea what had happened. I was concerned I could have helped him, but the police told me there was nothing I could have done. He died quickly, apparently.'

'You left at around one? Do you often stay so late?'

'Occasionally. As I told the police, there are plenty of teachers working silly hours at home. I just choose to do mine at school. They found it hard to believe I'd been slaving away all that time; they even asked me to go through what I'd been doing. Of course, it's hard to remember it all. I remember a quick call from Cerys in the middle of it, but it's hard to recall all the details. I must confess, I probably had a wee shut-eye at one point. The main thing is they could check on the CCTV to see when I left.'

'You have cameras on the doors?'

'Oh, aye, we've had trouble with vandalism. Only last month the governors used it to check what had been happening. The problem was it meant they saw how late I left. It was a Tuesday in May, the week of our SATs, ye know, the national tests for year six. I had a lot to do. We didn't catch the vandals, but they went on about how they weren't insured for me to be in the building that late. I told them in no uncertain terms that if I've jobs to get done, I'm staying and that's that.'

'Lawrence told me how hard you worked. After that choir committee meeting, he came into school before going up the bell tower with me. He went in to read an email; he seemed quite disturbed by it.'

'I didnae even know he was in the school.'

Susan was surprised. 'Oh, he told me he'd talked to you about the email. He was upset about it.'

Fiona looked away. 'No, as I said, we didn't speak.'

Susan changed the subject. 'So, Ross is staying. You must be pleased.'

Fiona nodded.

'Lawrence told me you were leaving. Will your plans change now?'

'I dinnae know why he said that. Don't repeat it. I've no intention of leaving.'

Susan could see tears in her eyes now, and her hands were shaking. 'I'm sorry. Of course I won't mention it.'

'I appreciate that. Now I need to get on. I'm taking Cerys round to see Hazel this afternoon. I need to find someone to help her tomorrow. It's the only day she doesn't have an assistant in.'

Susan hesitated. 'You really need help?'

'We do—'

'Would you like me to come in for the day?'

Fiona blinked. 'Ye could do that?'

'Yes, of course. Lawrence had already got me to complete a DBS check. I can come in any time.'

'Brilliant. Right then, could you be in school about half eight? We'll be having a staff meeting beforehand. It's important everyone's there.'

Susan hid a smile; Fiona was already treating her as a member of staff.

'I'll let Cerys know you'll be in,' continued Fiona. 'I have your mobile on that choir list. It was good to see Robert again last night. Have you been friends a long time?'

'A few years. He sounded keen on taking up tennis again.'

'Good, I hope he does.'

Susan looked down at the dogs. 'These two have been very patient, I'd better get off.'

As she walked away, she realised that Fiona had contradicted Lawrence. He had said he'd spoken to Fiona when he had gone over to the school. She couldn't think of a reason for Lawrence to make that up, but why would Fiona deny it?

Susan went to the park and walked around it at a brisk pace, before making her way home. On her way back, she crossed the road to read a plaque she could see on an ancient oak tree opposite the school. It said: 'Planted to commemorate the coronation of King George V and Queen Mary on 22 June 1911', meaning it was over a hundred years old. Of course, St Jude's had been here eight hundred. Susan found their presence comforting. They grounded the community, gave it roots.

She was about to walk on when she saw Jessie standing on the grass area that lay between St Jude's and the gate to the vicarage. She was tutting, looking down at her phone.

'Morning,' Susan called.

Jessie looked up, but her face was creased in concern. Susan walked over to her.

'Are you all right?' she asked.

'I don't suppose anyone is at the moment. There was that horrendous row over Ross, but more devastating, this terrible accident. I can't believe Lawrence is dead. I wish Daniel was here. We all need him.' Jessie's voice was cracking as she spoke. She tapped the long fingernails of one hand rhythmically on her chin.

'Where is he?'

'Still over at the prayer centre,' Jessie went on to explain. 'He goes every

Friday. It's a kind of retreat over in Castleford. I left a message as soon as I knew about Lawrence, and he rang back. When I told him the church was all closed off, he decided to stay last night as well. He'll be back later today, thank goodness. There were points yesterday when I really could have done with him here. The phone hasn't stopped ringing. People want to speak to him.'

It seemed very unfair to Susan that Daniel should be hiding away, leaving Jessie to handle everything here. 'If he's only in Castleford, why didn't you go and make him realise he was needed?'

'I did send another text but he felt he could do more praying for us all. In any case, I can't just go over there. Daniel would hate me to just turn up. Also, Martha who runs the place would be most put out, probably refuse to let me in.'

'She can't stop you seeing your husband.'

'Wanna bet?'

'That's crazy.'

Jessie shrugged. 'I know, but it's the way it works, and Daniel seems to see Martha as some kind of saint.'

'So, he goes there every Friday?'

'Yeah, usually comes back on Saturday morning or maybe in the evening if he's not got any weddings.'

'But every Friday? That's a lot.'

'He says he needs it. I get my break on a Wednesday – not so spiritual.' She smiled. 'I go to car boots over here or on the mainland. It's like my hobby.' Jessie flicked back her hair. 'Anyway, he'll be back later to plan the assembly for school tomorrow. This workman returned Daniel's keys yesterday,' continued Jessie. 'I was all over the place, I'd forgotten he had them.' She paused, took a deep breath. 'Sorry, I'm rambling. Now, I need to get back to Cerys, make sure she can manage the shower.'

'How is she?'

'Worried about school. I notice her flinching sometimes. The painkillers aren't completely knocking out the pain.'

Susan told Jessie about her offer to go into the school.

'That's good of you. You'll need one of those current police checks, a

DBS. You can't do anything these days without them. Lawrence even made me and Daniel go through it all. I was so cross.'

'But surely they have to be careful with who goes into the school? Everyone has to go through it. Anyway, I've already completed one. As soon as Lawrence realised I used to teach, he had me filling in forms, ready to go in and help.'

'That's lucky for them. Right, I'll go and check on Cerys, she'll be so pleased you are going in.' Jessie gave a fleeting smile and went back into the vicarage.

Susan returned home, ready for her regular Sunday morning phone call with her daughter Zoe. Since the baby had arrived, Zoe now initiated the call to fit in with the baby's feeds and they now made a Zoom call, so that Susan could see Jamari.

As she was making a drink, she received a text, checking if she was ready. Excited as always to see her new grandchild, Susan turned on her laptop.

Zoe answered. She looked very like her father, Steve. Pale, fair, with short hair and delicate features. However, she had a far more outgoing and emphatic personality than her father, which Zoe claimed came from her mother. Before her maternity leave, she had certainly been an extremely successful deputy head in a difficult school. Some of that resoluteness, however, was missing today and Susan saw black circles under her eyes.

'How are you?' Susan asked.

'Absolutely knackered, Mum.' Zoe blinked away tears. 'Why didn't anyone tell me that a good night with a baby is getting three hours' unbroken sleep? And I've not had that all week.'

'Oh dear, how is the feeding going?'

'Good, but Jamari is always hungry. I am trying to get better at expressing and we'll try to help her get used to bottles slowly, as it's only six months until I go back to work and it's flying by. How on earth am I going to work feeling like this?'

'Six months is a long time in a baby's life. You'll be in more of a routine by then.'

'I tried to go to our local NCT group on Tuesday but by the time we were both ready, it was too late to go. I've not been out of the house for days.'

'Oh dear, it sounds very tiring, love.'

'It is, but at the same time, I don't want to see anyone. How can something so little become my whole world?'

Susan smiled. 'That's how it's meant to be.'

'Honestly, I had a group of single friends arrange a Zoom meeting the other night. They were all sat there with their glasses of wine, laughing and nattering, and I was just listening out for Jamari. At one point I turned off the mic and camera, went and fed Jamari. Still, when I came back twenty minutes later, no one had missed me.'

'It will get better, love, I promise.'

'Thanks, Mum. Enough of me moaning on, let me take the camera for you to see Jamari. She's fast asleep, looking absolutely angelic.'

Susan's screen became a blur of images as Zoe manoeuvred the camera.

'Say hello to Nanna,' Zoe said to Jamari, and Susan watched, enraptured by the sight of her granddaughter, longing to touch the tiny fingers and hold her.

Once they were back chatting, Zoe brought up her father's visit that week.

'He was so sweet, Mum, quite emotional. I'd not expected that.'

Susan felt a pang of regret. Having grandchildren had been something she had always imagined doing with Steve. It was one of the things that hurt deeply about their break-up.

'I did wonder if he'd go into doctor mode, advising me about feeding or something, but he told me she looked beautiful and left it at that.'

'That's good. I'm glad it all went well. Did, um, Hester come?'

'Well, yes, it was a shame. I wish he'd left her at home. She was quite good for her, didn't talk quite as much as she usually does. She brought the most beautiful first babygrows, a brand I'd never heard of but obviously cost a bomb, and also a first teddy bear.'

Susan bit her lip. Buying Jamari her first teddy bear was something she'd been planning, but she simply replied, 'That's kind.'

Zoe, however, frowned. 'She did say something that worried me, though.'

'What was that?'

'She told me to make sure I worked hard at getting rid of the baby fat.' Susan saw tears again in her daughter's eyes and immediately felt angry and defensive. How dare this woman say that to Zoe? However, she tried to respond calmly.

'You do know that's nonsense, don't you? Just concentrate on looking after you and the baby. There is far too much pressure on new mums to diet, it's all wrong.'

'You don't think I look terrible?'

Susan shook her head. It was so unlike Zoe to be as sensitive as this, and she put it down to lack of sleep, hormones and the huge adjustment of a new baby. 'Of course not, you look gorgeous. At this stage when you were a baby, I wasn't out of my nightie before midday.'

Zoe laughed. 'Thanks, Mum, I needed to hear that.' She hesitated and then said, 'Actually, Mum, I wanted to ask a favour.'

'Anything, what is it?'

'Fay and I were wondering if you could cope if we came to stay next weekend with Jamari? You can say no. I know you've only just moved in.'

'Of course you can come. It would be smashing to have you here. What do I need to get in for Jamari? I'm out of touch with baby equipment. I don't have a cot.'

'Don't worry. We'll bring everything we need. How is the house, though? I can still see lots of boxes around.'

Susan laughed. 'I've still got a few to unpack, but some are in the garage. Robert has put up some shelves. If you're coming, I'll get things as organised as I can. We have a decent pub down the road. We could go there for Sunday lunch.'

'You're still seeing Robert, then? When am I going to meet him?'

'It's not like that. We're just friends.'

'Does he know that?'

'Yes,' replied Susan firmly.

Zoe smiled. 'Subject closed, I guess. I'm glad we're going to see you. I've something to ask you and it would be better face to face. It's to do with Dad.'

Susan felt a wave of panic. 'What's up with your father?'

'Nothing to worry about. We'll talk properly when we come. I'll be in touch before the weekend obviously to let you know what ferry we are on. Oh, Jamari is crying, better go—'

And with that Zoe was gone.

Susan's head was spinning, both with the plans for the coming visit and wondering what was up with Steve. One of the reasons she knew she wasn't ready to start a relationship with Robert was that, despite everything, she was still confused about her feelings for Steve. She couldn't just erase forty years together. She knew part of her was hoping Zoe was going to tell her he'd split up with his new partner Hester, but time alone would tell.

Susan tried to concentrate on getting the house ready for the family. She had three bedrooms here, two large and one just big enough for a double bed. She guessed the baby would be in with Fay and Zoe and started to consider buying a cot in preparation for the visit.

Much later that evening she took the dogs out. The sky was splattered with stars and everywhere was very still.

As she approached St Jude's, she noticed the police tape had been taken down. Glancing down at the vicarage, she wondered if Daniel had returned.

Most of the church was in darkness apart from a light over the main door. Susan decided to go and sit quietly at the place Lawrence had fallen, take a moment to remember him.

She went into the churchyard, walked down the path that led to the main door. Last time she'd been here she'd stood listening to Lawrence closing the door, locking it behind him, and she recalled the unsettling feeling she'd had.

Turning left, she made her way around the side of the church to where the bell tower stood. Lawrence had fallen onto the slabs at the base of the first exposed side. The area had a seat and planters, and she'd always thought it a pleasant place to sit. But it would never be the same again. Maybe people would avoid it, maybe it would even hold some kind of morbid curiosity for others. As Susan approached, she was surprised to hear someone crying. She paused, peering into the darkness.

9

Susan could make out a figure sitting on the bench and was about to creep away, leaving Hazel to grieve alone, but the dogs were in front of her, pulling on their leads, and Rocco was sniffing Hazel's knee. Hazel looked up, clearly shocked.

'It's me, Susan,' she said in the darkness.

'Oh, God, I didn't expect anyone to find me here,' replied Hazel.

'I'm sorry. I didn't mean to intrude. We'll go.'

'No, please stay. I thought coming here would be some kind of comfort, but it's made it so much worse. Come and sit on the bench.'

Susan sat down, holding the dogs on loose leads as they sniffed at the grass. Her eyes were quickly adjusting to the darkness, and it was a very still evening. They sat quietly together for a few more minutes and Susan could make out the silhouettes of flowers in some pots. Suddenly she saw two tiny bright spots peeping out and wondered what nocturnal mammal was watching them.

'The police returned the church keys to me today. I thought about going inside to pray but I knew I really needed to be where he died,' explained Hazel.

'I understand. I hope you don't mind. I just wanted to come and pay my respects. There has been so little time to think.'

'I know. Only last Tuesday Lawrence and I had our usual argument about a summer holiday. I know I moan about all the time he spent in work, but we were happy here. We both watched TV on a Sunday evening, liked to have takeaway on a Saturday, all those routine things we did together and now it's all ended. I will never do those things with him again.'

'It's a terrible shock.'

'I don't want to be on my own, but I don't want other people either. I just want Lawrence. I've hardly spent more than a night without him in thirty years. The bed feels huge. His end of the sofa looks so empty—' She started to cry.

'I'm so sorry. Is your sister still with you?'

'No, I told her to go back to the family. She has children and I have good friends here to look after me. And to be honest, she can be exhausting. She is remarkably successful, has set up her own business creating a range of self-care products for new mothers.' It was clear that Hazel and her sister were quite different personalities. 'Anyway, it was kind of her to come, but her business and young family need her.' Hazel threw a faint smile at Susan.

Susan heard a young couple chatting as they walked past on the pavement the other side of the church wall. They were laughing about their evening at the pub the night before and how much a friend had been drinking. To Susan it sounded brash and insensitive, yet of course, even in a village as close as this, normal life was carrying on.

'Daniel came to see me earlier this evening,' said Hazel. 'He was kind. He didn't come out with a lot of platitudes or, God forbid, say God had a reason for this to happen. He simply sat with me and told me he would pray for me.'

'I'm glad he was some comfort.'

'He was. He also told me not to worry about my warden duties.' Hazel looked up at the bell tower, which seemed to loom over them in the darkness. 'It's a long way to fall, isn't it? They say they think he died instantly. One moment he was alive and then it was the end.'

'It was all so sudden. It's very hard for you to take in.'

'I realise all those questions about his state of mind are the police checking whether he might have taken his own life, but I'm sure that didn't happen. Like I said to you, Lawrence was the eternal optimist. Mind you, I find the alternative, that he just fell by accident, hard to believe too.'

'Accidents are always hard to come to terms with. They come out of the blue.'

Hazel shrugged. 'I know that but there is usually an explanation of why it happened. I don't understand how this happened with Lawrence. He never ventured close to the edge of the tower. He was scared of heights.'

'He told me that. He had a blanket set up in the centre of the roof and stayed there.'

'Exactly. Why did he go near the edge at all?'

'Maybe he heard something from down here?'

'I suppose so, but if he did go to the edge he would have been holding on tight.' She pulled on her sleeves. 'There are other things I don't under-stand...' Her words were passionate, desperate. 'Why weren't his binocular cords clipped into the pouch of the harness? They found them away from his body, as if they'd flown out of his hands when he fell. He never took them off. The cords were long, there was no need. And the clips were very secure, they weren't broken.'

'Actually, he unclipped the cords so that I could use the binoculars, but then I'm sure he reattached them to the pouch of his binocular harness afterwards.'

Hazel looked down at the flowers lying on the cold slabs. 'It made me wonder if someone else was up there with Lawrence, but no one has admitted that to the police.'

'It's early days. The police are investigating. They'll be able to answer these questions, I'm sure.'

'Yes, you're probably right.' Hazel clenched her fist and pressed it tight into her stomach. 'I just wish I could get rid of this feeling deep in here that something is wrong.' She stood up. 'Sorry, I'm just getting in a muddle. I'd better get home; the phone is ringing all the time.'

Susan stood up next to her. 'And I need to keep walking the dogs.'

'Thank you, Susan, it helps to talk.' Suddenly there was a screeching sound and both Susan and Hazel looked up. 'Bats,' whispered Hazel. 'I used to be scared of them, you know, but Lawrence helped me overcome that. Some people say their loved ones who have passed on visit them in the form of robins and feathers. If Lawrence wants to talk to me, he will come as a bat.' She smiled shyly.

'What a lovely thought.'

After saying their goodbyes, Susan went back to walking the dogs, thinking about Hazel. It was natural she was struggling. She'd had no way of preparing for this, no way of foreseeing it. Everyone craves certainty, and any sense Hazel would have had that she was in control of her life must have been shattered.

However, Susan didn't want to dismiss that gut instinct of Hazel's; such feelings were too often proved right. She remembered that awful sense of foreboding before the choir committee meeting. Something had been very wrong that day and she had a terrible feeling it wasn't over yet.

* * *

The next morning, Susan realised she needed to get organised early, she was due in school. The dogs had a shorter walk than usual, but seemed happy to settle down when she left them.

At the school, the receptionist was managing to maintain a cool and controlled demeanour in what were exceedingly difficult circumstances. She greeted Susan warmly, and directed her to the staffroom. As Susan approached the room, she could hear muffled voices and her stomach clenched with nerves. Her instinct had been to offer help but now the reality of it hit her. She didn't really know anyone in there. How would they react to her coming, a stranger intruding on their grief?

The small staffroom was crammed with people. Fiona had clearly invited every member of staff, including all the assistants, as well as everyone who worked in the office and the kitchen. It brought home to Susan how many people were involved in the running of a school and how this tragedy reached out into the larger community.

Daniel was sitting in his dark clerical clothes, gnawing at the side of his thumb, looking very ill at ease. Cerys looked subdued and sat with her left foot in its orthopaedic boot resting on a makeshift footstool. It looked like a kneeler from St Jude's and Susan guessed Jessie had supplied Cerys with it.

Fiona, in her usual tracksuit, was in charge of the meeting. She started by laying out the facts she knew about Lawrence's death. Her manner was calm and reassuring.

'I know we are all grieving and distraught, but I thank you so much for coming in. Our children and their parents need us more than ever today. I am grateful to Daniel and Jessie for joining us, and before I continue, Daniel is going to lead us all in a prayer.'

Daniel stood and said a short but heartfelt prayer and then quietly sat down.

'Thank you,' said Fiona. 'Now, the first thing I would say is that the children will obviously be asking questions. I will suggest some guidelines and then set out the programme for the day.'

They listened to the carefully planned day. Susan was impressed at the foresight and sensitivity Fiona showed.

'Finally,' concluded Fiona, 'take care of yourselves as well. It's been a very difficult time for us all.' Slowly people started to leave the room.

Susan could see Cerys struggling to get hold of her crutches and went to help her. She was very pale, with dark rings under her eyes.

'How are you?'

'Exhausted. What with the nightmare over Lawrence and now this foot. What a terrible time to put myself out of action like this.'

Susan walked besides Cerys, opening doors for her.

Fortunately, it wasn't too far and soon Cerys said, 'This is my room, let's go in.'

The classroom was neat, bright and welcoming. The room showed the professional side of Cerys, someone competent and committed to her work.

Susan helped Cerys to her chair and found a spare infant-sized chair for her to rest her foot on.

'That's great, thank you so much for coming in,' said Cerys. 'I would have had to pinch someone else's assistant to help me and that wouldn't have gone down well, particularly on a day like this. I do hope you won't find it too hectic; they're very sweet kids, but I have no idea how they will be after everything that has happened.'

'I'll do my best to help you,' said Susan. She looked down at Cerys's foot. 'I didn't realise how badly you'd injured yourself. I should have taken you straight to the hospital.'

Cerys held up her hand. 'Oh, no, don't worry. It really didn't seem to be that bad at first. I had a quick chat with Fiona, and I was fine through that. But it got worse as time went on. I was glad when Jessie came home.'

'I'm surprised Ross didn't take you to the hospital sooner.'

'Sorry?' Cerys blinked in confusion.

'I wondered why Ross didn't take you to the hospital as he was there with you all evening.'

'Oh, he doesn't own a car at the moment. He has to walk everywhere, can't even cycle. Anyway, I was embarrassed, I didn't want to make a fuss.' She blushed slightly. 'We've not been together long, I don't want to appear too needy, you know. Anyway, I only went because Jessie insisted. She's so kind. I am relieved I could come in today. Now, it would be best for the children to call you by your surname, if that is okay with you?'

'Of course, that would be Mrs Flynn.'

'Great. I'll quickly go through the routine.'

As Cerys came to the end of her explanation, she glanced out of the window, where the parents and children were gathering in the playground outside. There was a subdued air among the parents, although the children were chattering and running around.

'Could you open the doors and let the children in? They have their own cloakroom through there, their lunchboxes go on the table over there.'

Susan helped the children sort out their coats and lunchboxes. Seeing the unease on their faces, Susan explained to the parents about Cerys's accident and was impressed with their offers to help.

Susan noticed a woman about her own age, and she was sure she recognised her.

'Hi, I hope you don't mind me asking, but are you Alice's daughter?' Susan enquired.

The woman's face broke into Alice's gentle smile and her grey eyes shone. 'I am, I'm Jo.'

'I'm Susan. I've seen a photo of you. Alice and I became friends when she was in the nursing home over in Ventnor.'

'Of course. Mum told me about you. I am so pleased she has moved over here. She thought it was better for us to have her all the way over in Ventnor, but she was wrong, not that she'd ever admit that.'

'I'm going to see her tomorrow, lots to catch up on.'

'That's great. I bring my grandchild two mornings a week as I'm working part-time now. I'm going to retire in September, can't wait.' Jo smiled down at a serious little boy with jet-black hair. 'Jacob, this lady knows Nanny Alice.'

'Oh, hello, Jacob. I saw you in choir, didn't I?'

Jacob nodded. Susan gave him a big smile, and again there was a brightness in his grey eyes that reminded her of Alice.

Susan could see another child about to panic as his lunchbox snapped open and the contents started to fall over the floor.

'I'd better go,' she said, and hurried over to help.

Cerys stayed inside but the children rushed to her and were soon sitting on the mat in front of her, ready for registration and morning greetings. Susan saw the weariness and stress on Cerys's face replaced by a brighter, sunnier, familiar smile.

As they settled, Cerys greeted them initially with, 'Good morning,' and then, in Welsh, '*Bore da,*' and the children replied in the same way.

The children were full of news of their weekend. Susan found their excitement over simple things, a visit from an auntie, a trip on the Red Jet to Southampton shopping, refreshing after the intensity of the past few days. It was wonderful to see Cerys's enthusiasm and the joy she shared particularly when one little girl gave her a painting of a lopsided Welsh dragon.

'A Welsh dragon, a *draig Cymru*, well done, *da yawn.*'

The child glowed with pride.

Time passed quickly and Susan was surprised when break came. She went out with the children and after this, as there was fifteen minutes before the assembly, Cerys suggested Susan go and grab a cup of coffee while she read a story to the children.

Susan made her way to the staffroom. She had brought her own mug and some coffee granules, all she needed was to fill it with water. Most of the staff had returned to the classrooms and she was glad to have a few minutes' quiet to herself.

However, as she sat sipping her coffee, Daniel came in. He glanced around and she caught the quick grimace. Clearly, he'd thought the room would be empty, he'd come in here to escape.

10

Daniel quickly regained his composure and forced a smile as Susan explained she had come in to help Cerys. As she was talking, she watched him pour a glass of water for himself, noticing his hands shaking, his face pale.

He chose a seat a few along from Susan, sipped his drink and, in a slightly embarrassed way, asked her how she was feeling.

'Shocked, like so many people.'

'Of course, it's devastating. I considered Lawrence a good friend. I regret now getting so upset with him at the choir committee meeting. Heaven knows he had enough on his plate, with this complaint and everything...'

The description of good friends seemed a bit odd to Susan, but she wanted to pick him up on the complaint.

'Lawrence mentioned that to me when we were up the bell tower the night he died. Do you know what it's about?'

'Oh, that's school business. As a governor I am told about things. Anyway, it's very kind of you to come in and help Cerys.'

'I'm pleased to help. Your Jessie was amazing on Friday evening, first taking Cerys to A & E and then visiting Hazel in the early hours. I don't think she could have got any sleep that night.'

'She is very conscientious. Ours is such a difficult job. We're on call twenty-four hours a day, always available, always working.'

Susan noticed how the words rushed out. 'It's a heavy responsibility.'

'It is. Jessie has a day off on Wednesday, goes to the mainland sometimes. She has a small online business on something called Flexee, I think it is, selling toys and collectibles.'

'And you have your time at Shiloh, the prayer centre, on a Friday. I am sure that is helpful.'

'Yes, we are so fortunate to have such a place here on the island. Martha set it up and she is amazing. I spend my Friday evening in prayer and reading.'

'So, you are on your own a lot?'

'I am. Apart from mealtimes, I stay in my room. There is one chap called Alan. He goes out for a few hours. I heard he even sometimes eats in the local pub,' said Daniel.

'Have you ever gone with him?'

'Oh, no, but we are both trying to take time out to be with God in our own ways. It's not some kind of holiday, it's work.' He continued defensively, 'I go to pray for my parish. Prayer isn't easy. Sometimes you feel you are shouting down a cold, empty well, your words echoing back...' He paused, his voice cracking with emotion.

Susan responded gently. 'I guess a lot of people don't quite appreciate what is involved in your job. People have very old-fashioned notions about vicars: gardening, afternoon teas and popping in to do the odd sermon.'

Daniel nodded. 'I know, and let's face it, the job was never that. But people like to imagine a time when the vicar was someone with all the time in the world to listen to their problems, someone safe, reliable, a steady hand through the crises in their lives. And who can blame them? They don't want us to be some kind of burnt-out social workers. I guess we all have to hide a lot of the stress, put on a face, appear strong at all times. We have to play a part, don't we?'

'I guess we do. It's tough, though. My ex-husband was a doctor, and it was a bit like that for him. People with problems don't want to go and see someone clearly stressed and exhausted.'

'It's hard. I was trying to explain this to someone who also does, I mean did, a very stressful job. I thought he'd show some empathy, step back. But he showed no understanding, he was totally oblivious to the chaos he was going to cause—' Daniel lifted clenched fists to either side of his head, screwed up his face in frustration. Susan held her breath, waiting: was he going to scream or cry?

However, they were interrupted by the staffroom door being flung open, and Jessie appearing. She was wearing her usual high stilettoes and skinny jeans, huge hooped earrings swinging. 'Daniel!' Daniel dropped his hands, stared at her as she continued, 'There you are. Come and sort out the seating for assembly. I've done the letter for the kids to take home. I wanted them and their parents to know they can come to either of us any time. Oh, and I've found a place for the Hope Garden that we're going to create in memory of Lawrence.' She turned to Susan and spoke earnestly. 'One of the mums who runs a plant nursery is going to give us the right plants and seeds. Just as well, I know nothing about gardening. Right, Daniel, let's get to the hall. I asked Fiona about lighting a candle, you know how many smoke alarms there are here.'

Daniel followed Jessie out, walking as if he was in a dream. Susan caught her breath, taken aback by Daniel's outburst. She was sure he'd been referring to a conversation he'd had with Lawrence. What had gone on between the two men? What hadn't Lawrence understood? Daniel had not only sounded upset but more than that, he seemed scared. What on earth had he thought Lawrence was going to do?

Susan realised it was time to go back to the classroom. A lot of parents were arriving for the assembly. There was a subdued air, but also a kind of excitement, picked up by toddlers who were running around the reception area.

She saw that Fiona, though, had everything in hand. She had arranged a crèche in the preschool for the young children and was encouraging parents to take their children there.

Susan joined the assembly with Cerys and her class. As the service progressed, Susan saw Daniel relax into his role. He addressed the parents and children gently and in a reassuring way.

At the end, everyone left looking thoughtful but more settled than they had done when they arrived. It was a job well done and Susan caught a look of encouragement and appreciation pass from Jessie to Daniel.

At lunchtime, Cerys decided it was easier with her injured foot to stay in the classroom, so Susan joined her.

Sitting awkwardly on one of the tiny chairs, she stretched out her legs and sighed. 'I'd forgotten how tiring children are. They never stop.'

'You're right. I understand now why my mam was so exhausted at the end of the day.'

'Your mum was a teacher as well?'

Cerys twisted the pink chiffon scarf around her fingers. 'She was.' She paused. 'Did you say you were a foster parent?'

'I was. I'm still in contact with some of the children who lived with us even now.'

'That's lovely. I was fostered for a while and my foster carers were great. I went to them because Mam, although she loved me, couldn't always cope with raising me on her own.' Cerys smiled sadly; her hand drifted to the necklace with two pendants: one was a white enamel-glazed flower with the word 'MAM' engraved on it, the other etched with an elaborate cross.

Susan looked at the pendant thoughtfully. Catching her eye, Cerys touched the white flower and said, 'I had this one engraved when Mam died.'

At that moment, two children came into the classroom; one was carrying a scruffy piece of A4 paper.

Cerys greeted her with a smile. 'Ah, Lily, you've come for your sponsorship money?' Glancing at Susan, she said, 'Would you mind passing me my purse, it's in my bag over there.'

Susan took the leather purse from Cerys's bag. It was unzipped and she could see it contained the usual collection of photographs, driving licence and shopping receipts.

Susan handed it to Cerys, who started chatting to Lily. 'So, you swam twenty lengths of the pool! *Da yawn*, well done.'

Lily grinned. 'It was ever so hard, but my teacher said I did very well.'

Cerys pushed a five-pound note into a tin Lily was holding. Lily carefully laid down the piece of paper and slowly wrote 'paid' in the right column.

'Thank you, Miss Evans,' she said and, blushing, left the room with her friend.

Cerys handed her purse to Susan. 'I'm sorry, could you put it back? I don't want to lose it again.' Once Susan had sat back down, Cerys said, 'One of the hazards of teaching. Honestly, I spend my life sponsoring children, buying raffle tickets. We've the school fete coming up soon. It's ironic. It's for school funds and us teachers end up paying out much of it.' She laughed. 'Still, that's the way it goes, and I love teaching here. Fiona is my mentor, and she has so much experience.'

'She works very hard.'

'I know she can seem formidable, but she has been wonderful to me. It's always been such a happy school, which makes what happened to Lawrence so awful.'

'Of course, although I spoke to Lawrence the night he died, and he was quite upset about an anonymous complaint that had come in. He didn't expect anyone to cause trouble like that.'

Cerys went very red, and her eyes burned with anger. 'That should never have happened.'

'So, you know what the complaint was?'

'Fiona mentioned it briefly to me yesterday, but it sounds petty and should have been ignored.' Her voice trembled with strong emotion. She looked over at the time and took a deep breath. 'Right, I thought we'd have art this afternoon. After such an emotional morning, it would be good for the children to do something creative. Could you help me sort out the materials we'll need?'

Susan enjoyed her day but was glad to return to Rocco and Libs after school and the quiet of her home.

With a clear evening in front of her, Susan opened her laptop. She started by replying to two emails from young people she used to foster and then sent emails for two charities she supported, one supporting victims of domestic abuse and another that was raising awareness of pollution in the sea.

Once she'd finished, Susan sat down to try to relax with her knitting and the TV. As she sat knitting blankets for the local dog rescue and watching *Bake Off* on catch-up, she remembered that she would see Alice the next day. She was relieved. Alice had been her touchstone of reason when they'd been involved in the murder case over in Ventnor. Not, of course, that she was saying this was a 'case' but there were questions around Lawrence's death, and she was desperate to talk about them to Alice.

* * *

And so Susan arrived at Alice's nursing home after lunch the next day. She could smell the remains of a roast dinner.

The nursing home was light and bright, and she enjoyed visiting here. After she'd signed in, she made her way along the corridor, passing one of the nurses she recognised.

'Hello, Susan. Come to see Alice? She's in the main room.'

She found Alice sitting in the lounge, slightly hunched over, wearing comfortable but smart black trousers and jumper. Her soft white hair was neat, and her paper-thin skin had a slight pink blush. Her arthritic hands grasped her iPad. Susan guessed she was doing a crossword.

Her face broke into that familiar warm smile when she saw Susan, and bright, intelligent grey eyes shone from behind her glasses. Susan sat down in a chair next to her.

'My dear Susan. How wonderful to see you. How are you? How is your house coming along?'

'Oh, still a mess, you know how it is.'

Alice put her iPad down on the small table next to her. 'I'm sure once you know exactly what you want to do, it will be perfect,' she said, giving her a hint of a smile. 'How are Zoe and the baby?'

'Zoe, and I guess her partner Fay is the same, is very tired. No one really has any idea in advance how exhausting a new baby is, do they? They're coming over to stay for the weekend. I'm considering getting a cot ready for them.'

'Good idea. I know there are all kinds of travel cots now,' said Alice. 'My daughter had so many bits and pieces, and then my granddaughter had even more. Very handy they were too, but her house seemed full of equipment.'

'That reminds me, I met your daughter, Jo. I was in the school helping and she brought your great-grandson, Jacob, to school.'

'Ah, he's a lovely lad, isn't he? Very bright.'

'I'm sure he is.'

Alice paused. 'I'm guessing they were glad of some extra help at the school after what has happened. It must be such a shock for everyone.'

'Ah, you heard about Lawrence.'

'Tracy from the shop keeps me abreast of all the news. She came over yesterday, brought me some jelly sweets. I met Lawrence not long after I moved in, back in February. He came with some children and that nice young teacher to visit. Of course, Hazel comes in regularly.'

Susan grinned. 'Hazel told me you'd mentioned our investigation over in Ventnor.'

Alice gave a sweet smile. 'When I found out you were neighbours, I couldn't resist it. Tell me, how is she?'

'Devastated. It's such a shock. I've had a few chats with her. She's quite shy, isn't she?'

'Yes, she was very quiet at first, but now she chats away. I've heard about her time in Cardiff, her singing and her twenty years in Bristol. She seems to have settled well on the island in the three years she's been here.'

'She does have the most wonderful singing voice, exceptional.'

'I love opera, and Hazel brought in photos of all the ones she'd been involved in. She was so lucky to have a friend introduce her to the company. A wonderful opportunity, but still, I think after they left Cardiff, Hazel's life revolved around Lawrence. One day she let it slip that he had a blood disorder, which worried her. He kept that from people, though. Hazel made me swear not to tell anyone. Still, it didn't stop them doing anything.'

'She told me about all her plans to spend their savings travelling. So sad they won't be able to do that together now.'

Susan heard the rattle of a tea trolley and heard a member of the care staff asking one of the residents, several times, if they would like a drink.

Alice grinned. 'He's turned his hearing aids off again; he's quite naughty. I've seen him switch them off when his family come to visit as well.' She paused and spoke more firmly. 'Now, this accident. Was Tracy right in saying you'd been up there with him that night? Is it right he was looking for bats?'

Susan smiled. 'I did go up with him and yes, he was looking for bats.'

'My dad was a bell-ringer at St Jude's and sometimes he would take me up to the roof. Mum didn't like it, but we were careful.'

'Lawrence was actually quite frightened of heights and stayed sitting in the middle, which I was glad about. It's a long way up.'

'Tracy said she thought you might have been the last person to see him alive.'

Susan had no idea how Tracy had heard that but confirmed this to be true.

'She wasn't able to tell me a lot, of course—'

Susan could see Alice was dying to hear all the details. 'I'll tell you what I can. Earlier that evening, we'd had a pretty fraught choir committee meeting.'

'Now who is on that choir committee?'

'Well, I am now, of course, but apart from me, there was Lawrence and Hazel, the vicar, Daniel, and his wife, Jessie, Ross, the choirmaster, and two teachers from Lawrence's school, Fiona, the deputy head, and a young teacher, Cerys.'

'What happened?'

Susan began by describing the row at the meeting.

'I see, that must have been very unpleasant,' said Alice. 'That was shocking news to spring on the musical director, Ross. I'm surprised Lawrence had not spoken to him privately before the meeting.'

'Lawrence had literally just made the decision before choir practice. He was anxious to tell us all as quickly as possible. But I agree, it was tough on Ross.'

'I wonder what Ross will do now?'

'Oh, Ross is to keep his job. Fiona agreed it with the governors on Saturday.'

'Ah, well, that is interesting and of course good news for him, and others, I'm guessing. So, after Lawrence delivered this news, did he seem stressed, worried about it?'

'No, I'd not say that. He assumed people would come round to his way of thinking.'

Alice gave a tiny nod, pursed her lips, and tapped her fingers on her knee. 'Yes, that fits with what I've heard about him. My granddaughter, Laura, who as you know is a teacher like her mum, has heard him speak several times and says he was inspirational and had made a lot of changes at the school. However, I got the feeling from Hazel that, as is so often the case with people who are so driven, he could be very single-minded, blinkered in some ways to the feelings of other people. Now, what happened up the bell tower?'

Susan went through the rest of the evening, from her chat with Lawrence to the moment she saw the police cars in the early hours of the morning.

Alice shook her head. 'And are the police treating this as an accident?'

'Yes, that's what they are saying.'

Alice put her head to one side in that little birdlike gesture Susan recognised. 'You look like someone who has something on her mind. What's up?'

11

Susan turned to Alice. 'It's some things Hazel said.' She told Alice about the binoculars, and the question about why Lawrence would go near the edge of the tower.

'I see, yes, they are good questions. I must admit I was concerned about the idea of him falling over the wall by accident. I mean, you would naturally be incredibly careful. It's why, in all the hundreds of years the tower has been there, no one has ever fallen before. I assume they are sure no one else went up after you?'

'No one has said they did.'

'Who had the keys for the front door of St Jude's, by the way?'

'Only Hazel and Daniel. There were just the four keys altogether. Hazel had two on a bunch. Daniel had two on another bunch. The night he died, Lawrence had Hazel's. Daniel's were with a workman on the mainland. And so, if someone wanted to go up after I left, Lawrence would have had to let them in.'

'Unless they had the key to the side door – we used to go in that way to arrange the flowers. The previous vicar didn't like the mess we ladies made.'

Susan nodded. 'Hazel showed me that old key. There is only the one, but she said that that door hadn't been used for years.' Susan frowned.

'That's odd, actually. The police asked about the old key for the side door, and we looked for it. It wasn't there, but it had been in the drawer earlier in the evening. I'm sure of it.'

'Didn't the police wonder where it was?'

'Not really. They didn't really seem too bothered. They were mainly concerned about the front door. It was the main entrance.'

'But I don't see why someone shouldn't have gone in through that side door.'

'You're right, and if the key to that door has disappeared, it's very odd.'

'You say it was there after that choir committee meeting but you couldn't find it when the police came in the early hours? If it had been removed, it had to be during that time. Who would have had access to it?'

Susan blinked. 'Well, I suppose only the people at the meeting. That was the vicar, Daniel, his wife, Jessie, Fiona, the deputy head, Cerys, the young teacher, me and Hazel and Ross.'

'And who else would have known Lawrence was going up the tower?'

'I don't see how anyone else would have known. Hazel only found out shortly before the committee meeting that the bell tower was now safe to go up. She told us at the meeting and it was then Lawrence decided to go up.'

They paused as the member of the care staff with the trolley approached them. 'Usual, Alice, milk, one sugar? And what about you, Susan?'

Susan was grateful for a cup of coffee, but soon they were able to resume their conversation.

'And so, the people who were at the choir committee meeting were the ones who knew he'd be up the tower and also had access to that side door key, as it was at that point in the drawer at Hazel's house?' said Alice.

'Exactly. Although why steal the key? They could have just called up to Lawrence to let them in.'

'Yes, but you know how it is around that church at night. Sound travels. Anyone passing would have heard them, and maybe they didn't want their visit broadcast around the village.'

'But why all the secrecy?'

'From what you have told me, there's a number of reasons why people at that meeting could be angry with Lawrence. There was obviously the row about Ross. Were there any other disputes with Lawrence?'

'I didn't mention what he said about Jessie and Daniel,' said Susan. 'He told me something had happened around Christmastime, and he'd been upset with Jessie and then he'd been shocked by Daniel much more recently. I think he had talked to them both, but they weren't too pleased. In the same way, he had told Ross that him and Cerys weren't suited.'

Alice tutted. 'Oh dear, he really did have a habit of interfering, didn't he? People don't like it, and you can't really blame them. I can't imagine a grown man like Ross would take any notice, but it could be different with Jessie or Daniel depending on what they had done. If it was a serious misdemeanour, and with them so involved with the school as well as the church, he might have felt he needed to act, and that could have been quite threatening.'

'You have a point there; he did say they were important people in the community.'

'Exactly, and of course there is this complaint – do you know any more about that?' asked Alice.

'No, nothing. There seem to be a few reasons why someone might want to talk to Lawrence, so they may have taken that key, but in the light of what happened, surely they would admit to having been there? I know it's not exactly something you'd want to shout about, but it's important information.'

'It would depend how that meeting went. If the argument had become heated and Lawrence had come to some harm, they are certainly not going to admit to being up there.'

'Oh, no!'

'But why not?' As so often in the past, Alice's bluntness shocked Susan as she continued. 'We have three possibilities. First, that it was an accident. This is what the police appear to accept, but we have questions about that. Then there is the possibility he took his own life.'

'I don't think so, and neither does Hazel.'

'From what you've said, it doesn't sound likely, although we need to know more about this complaint, I think. That only leaves one other alternative, and that is someone was involved in his death, either accidentally, or purposefully pushing him off the bell tower to a certain death. It would explain why no one has confessed to being up there with him.'

Susan pursed her lips, put her head to one side. 'I can see your logic. It would have to be a violent fight to push someone off that tower. Lawrence would have done anything to avoid going close to the edge. I suppose we'll know more when they've done the post-mortem. The idea that someone went up with intent to kill him is so, well, so extreme.'

'Yes, and fortunately premeditated murder is rare. But there are some people who are prepared to see it as an option. They will carefully plan to end the life of someone else.'

Susan glanced at an elderly lady dozing in the chair next to her. All so normal. And yet she and Alice were sitting here talking about the heart of a killer. Susan realised that while Alice might appear to have had a sheltered life as a shopkeeper in a small village, she had been observing, listening all these years. She had developed a real understanding of human nature, and she'd had the courage to face the darker and more disturbing sides of people.

'But is it really possible that someone in that group of choir members, teachers, health workers, a musical director, a vicar and his wife, would have killed a highly respected head teacher?' Susan asked.

'I am not saying it happened, but of course it's possible. Lawrence was respected but, on the day he died, he'd upset a lot of people.'

'True. He'd taken away the job of one of them, Ross, which in turn would affect his girlfriend, Cerys, and his stepmother, Fiona. Then there is the vicar, Daniel, and his wife, Jessie, who have so much invested in their work. Losing Ross was going to have a significant impact on their success at St Jude's.'

'Yes, you see there are possibilities. However, maybe we need to do a bit of checking around before we jump to that conclusion. Firstly, we need to know if that side door key was stolen. You need to check the key really is missing.'

Susan bit her lip. 'Robert told me not to make this into a case, but it wouldn't hurt to check about the key—'

'Of course not. I don't consider this a case either, but it won't hurt to ask a few questions. I shall be able to have a little dig around as well.'

'Really?'

'I'll have a chat with my cleaner, Barbara. As well as coming here, she also cleans the primary school. Most days she goes in about four but on a Friday, I believe she goes in much later, about half seven to half nine. Barbara likes it because, apart from Fiona, she has the place to herself, and she gets on better with her work.'

'So, she could have been in there the evening Lawrence died?'

'I happen to know she was and that she overheard some discussion between Lawrence and Fiona last Friday,' said Alice. 'I'd like to know more about that.'

'Goodness, how on earth did she come to tell you about that?'

'We always have a good chat. I admit I do love to hear all the gossip and she knows that. Of course, she was full of the news about Lawrence when she came in yesterday. She said something like it was sad that the last conversation Fiona had with Lawrence had been an argument.'

'Did she? Fiona said she didn't speak to Lawrence after the meeting,' said Susan.

'Well, Barbara told me she did. Barbara also told me that she'd seen that young teacher, Cerys, crying with Lawrence last Thursday after school. She said there seemed to be a lot of tension around.'

'Hang on, why does that ring a bell? Last Thursday? Oh, yes, on Friday, when we were walking to Hazel's after choir, I heard Ross ask Cerys if she'd found her purse and she said Lawrence had returned it to her the night before. I wonder why she'd been crying?'

'I'll try and find out a bit more about both conversations,' said Alice. 'And, of course, I could talk to my daughter and granddaughter. They are both teachers. My daughter is at the high school so won't know much of the gossip about the primary school here, but my granddaughter, Laura, is teaching in the primary school close by. Yes, she may have heard things on the grapevine.'

'Could you ask her if she knows about any sort of rumours of a complaint against the school?'

'I certainly will. It's the sort of thing that gets talked about in staffrooms.' Alice sat forward. 'Oh, of course there's a church service coming up on Friday, here at the home. I don't usually go but it will be a really good chance to meet Daniel and hopefully his wife, Jessie. I've heard she comes as well.'

Susan smiled. 'It never ceases to amaze me how you manage to bring the world to you.'

'I try. Now, do send Hazel my condolences. I'm so sorry. And we'll have a chat next week. It will be very interesting to hear if you can find that key.'

Susan's opportunity to find out more about the key came the next morning when Hazel asked her to call round.

12

Susan went to Hazel's early in the morning. Hazel had a police officer coming to see her and she had asked Susan to be there with her. While they waited, they had coffee and chatted.

'By the way,' said Hazel, 'I don't know if I mentioned it to you, but I've been worried about Lawrence's silver pen. I'd asked the police to look out for it as it's valuable.'

'I remember seeing it. Lawrence showed it to me.'

Hazel eyes widened. 'He did? Gosh, I'm so glad you saw it because I've now been told they can't find the pen. They said I must have made a mistake. I had to admit I hadn't seen Lawrence actually put the pen in his rucksack that night, but he always had it with him.'

'I'm sure he did. I saw him write with it.'

'But that is so odd. Where is it then? The police officer told me there were other cheap pens in the rucksack. They said he must have used one of those.'

'They're wrong. I saw it.'

'Oh dear. It's like this side door key. I told them that's missing. I keep checking the drawer.'

Susan went over and checked again. 'It's definitely not in here.'

Eventually, DC Kent arrived. After a short chat, they returned to the matter of the key. The police office looked in the drawer.

'There are a lot of old keys in here,' she commented. 'Are you sure the one for that door is definitely not one of these?'

'Yes, I'm positive,' said Hazel. 'It was more elaborate, had a Celtic cross on the top, enclosed in a twisted metal circle.'

'And so, when was this side door last used?'

'It's not been used for years.'

DC Kent suggested they go over to St Jude's, and checked the front door keys had been returned to Hazel by the police. Hazel assured her that she had them.

Susan could see the stress on Hazel's face, and smiled kindly. 'Come on, I'll be with you. Don't worry.'

She put her arm through Hazel's, and they left the house. They went into the churchyard, towards the main door, and then left, past where Lawrence's body had been found. On the other side of the bell tower was a small wooden door that Susan had never noticed before. Although the path was quite clean gravel, there was a large muddy patch before the stone slab in front of the door.

'We won't walk on the mud; I'll take some photographs for now. You could show me inside the church.'

They went inside and walked down to the side door. There was no mat in front of the door, but the stone slabs were clean.

'Have the cleaners been in since Friday?'

'No, no one has been in.' Hazel looked down at the floor. 'I suppose it's surprising there's no mud if the door was used.'

'Yes, it is odd.'

'But the only reason the key could have disappeared is because someone took it, and why would they take it if not to use it?' asked Susan.

'I agree it seems odd, but things go missing and turn up again. Look, why don't we sit down, I have something I need to tell you.'

The police officer sat on a pew. Hazel sat next to her. Susan remained standing opposite them.

'As you know, Hazel, the post-mortem was carried out yesterday. I managed to get hold of the initial report before coming here. We hadn't suspected it, but it confirmed for us that Lawrence had not taken any form of drugs or alcohol. There were no injuries to suggest a fight or confrontation and we have no physical evidence to suggest the presence of anyone else up in the tower with your husband. No drink cans, no cigarette butts, nothing that did not belong to Lawrence.'

Hazel frowned. 'But I'm still worried about some aspects of this. I keep thinking someone else must have gone up there after Susan.'

The police officer continued. 'I promise you we've looked into everything. The front door was locked, and Lawrence himself had the front door key to the church, the only key available that evening. We found his torch by the lower part of the wall where he fell, and it would be a fair assumption he'd gone to the edge to look down at some kind of wildlife. I know he didn't normally but if it had been an unusual sound, he might have been tempted. We can't explain why the binoculars were not attached to the pouch, but there could be all sorts of explanations for that. Maybe he'd not hitched them on properly after Susan used them, something like that.'

'But what about the pen? That's missing.'

'As we explained, there were other pens in the rucksack, so perhaps he'd lost the silver pen a while back and didn't like to own up. Hazel, you told us you hadn't actually seen the pen for a few weeks. Isn't that right?'

'Well, yes, but Lawrence told me he had it with him and Susan saw him using it.'

'But Lawrence didn't take it out and show you?'

'Well, no.'

'He may not have realised he'd mislaid it. As for Susan seeing it, well, it must have been hard to see in that light. He had an assortment of pens, not just cheap plastic ones either. One was a golden colour, it would have shone in the torchlight. Now look, superficial examination of the door this side suggests the door wasn't used. However, I will organise for scene of crime officers to come along, check the area, dust for prints.'

'But where is the key?' asked Hazel.

'Maybe it will turn up. I think I've seen everything I need to today.'

Susan glanced around, remembering walking down the aisle with Lawrence, the blackened windows, the only sound their feet on the cold, hard stone. It was still quiet today, still cold, but light shone in through the stained-glass windows, the brass cross on the altar glistened, and, although the flowers were wilting, there was no sense of threat, no sense that some terrible tragedy had happened. Maybe they had been letting their imaginations run away with them.

DC Kent stood up and they left the church.

Once they were outside, she turned to Hazel and spoke more softly. 'Try not to worry or let others put ideas into your head. We have everything under control. You need to trust us. Remember, you can get in touch any time.'

With this, she left. Susan winced. 'Well, she put me in my place.'

'I don't care. She didn't answer our questions, did she?'

'I don't know. She had a good go at it, and some of the things she said made sense. Maybe Lawrence didn't attach the binoculars properly, and he might have heard something unusual, I suppose, and leant over—'

'But we know the key has been taken and the pen has disappeared. I'm sure Lawrence would have known if he'd lost it, and you were so certain you'd seen it. I know I'm right about this.'

Susan blinked. 'Goodness, you've not been thrown by what she said at all, have you?'

'No. I guess the initial shock has worn off and I'm less numb,' said Hazel. 'The side door key was stolen, and it must be by someone going up to Lawrence. To me, the questions are: who that was and what happened when they were in the tower?'

'But the detective seemed pretty convinced no one had used that side door.'

'I know, but that was only because there was no mud on the floor. Maybe it had been cleaned up somehow.'

'But she also said there was no evidence of anyone having been up there, and no injuries to Lawrence.'

'Yes, I realise that, but say the person who went up had been careful, not left anything behind, not even had a physical fight... they could have pushed Lawrence without marking him...'

Susan sat, wide-eyed. Hazel seemed to be rushing ahead of her now. 'You make it sound almost premeditated, as if someone knew what they were doing.'

Hazel nodded. 'I know, and that's a terrible thing to imagine someone doing, but the more I think, the more likely it seems to me that that is how it happened.'

'But who do you think would have done this?'

'I hate to admit it, but it must be someone in the committee meeting. There was a lot of anger at that meeting, and maybe someone was even more upset than they appeared.'

They wandered over to a small wooden bench in a patch of sunshine that had come out from behind the clouds. The bench was among the old gravestones and Susan was struck again by how different it felt here today. Now she could see brightly coloured wildflowers growing, bees and butter-flies flitting among them; a thrush sang in the old elm.

Hazel sighed. 'I hate thinking like this. These people are my friends. They're good people, and yet I have to suspect them.'

'It's not easy. I understand that.'

'I mean, if I go through them, it seems impossible. It can't be Fiona. She has always been so devoted to Lawrence. Despite this decision about Ross, I can't see her ever hurting him. There's of course Daniel and Jessie, but what motive could they have?'

'Well, Lawrence ending Ross's contract affected their work. Jessie was very passionate about them doing the work on the church hall. It was going to make it a lot harder not having Ross to support the fundraising.'

'But no one is going to kill over something like that, are they?'

Susan turned to face Hazel. 'When we were up the tower, Lawrence seemed to know things about both of them that concerned him. Have you any idea what it might have been?'

'Now you mention it, Lawrence did tell me he'd found out something about Daniel the Friday before he died, and I know that worried him. They'd had a meeting about money at school. I don't know if it was anything to do with that.'

'Lawrence was the church treasurer, wasn't he? Were there any prob-lems with the accounts, anything like that?' asked Susan.

'Not that I know of.'

'Lawrence said he was going to have a word with Jessie. I've no idea what was going on.'

'Ah, I think he'd tried to talk to Jessie, but I don't think he got very far. They've never had a very easy relationship. I know they crossed swords when Daniel and Jessie first arrived, over some form Lawrence needed them to fill out. Then, well, it must have been at Christmastime, Lawrence had a meeting with Ross and Jessie about some service they were putting on for Christmas. He came back in a foul mood. He wouldn't tell me what it was about. He just said he was upset with Jessie. That was it. He did also say to me that Jessie seemed to have expensive tastes for a vicar's wife, asked me details about her online business.'

'He obviously had his issues with Jessie then, and she was the most vocal at the committee meeting when he told everyone about Ross. I think there's more to find out about her and Daniel.'

Susan saw a delivery van drive into the school grounds. Further down, an elderly couple turned off the path walking towards the doctors' surgery, life carrying on as they talked.

'And what about Cerys?' Susan asked.

'I can't imagine she had anything to do with Lawrence's death. She is very sweet.'

'And she had hurt her foot. I can't see how she could have gone up a tower. What about Ross?'

Hazel shrugged. 'I suppose he does look a bit rough and ready, and he was going to lose his job because of Lawrence. I really don't know. Now I think about it, it seems mad to be suspecting any of them of anything. Maybe I should just listen to the police.'

'That's your choice, of course, Hazel. There may never be answers to your questions anyway.'

'I would love to ignore them, but I know I can't find any kind of peace if I've not at least tried to find some answers.' Her hand went to the wedding ring hanging on a chain around her neck. 'I have to do this for Lawrence. You understand, don't you? It's how you felt with that girl over in Ventnor, isn't it?'

Susan grimaced. 'It is, but trying to get answers was hard. You can end up offending friends, even losing them if you start asking uncomfortable questions. And this is your community. You need their support now. All the goodwill you need to heal and settle back into life here could be lost.'

Hazel sat upright. 'Lawrence was my soulmate.' Her voice broke. 'He was my world. I have no one else. No children, no close family.' She covered her face with her hands and sobbed. 'I must do something. I just don't know where to start. I have never felt so tired and so alone.'

Susan put her arm around Hazel. 'You are not alone—'

'Will you help me?'

Susan took a deep breath. She'd sensed this question coming and she'd known since talking to Alice that she wanted to find answers to some of these questions. 'Of course I will.'

'Thank you. But what can we do?'

'It might be better for you to step back. I can chat to people, maybe look at what they were all doing after the choir committee meeting.'

'You would really do that?'

'I can't promise anything, but I can try.'

Hazel grasped her hand. 'I don't know how to thank you.' She looked over at the gate. 'I should be getting back. Thank you.'

Susan watched Hazel walk away, but she stayed on the bench a little longer, mulling over what she'd heard, trying to decide what she should do next. She didn't regret offering to help Hazel. She understood her need for answers and felt she deserved to feel someone was listening to her. After her experiences in Ventnor, she also knew that if by any chance there was a killer here, then what she was embarking on could be very dangerous indeed.

She left St Jude's and walked home. Once there she sat on the sofa, the dogs either side of her, and her mind went back to Hazel.

'This has been quite a morning. How am I going to help Hazel?' she asked them. 'Robert is not going to be happy. However, he could be useful. I really could do with a bit of inside information here.'

She picked up her phone and sent him a text.

Are you able to check what Daniel (vicar) and his wife Jessie, Fiona and Cerys (also a teacher) and Ross told the police they were doing when Lawrence died? Also, can you check if any of them have a criminal record?

Almost immediately after she'd sent the text, her phone rang.

'What's going on?' asked Robert.

Susan explained about Hazel's request.

'Does Hazel really need you stirring things up like this?'

Susan tutted. This was just the kind of thing that irritated her about Robert. Steve seldom questioned her actions, seemed to trust her judgements on most things. Robert was far more likely to interfere.

'I am not stirring anything up. I am not putting any ideas in her head that she's not thought of already. I am simply listening to her and I respect the fact she has questions. She has asked for my help, and I will give it.'

She heard a brief sigh, but Robert replied in a more conciliatory tone. 'Look, I'll have a chat to one or two mates, see if I can find out anything, but don't go getting yourself too involved in this.'

She mumbled a reply and then ended the call. She had one more call to make. This was to Shiloh, the prayer centre Daniel went to on a Friday. She made an appointment to visit the following Monday.

13

FRIDAY

At the nursing home, Alice had a busy day ahead of her.

It started with the arrival of the cleaner, Barbara. Once they'd swapped the usual bits of news, Alice steered the conversation round to the Friday night Lawrence had died.

'I was thinking about you in the school. Did you hear anything that Fiona and Lawrence said to each other?'

Barbara drew herself in. 'I'm not one to listen at doors.'

'Of course not,' said Alice quickly. 'But if people shout you can't help but overhear them.'

Barbara appeared mollified. 'Oh, well, yes. I did overhear one or two bits, I have to say. It was Fiona that sounded upset and he was trying to calm her down. He said something about a fresh start, that was it, really. It was strange to hear them having words. They've always seemed so close.'

'They were close?' Alice raised an eyebrow.

'Not like that. No, we all thought it when he first came, what with him being good-looking, her single and up that school all hours. But no one saw him coming out that late. As far as we all knew, he left at a sensible time, no later than seven. No one has seen so much as a wistful glance between them, and he does seem to be very happily married.'

Alice smiled. Clearly the village had been waiting and watching, and no doubt secretly disappointed when that potential gossip dried up.

'You mentioned you'd seen the young teacher crying in Lawrence's office the day before?'

'Yes, she was, but she's so young. Maybe the kids had been playing up. I wouldn't want to teach some of them now. Children don't respect teachers like they used to.'

Alice interrupted. 'But you don't know what they were actually saying?'

'No, the office door was closed. There's a glass panel in the door so that's how I saw them. She looked a lot happier when I saw her later, excited even. I was cleaning her classroom and she asked me if I knew anything about those new flats they're building up the other end of the village. I wondered if she was planning to buy somewhere with her young man, Ross, the music master.'

Alice took her time to digest all she'd learned. It was impossible to know what would be important, and she had to try to remember as much as she could.

After lunch, Daniel and Jessie came to take the service and Alice tucked herself in a corner. She'd been to church often when she was younger and enjoyed the familiar hymns and prayers.

When the service had finished, Daniel and Jessie stayed for a cup of tea with the residents. Alice noticed Jessie happily mixing, laughing and chatting. Daniel looked more at a loss, and once he caught her eye, he seemed grateful to go and sit with her and stay in one place.

Once they'd covered the usual pleasantries, Alice found it quite easy to manoeuvre the conversation around to Daniel's own life.

'I, of course, have seen many vicars come and go in the village,' said Alice. 'I'm always so interested to know what brings people here. Do you have family on the island?'

'Oh, no, they live in Kent. I went to boarding school there.'

'How interesting, did you enjoy it?'

'I did. I wasn't sporty but I was always very academic and so it suited me down to the ground. My parents were very supportive of me, they came to all the awards days. I left, went to university to read chemistry. I enjoyed it, but the best part of university for me was being part of the drama society.'

Alice was surprised. 'You enjoyed acting?'

'I did. Anyway, I was thinking of going into research when I left university but instead I went to theological college,' said Daniel.

'I should imagine they would demand very high grades for research.'

She noticed his face go quite pink in indignation. 'I didn't become a vicar because I couldn't get into research. I graduated with a first. I would have had no trouble in moving on to do a PhD.'

'Sorry—'

He smiled. 'It's okay. I became a vicar because I wanted to do something meaningful with my life. My parents have always worked with people in need. They work for a charity. I wanted to follow in their footsteps, and they were thrilled at my choice. I have to say I struggled, but then clergy are not called to an easy life, are we? It's all about service. And through it, of course, I met Jessie.'

'You met her at church?'

He grinned. 'No, at a café. I went in for a drink regularly and we got talking. She came to our church and slowly her faith grew. When I asked her to marry me, she was unsure: not about me, but about her role as a vicar's wife. But I persuaded her and I'm so glad I did. People love her and, of course, so do I.'

He smiled over at Jessie, who was sitting with an elderly gentleman who was laughing at a story she was telling.

'A lot of partners of vicars nowadays have other jobs, but Jessie seems to just work with you.'

'Oh, she has her small business online, selling things she has picked up at car boot sales. She has her own account, just spending money, gives her a bit of independence.'

'Now, I have an idea,' said Alice. 'I understand that new teacher at the school, Cerys, sings, doesn't she, with the musical director, Ross?'

'I believe they sing in pubs together.'

'Yes. Now, I was wondering if they would come here, sing to us oldies. It would be such a treat. Could you ask them?'

'Of course,' said Daniel. 'Um, I'd better check with the manager first.'

'Oh, yes, though she's always trying to come up with activities for us.'

'Maybe Cerys could come and chat to you all about a visit from the children. I could ask her; would that be helpful?'

'That would be perfect. I'd love to meet her.'

'You know, that could be a great idea. Yes, I'll have a word with the acting head teacher about it.'

He left Alice, walking quickly away, missing the satisfied look on Alice's face.

Alice had one more visitor that day and that was her granddaughter, Laura, who usually popped in on a Friday when her children were at their after-school clubs.

'I'm sorry I'm late, Gran. I dropped the kids off, but would you believe it, a parent of one of the children I teach nabbed me and was asking me if her child could have more homework, poor thing. Anyway, how are you?'

'I'm very well, love. How are the children?'

They settled back for their usual chat, but it wasn't long before Alice was able to bring up the subject of the complaint at the village school.

'I was just wondering if you had heard anything on the grapevine?'

Laura laughed. 'You never did like to miss out on the gossip, did you, Gran? I don't know how you picked that one up. They are trying to keep it all very hush-hush. Funnily enough, the deputy head at my school mentioned yesterday that she had heard a rumour that they were investigating an anonymous complaint about the SATs testing.'

'Sorry, SATs?'

'Those are the exams they make children do now in year six. It's all very official. The papers are delivered to the school. The head is not allowed to open them until the day of the test and there are very strict regulations about how they are carried out. I've no idea what they are meant to have done wrong.'

'I see. So maybe somebody thought they were fixing the results?'

'I guess so, but as it's Fiona's class, I find that highly unlikely. She's a real stickler for doing things properly.'

'Well, I expect we'll know more soon enough.'

'You will, Gran, probably before me.'

* * *

Susan's daughter, Zoe, her partner, Fay, and baby Jamari arrived mid-morning the next day.

Susan was nervous, not only for her first visit from the family to her new home, but also to hear this news, whatever it was, about Steve.

As she helped them in, Susan was amazed at the amount of stuff they had brought with them and watched as they made numerous trips back and forth to the car.

Zoe was very slim and athletic, could be frighteningly direct, and always seemed to be dashing about. Fay was much calmer, took things quietly. She had long brown hair, was curvy, soft and gentle.

Fay handed Jamari to Susan. 'There you are, Nanna.'

Susan held Jamari gently and sat down, overwhelmed again at her feelings for this little one. As she gazed on her she recognised Zoe's large, watchful eyes, and it took her back to the days of holding Zoe as a baby.

'This is so sweet, Mum,' said Zoe, looking around the room. 'But how are you going to cope with somewhere so small? Are you sure about this? Those stairs look pretty steep.'

Susan sighed. 'Of course I'm sure. I will be fine on the stairs for a long time, and I am just going to have to keep my stuff to a minimum. Speaking of which, I have boxes for you to look through in the garage.'

Once they'd all had a drink, they decided to take Jamari for her first visit to the beach. As they drove, memories of taking Zoe down to the beach came flooding back to Susan.

In the car park, Zoe carefully took Jamari out of her car seat and strapped her into a baby carrier. Susan could see Jamari was awake and her eyes wide, peeping out. Fay and Zoe talked to her all the way down the path, telling her about the sea and the sand.

Once on the beach, Jamari's eyes were even wider as she took in all the new sounds, smells and sights around her. This was one of those baby 'firsts' that Susan felt honoured to be part of.

Fay had not grown up by the sea, and although she'd been to the beach many times, you could see that excitement, that special 'we're on holiday' feel.

Watching Zoe was quite different. Susan saw her shoulders relax. She lifted her face to the sky. She was at home. The beach had always been a special place for Zoe. She'd loved it from her first visit. Susan had seen so many reactions from the foster children she and Steve had brought down over the years. Some were quite frightened, and she could understand that. The sheer scale of the beach, the crashing of the waves, could be overwhelming. But Zoe was like Susan. She loved to be immersed in the sounds and smell of the beach.

'I can't wait for Jamari to take her first steps down here,' said Zoe. 'I want her to feel the sand between her toes. Dad used to hold my hand and we'd walk up and down together. Then we'd dig deep holes, look for Australia. It was such a lovely time.'

'It was wonderful,' said Susan, and she looked around. 'You know, all our beaches on the island are so special. You will always find fossils. The island remembers everyone who comes here, I am sure of that, and those who are born here, and their children, are even more part of its heritage.'

They walked on.

Zoe placed her hand on Susan's arm. 'Mum, you know I had something to tell you about Dad?'

Susan held her breath and Zoe continued.

'Well, you know Fay and I don't go to church, well, we'd still like to hold a celebration for Jamari. Our idea is to actually hold two celebrations, one in Scotland and one on the island.'

Susan screwed up her eyes, waiting to see where Steve came into this. 'That's a lovely idea, and your dad?'

'We need to organise things on the island soon as Dad and Hester are off on their travels for the summer. It would have to be in a fortnight, two weeks today. Would that be all right with you?'

Susan felt a rising panic but, seeing the concern on Zoe's face, replied as calmly as she could. 'That's rather short notice, but I've nothing planned.' She was speaking with that forced casualness that all parents have used as their child springs events on them. Behind that hopefully calm exterior, her mind was rushing. What really bothered her was the thought of Steve and his partner Hester coming to her house. This was her space now. Everything in it was her. It was very personal. She'd never imagined Steve there. Suddenly she had to picture him walking around, judging her. And then there was Hester. So loud: too big for her cottage. She hated the idea of Hester in her home.

'Are you okay, Mum?' Zoe asked. 'If it's too much, Fay and I could hold it at our house.'

Susan realised the smile had slipped and that Zoe was looking at her with a mixture of concern and disappointment. At this point, she knew that she had to do this for her daughter. Steve and Hester's opinion of her house shouldn't matter any more. Fear of it certainly shouldn't be stopping her hosting the celebration of the birth of her granddaughter.

'Sorry, you know me. I was thinking of all the housework. It will be good for me, make me get on with sorting out the house.'

'It's Dad really, isn't it?' said Zoe. She was like her dad in a lot of ways. She didn't miss much.

'I admit it will be a bit of a challenge having him in the house, but it's got to happen sometime. Seriously, Zoe, this will be fine. Tell me what your plans for the occasion are.'

'Okay, well, we'll have family, and I thought you might like to ask people from the village. It will be a way of getting to know them. Hopefully, it will be sunny, we can just have food and drink, and then a short ceremony when we say words of welcome to the world for Jamari. I'd love to find someone who is used to holding this celebration, you know, to make it special, but it's very short notice.'

'The vicar in the village is young and I've a feeling he'd be open to a non-religious ceremony, if that is any help.'

'You don't think he'd mind? We're not having godparents or anything.'

'I'll text him first and give him time to tactfully decline. Let's see what he says.'

Zoe grinned. 'Okay, thanks. I'd like to ask some of my island friends.' Zoe mentioned some old school friends. 'And you could ask a few friends as well. You could invite Robert, and there must be others.'

'I guess so, yes, thanks.'

'It's a way of you getting to know them and, well, part of welcoming Jamari to the island. Oh, do you know anyone who could provide music?'

'There is Ross, our musical director. He plays and sings with a young teacher, Cerys.'

'That sounds great. Could you give me Ross's mobile? I'll see if they're free.'

They continued their walk; the dogs were off lead and having a wonderful time, but Jamari started getting restless.

'We're coming up to feed time, could we go back now?' asked Zoe.

Back at Susan's home, Fay and Zoe disappeared upstairs together with Jamari, while Susan prepared lunch. At the same time, she composed a text to Daniel. Susan reread the text a few times. It said everything she needed and if Daniel had any problems at all, she had given him a way out. She pressed send.

14

The reply from Daniel came quickly. He would be happy to be part of the celebration and, as he was gardening that afternoon and welcomed an excuse to have a break, he suggested popping around about two.

And so, after lunch, Susan, Zoe and Fay walked through the village with Jamari to the vicarage. 'You know, this is quite idyllic,' said Fay. 'I'm not surprised you wanted to move here. Mind you, Zoe told me about that accident the head teacher had. That must have been a terrible shock.'

Susan looked at St Jude's ahead of her. 'It was. The village is still coming to terms with it.'

'So, what side of the tower did he fall off?' asked Zoe with her father's characteristic bluntness.

'The one closest to us, although it's hard to imagine on a day like this.'

So far, Susan had resisted telling Zoe anything about her investigation. Zoe's world was completely consumed with Jamari, and that was quite enough to occupy her for now.

Daniel was out in the front garden and stood up as they approached.

'Ah, Susan, hello, and this must be Zoe and Fay?' He took off his gardening gloves, held out a hand self-consciously. Zoe grinned and shook his hand.

'Good to meet you, Daniel.'

'We'd better go into the back garden; Jessie is there.'

They followed him into the dark interior of the vicarage then through into the rear garden.

Jessie was wearing a short denim skirt, her signature large hooped earrings, gold chains and a pink cropped T-shirt, sitting in an old garden chair in a square of sunshine. For once she was missing her stilettos, but flip-flops displayed her carefully pedicured feet and immaculately painted toes.

She jumped up when she saw them. 'Hi, great to meet you. Um, we'd be better off sitting in the kitchen, one day we'll get enough garden chairs to sit out here with people.'

They all went back into the kitchen and sat down.

Susan introduced them all.

'I've got decent white wine in the fridge, or I've got some squash somewhere,' said Jessie.

Zoe laughed. 'I'm afraid I'm on the squash but I'm sure Fay would love a glass of wine.'

Daniel was standing at the edge of the group, holding a glass of water.

'I think Zoe and Fay want to talk to you about the celebration?' nudged Jessie.

'Yes, of course. Tell me what you had in mind.'

Zoe looked at Daniel and explained her vision for the day.

'I see exactly what you want, and I'd be very happy to act as celebrant,' said Daniel. 'You'd be surprised at how many requests I get like this. To me the main thing is to celebrate what must be the most special event in the world, new life. I have orders of service I have used before on my laptop. Do come and have a look.'

Susan thought it best to leave Zoe and Fay to sort out the details and they went off, taking Jamari with them, to Daniel's study.

She noticed some stuffed toys on a table behind Jessie. 'Are you collecting for something?'

'No, these are some of my purchases from the latest car boot sale. I sell them in my online shop.' Jessie stood up and picked up one of the toys. 'See this Minnie Mouse, she's a hand puppet. Now I picked her up for a fiver, but I reckon I will start the bidding on Flexee at fifteen pounds.'

'Really?'

'Yes, I've got to know now what sells. I've not had any big finds, you know, some rare Steiff bear, but I've had a few good finds.'

'That's great.'

Jessie sat back down. 'So, this is your first grandchild?'

'She is.'

'It's great you are so close to your daughter and her wife. It's a relief to talk about something happy after the week we've had, isn't it? The phone hasn't stopped, people needing to talk to Daniel. Everyone has been so affected.'

'Of course, and it's good they can turn to Daniel. He led the service at the school well.'

'Yes, he's really good at that kind of thing, knows what to say.'

'I love the idea of the Hope Garden.'

'Yes, it will be good for the children, something they can "do" if you know what I mean. I reckon even the adults are a bit stumped by that, and it must be awful for Hazel. I mean there is nothing she *can* do; she can't even organise a funeral at the moment.' Jessie took a long sip of her wine, winding the long gold chains around her fingers, before she continued. 'I heard about this business with the old side door key for St Jude's going missing. The police came and asked Daniel about it. He told them it was with Hazel, but that it's not been used for years. They said Hazel was worried about not being able to find it.'

'Yes, she'd shown it to me after the committee meeting at her house but hasn't seen it since. She thought she should tell the police.'

'But why? Why was she looking for it and why did she tell the police?'

Susan was aware of the intensity of Jessie's questions. 'Hazel has some concerns about Lawrence's death, and she wants to be sure that nobody, after me, had been up to see him. She wondered if someone could have used that side door to let themselves into the church.'

'Do the police think someone else went up there?' demanded Jessie.

'Not that I know of.'

'Right then, and this key – it's a bit mad that someone would have gone to all that trouble of nicking a key to sneak up to Lawrence. I mean, if they'd needed to see him, why not holler up to him?'

Jessie was sitting forward, glaring at Susan. Susan felt under attack, as if this was an interrogation.

'I suppose Hazel thinks it's possible someone wanted to go up there secretly to surprise Lawrence.'

Jessie screwed her eyes up sceptically. 'What? Someone crept up there. But why?' She sat back, laughed coldly. 'You're not thinking someone went up there to pick a fight or something?'

'I don't know,' said Susan. 'However, there are a few things that suggest it wasn't simply an accident. For example, Lawrence's pen is missing and, of course, the old church door key must be somewhere. I am just trying to help Hazel find some answers.'

'It seems to me that these questions are a bit petty and the way you could best help Hazel is to encourage her to accept what the police say. She needs to grieve for her husband.'

'I agree, but she doesn't feel she can do that yet. She asked me to help and I think she deserves the truth.'

'Well, you be careful digging around. You never know what you'll find.' Jessie shot her a look that was so unlike her normal persona. It was hard, defensive, cold. There was a definite feeling of threat in the air and Susan felt distinctly uncomfortable. She was very relieved to see Zoe and Fay return with Daniel and, as it was time for Jamari's feed, they were able to leave.

They had a quiet evening, life revolving around the baby's feeds and sleeps. The next day they went back to the beach, and then to the local pub for a Sunday roast. Zoe also went through her boxes in the garage and, given the alternative of taking what she wanted to her own home, it was surprising how much she was willing to throw away or be taken to a charity shop.

By the time Zoe was ready to leave, she looked a lot more relaxed. 'Thank you so much, Mum. This has been just the break we needed. I know all the routine continues, but it's great to do it somewhere else, and to spend time with you. We'll be back in two weeks.'

'And will you be staying?'

'Oh, no, I meant to say, we will only be coming over for the day. We'll bring the car, though. Fay is making the cake and we have so much stuff for

Jamari. Would you be okay to organise the food? Sorry, I should have talked to you properly about this.'

'As long as you're not looking for anything fancy, I can do it, but you need to give me numbers.'

'Great. Oh, and Dad and Hester will only be coming for the day as well, so you've no one to put up.'

Susan smiled. 'I'm relieved not to be hosting them, but if you and Fay change your minds, well, there is always a room for you all, you know that.'

After they had left, Susan slumped into the sofa. The visit had gone well, and she was pleased to be able to give her daughter and Fay a break.

She mulled over Zoe's visit. Despite what Zoe said, it might help to have a few bits and pieces here for them, maybe a cot, spare baby clothes or nappies, and hopefully this had only been the first of many visits. It was difficult, though. She wanted to make sure that Zoe and Fay were happy with whatever she bought. The only way to do that would be to go over to Southampton, get some ideas and then maybe text photos to Zoe to choose. Yes, she would go over next week.

It was early evening, when Susan was getting ready to take the dogs out, that Robert contacted her as he was over on West Wight and wondered if she fancied walking the dogs together.

They met down at Brook Beach. Susan arrived at the car park to find Robert waiting for her with Gem Gem and Dougie.

The dogs were all pleased to see each other. It was past eight now and the beach was deserted. The dogs ran off, Rocco and Libby keeping close to each other.

'What brings you over this way?' Susan asked.

'Oh, a few matters to attend to.'

Susan raised her eyebrows in surprise. It wasn't like Robert to be evasive, but glancing at him, she could see he wasn't going to elaborate, so she moved on to ask if he had managed to find out anything from one of his police officer friends about Lawrence's death.

'I was lucky. My friend Paul, who you met, is mates with one of the officers on the case. He was able to tell me a few things.'

'Are they accepting it was an accident?'

'It must be the most logical conclusion. However, don't just assume they are taking the easy way out here. They've been digging around a lot more than you realise, looking for motives and opportunity. They have taken on board the row at the choir committee meeting, and this side door key.'

'The key has to be significant.'

'They were interested, of course, but as there is nothing else to suggest foul play, they would take some convincing that someone had stolen the key and used it to go up the tower when Lawrence was there,' said Robert. 'Anyway, they did send SOCO along, but there was no evidence of fresh mud brought in, the floor was very clean, no footsteps in the mud outside either.'

'But where is the key? It's definitely not amongst the other old keys.'

'If there were a number, maybe Hazel made a mistake.'

'No, she knew which was the old side door key. It was very distinctive, with a Celtic cross on the top.'

'Without any other physical evidence, I don't think they're going to do much more about the key, to be honest,' said Robert. 'As for alibis, Cerys and Ross were together, and of course Cerys hurt her foot very badly. They checked the hospital records; she wouldn't have been climbing any towers. They went to Shiloh, the prayer centre. Daniel was signed in. Jessie's gym doesn't have anyone on reception, you swipe your membership card when you enter and leave. There is a record of her entering that night but not of her leaving. However, she says the machine wasn't working very well. They checked this and she was right, the machine has just been replaced. Fiona was at the school; CCTV shows she didn't leave the building before one.'

'I see.'

'He said that Ross had some involvement with the police a few years ago, but couldn't give any details. However, there was someone with an actual criminal record.'

15

'Really, who is that?'

'The vicar's wife: Jessie.'

Susan gasped. 'She has? What has she done?'

'Well, she's never been to prison, but she did receive a suspended sentence for shoplifting,' said Robert.

'When was this?'

'When she was twenty-one. She had been stealing things like expensive perfume and luxury make-up brands.'

'So, she has a record for that?'

'Yes, and that would show on a DBS form. It's not necessarily going to stop her getting employment as the crime wasn't violent or abusive, but it's there.'

'I see, and it might make her reluctant to apply for jobs, particularly here on the island. She'd be reliant on people's discretion, and we know how hard that is. Lawrence must have known. She told me he asked for her DBS form to go into the school, and now I realise why she was so upset about it. I'm guessing she has managed to keep this from Daniel. There's something that doesn't add up, though. Lawrence said he was upset by something she did at Christmas.' Susan paused, her eyes widened, 'Oh, no, you don't think he caught her stealing or something, do you? He said to

Hazel he thought she had expensive tastes. I know she has this online business—'

'Has she? That could be a cover for selling on illicit goods.'

'That hadn't crossed my mind. Maybe I should have a look at it. Daniel mentioned the name of the website. I shall look it up. By the way,' continued Susan, 'Hazel said they'd done the post-mortem; do you have any idea about time of death?'

'Ah, yes, surprisingly accurate. Someone actually walked through the churchyard and past that side of the tower at 9.50, and there was no body there on the ground. The autopsy indicated 9.30 to 10.15 based on digested food, so the time of death must have been between 9.50 and 10.15. This theory is further strengthened by the fact that the ground below the body was dry, we know the rain started about ten past ten.'

'I remember, it really was heavy, and it started from nowhere. That's a pretty narrow window then for someone to go up the tower.'

'Yes, but it doesn't seem very likely,' said Robert. 'There's no sign of a struggle, though granted the wall is quite low and it wouldn't take a lot of force to push him over. He wasn't a big man.'

'What do you believe happened then?'

'I would say his death was accidental. The police aren't cutting corners here. They do have a new case, a spate of awful attacks on homeless people, one killed at the bus station. Nasty, but I'm sure if they had reason to suspect anything with Lawrence's death they would carry on.'

'I can understand that, but I still believe there is more to this,' said Susan. 'I have promised Hazel I will investigate it, and I have to keep my word.'

'I know you don't like me interfering, but be careful. Don't go getting everyone's back up. You're new to the village, and there's probably nothing in this.'

She scowled but didn't reply.

'Look, Susan, I only say these things because I care,' Robert said quietly. 'I'm not trying to control you or take over. I've dealt with controlling men in my job. I'd be really upset if you thought of me like that.'

She looked up at him, she could see he was serious, and she'd hurt him. 'I don't see you like that, but I need to make my own decisions. In this instance, I believe finding out the truth for Hazel matters more than what people think of me, and I'm sure you'll agree that is my choice to make.'

His face relaxed. 'Okay, I can see what you are saying. I'll try to stand back—'

Susan nodded. 'Thank you.'

His face burst into a grin as he put his arm around her shoulders, gave her a quick hug, and then let go. 'There we are then, friends again.'

They continued to walk along the beach around the point to the eastern end of Compton Bay. Susan's irritation started to melt away, and she began to take in the beauty of the evening.

They sat together watching as an invisible hand painted the sky with streaks of yellows, orange and pink. The sun itself was transformed into a burning globe on the horizon.

'It's a long time since I've seen such a stunning sunset,' whispered Susan.

She looked at Robert and could see the reflections of the colours glowing on his face. He turned to her; their eyes met.

'I miss you,' he said quietly. 'It's not the same now, going down to the beach or up the downs with the other dog walkers.'

'I had to move; you know that.'

'But right over here? Have you seen anything of Steve?'

'Not since Jamari was born. He'll be coming over in two weeks' time. We're having a sort of baby welcoming party. It will be strange for him; he's not been back on the island since he left to go sailing.'

'Is he still with that woman?'

'Yes, still with Hester, and she will be coming over as well. You must come, you're part of the family now.'

'I hope so.' He leant forward and, for the first time, she didn't move away. His fingers gently traced the outline of her cheek and slowly his lips brushed against hers. He pulled back but their eyes remained locked together.

Dougie broke the spell by dropping a rotting fish at their feet. They both laughed and began to walk back towards the cars.

Susan was waiting to see if Robert would hold her hand or put his arm around her, but he did neither. Instead, he chatted and threw a ball for the dogs. She was relieved, the kiss was taking her time to process. It wasn't something she'd foreseen, and she wasn't sure how significant it was.

When they arrived at the car park, they wiped down the dogs and settled them in the cars. Susan was wondering if Robert would come over to her and maybe there would be another kiss, but he simply thanked her for a great walk, said he'd be in touch and got into his car.

However, when she arrived home, she was greeted by something so disturbing that all thoughts of Robert were driven from her mind.

Susan stared up at her house. She couldn't believe it. The evening was drawing in, but she could see the mess covering the cottage. Someone had thrown about a dozen eggs at it. Who would do something like that? Was it just kids messing around?

She glanced over at Hazel's. The house was in darkness, and when she knocked there was no answer.

It seemed too petty to be bothering the police about. Susan found her hosepipe reached through the house and so was able to use it to wash most of the egg off.

A car drove into the close as she was finishing off, and Hazel emerged from it.

Susan explained what had happened.

'That's awful, we don't have things like that happening here. Tracy from the shop invited me for a meal, otherwise I'd have been here to see who did this. Are you okay?'

Susan blinked. 'Yes, um, of course, just a bit shocked. Still, it's all sorted now.'

'Come and have a drink?'

'Um, I'll give it a miss if you don't mind. I need to get the dogs out of the car and settle them down. Thank you, though.'

Later that evening, Susan sat with the dogs, watching TV, but her mind kept going back to the mess on her house. Maybe it was a childish prank, but something inside made her feel it was more than that. But who else would have done such a thing?

* * *

Susan was glad she had the visit to Shiloh, the prayer centre, to take her mind off the events of the evening before. She had never been to a place like it before and had very little idea of what happened there.

She had planned carefully how she was going to approach the people at Shiloh. Unlike the police, she couldn't just turn up and question them about the organisation. Instead, she decided it would be better to look at it as a person interested in going to stay there.

The drive took her about fifteen minutes, and she parked in a small car park opposite the centre, next to the fields surrounding the beautiful motte-and-bailey castle.

As she stepped out of the car, she promised herself to bring the dogs over here soon. She could see plenty having their evening walk even now and it was a wonderful place for them to run. Apart from the splendid castle walls, she could see wonderful views across the valley. Looking back at her car, however, she knew she wouldn't want to leave it here overnight.

Coming out of the car park, she could see the old priory further up the road, a large, rambling Gothic building which she knew had once been a home for Dominican nuns.

To get to Shiloh, she had to go further down the hill and then cross the road.

She walked up the long gravel driveway to a large, old grey stone house, with turrets and arched windows. It was dusk now and the place felt rather creepy. She pressed a large bell and waited.

Eventually a woman answered the door. Despite her old-fashioned appearance, the plain skirt and blouse, the make-up-less face and owl-like glasses Susan hadn't seen for a decade, Susan guessed she was about thirty.

'I'm Susan, I have an appointment.'

'Ah, yes, come in. I'm Martha.'

Martha flashed a fixed smile, but Susan felt uneasy, as if this woman was judging her and she hadn't passed.

So, this was Martha, whom Jessie had mentioned. Susan walked into a deserted reception area, with bookcases and a desk. A hush seemed to envelop her. It was the kind of room you felt would always be cold.

'I will sign you in and then I'll show you around.'

On the desk was a large registration book in which Susan signed her name, email address and the time she'd arrived. There were several columns for signing in and out after that.

'We'll start downstairs and then go upstairs to the guest rooms.'

Martha unlocked a large door that led into a corridor, off which were a number of smaller sitting rooms, each with bookcases and flowers in vases.

'You can come and read in any of these. Some people stay in their rooms most of the time, some prefer to come down here. Through here is the café.'

Susan followed her into a room with rows of pine tables and chairs.

'We supply a basic breakfast, cereals and toast. Apart from that, you can come and buy meals. We also have a chapel that is open most of the day. You can join in a service or if there is nothing happening use it as a place of prayer.' She waved her hand in the direction of the chapel, and Susan noted the absence of a wedding ring.

They walked back to the reception, where Martha unlocked the door to the sleeping areas.

'These are self-check-in as we're run by volunteers and don't have the people to man a reception. You need to book in advance, then the day before you arrive you will be sent a code particular to your day of arrival. Come over here and I will explain the system.'

Susan followed her over to a locker with a keypad.

'You punch in your code, open this and take the keys for your room number. There are a number of keys. One for the door up to the bedrooms, one for your room, one for the front door and one for access to the rest of the centre. The doors down here are all self-locking, just in case people forget to lock behind them. That way we keep this area as secure as we can.'

'I'd have a key to the main door so I could go and come as I please?'

'The rooms are comfortable, and you have use of all the rooms downstairs as well as the chapel. However, you can go over the road for walks around the castle fields or down into the village, where there are a few pubs and shops. We like guests to sign in and out every time so that we always know how many people are in the building.'

'That sounds very safe. If I stay here, do I have to park opposite? I couldn't see any parking here.'

'You don't need to worry; we have secure parking behind the building.

Fortunately, it's not visible from the road. We'd have all the walkers asking to park here otherwise! No, your car is quite safe.'

'Thanks. That's good to know.'

'So let me take you to the rooms. We need to keep our voices down. It's important to respect the space up there.'

They went up thickly carpeted stairs, which led to a long corridor.

'The vicar of my local church, St Jude's, comes here most Fridays. Daniel Green. Do you know him?'

Martha broke into a warm smile. 'Oh, yes, he comes most weeks, so devout. He has occasionally led prayers in the chapel. He's the kind of person we were set up for.'

'Yes, I know he values it.'

Martha took her into one of the rooms. It was quite plain, just a bed and side table, a cross on the wall. It reminded Susan of a monk's cell. Looking around, Susan could appreciate the appeal of coming here, to shut out the world.

'Do many people come weekly like Daniel?'

'No, he's the only person who comes that regularly. There are other islanders who come often, but Daniel is our most frequent visitor.'

Susan looked out of the window and saw the neatly laid out allotments to one side of the large garden.

'We grow most of our own vegetables,' said Martha.

'It's very peaceful.'

They left the room and started to make their way downstairs, where they talked prices, including the fact that clergy were given a discount.

'Daniel mentioned someone called Alan.'

The sunshine in Martha's smile crept behind a cloud. 'He's one of our more colourful visitors. He always wears a large kind of cowboy hat and bright tops. He's a regular Friday night visitor and likes to go out walking in the evenings.'

'So, are Daniel and he friends?'

'I've never even seen them talking.'

Once they'd reached the reception, Martha said, 'I do hope you have found the tour helpful.'

'Thank you so much for your time.'

'It's a pleasure, now if you'd excuse me, I need to go and set up the chapel for the next service. There are a few leaflets here that explain more of what we do, and also some courses we have coming up. I'll leave you to peruse them and then do let yourself out. Lovely to meet you, Susan.'

With that, Martha hurried off. Finding herself alone in the reception area, Susan went straight to the register on the desk and opened it.

16

Susan easily found Daniel's name, and he was signed in every Friday evening for the past six weeks. She found the night Lawrence died. Looking around, she saw Martha was busy and so took out her phone, and quickly took a few photos of the page. She could read that he had indeed stayed the two nights, signing out on the Sunday. She saw that Alan Smithee had stayed there that Friday night as well.

'All signed out then?' asked Martha, coming over to her. 'I hope this has proved helpful.'

'Yes, thank you.' Once Susan was outside the building, she had an urge to shout and run about, like a child let out at playtime. She understood the centre aimed to create an air of tranquillity, but she'd found the atmosphere stifling and was glad to be out.

She decided to walk down to the village and along to the pub. There was a garden leading down to a large stretch of water and on an evening like this, with the light fading and yet still early enough for people to be milling around, it was very pleasant. She went and bought herself a lemonade and lime and decided to order fish and chips.

Out in the garden, she found a seat close to the water. There were swans gliding along, with three large cygnets following. Although they were indisputably beautiful, Susan was glad they kept away from her. Close to, she found them quite threatening. On the opposite bank she saw a prehistoric heron taking off, a sight that always made her catch her breath.

Her meal was brought quickly. It was enormous, and she knew she'd never eat it all, but the fish was fresh, and very tasty. At the table next to her, two couples sat, sharing a bottle of wine and laughing, and it was only noticing them that reminded her she was sitting alone. She'd not eaten out much on her own since Steve left. In theory she didn't see why it should bother her, but she felt the need to be doing something other than just sitting looking around.

As the evening drew in, Susan was aware of a screeching sound over the water, and she realised that these were the bats Lawrence talked about coming to see. It was a long name beginning with D, but she couldn't remember what. It was quite a spectacle to watch them, though.

Her mind went to her conversation with Lawrence about Daniel – what had been so shocking? What was it Hazel had said... the meeting at the school that lunchtime about money... was that it? As the church treasurer, Lawrence would have seen the books. Had he discovered inconsistencies? Had Daniel been stealing money from St Jude's? If he had, was that a strong enough motive for Daniel to kill Lawrence?

Although it wouldn't have been easy, she had established that Daniel could have left Shiloh unnoticed. People came and went. He could have left, driven over to the village, killed Lawrence, and returned. If he had done that it might explain his odd behaviour the following day, staying away and not returning to the village until the Sunday. Had guilt kept him away?

Susan wondered who would be doing Lawrence's work as treasurer now. She could find out if there was any hint of a problem in the books to test out her theory.

* * *

Early the next morning, Susan went into the village shop to buy bread and some milk. It was quiet in the shop, so the shopkeeper, Tracy, was eager to chat. She started asking about Hazel and how she was getting on, but it was clear she had some news to share.

'Now, did you know that Ross from the choir was seen going into Newport police station yesterday?'

'No, I'd not heard anything.'

Tracy's face fell. 'Oh, I thought you might have heard something. You see, Ross came in here last Friday evening to buy a packet of cigarettes and some cigarette papers. I asked him if he was going up the downs like he had the week before. He mumbled "no" and seemed a bit off with me. And then I remembered I had heard he said he'd been with Cerys all night. I wondered what to do, but then I heard someone saw him going into the police station.'

Susan's mind was buzzing.

'Are you sure about that?'

'Oh, yes. One of the mums was telling me her daughter works in the council offices opposite the police station. She saw Ross going in and wondered what was up.'

Susan grinned – the actual mechanics of how gossip spread around the village was fascinating.

'I'm sorry, I haven't a clue,' she replied.

As she left the shop, she was wondering about Ross and Cerys. Ross had clearly said he had been with Cerys at the time Lawrence died.

As she entered her close, she was pleased to see Ross was just leaving Hazel's. He waved to her, and Cerys walked over to talk to them both.

'I was just dropping off some more music for Hazel,' he explained. He looked down at the shopping she was holding. 'I guess you've just been to the shop?'

'Yes, I was talking to Tracy.'

'I bet she mentioned that I went into the police station yesterday.'

'She did.'

He laughed. 'Good God, this place doesn't need a newspaper. As soon as she said to me on Friday that she remembered me going in for cigarettes, I knew I needed to go and clear things up. How the hell everybody got to know where I'd been I don't know, but yesterday evening someone in the pub mentioned I'd been seen.'

Susan waited. She wanted to know what he had been doing in there too.

Ross grinned. 'Okay, I'll come clean. I wasn't with Cerys all that time on the Friday evening Lawrence died. I left her about quarter to ten, and went up the downs nature-watching with my friend Dave. It's all very straightforward and Dave can confirm the times I was with him. It takes about half an hour to walk up there, and I was with him by about ten past ten.'

'Why didn't you just say that then?'

'It was a stupid lie. I didn't want a fuss. Lawrence's death was obviously an accident so where I was didn't matter. I just didn't want the police involved in checking up on me again. It was daft and ended up looking far worse. Anyway, it's all cleared up now and the police are quite happy with my story, although a bit annoyed that they have to do all the paperwork now to correct it.'

Susan remembered Robert telling her that there had been some contact between the police and Ross a few years ago. She wondered what it was. Maybe it explained why he didn't want to get involved with the police again, but it was foolish to lie like that. She simply replied, 'It's as well to get your story straight.'

Hazel interrupted. 'You ought to go up on the downs with Ross one night. Lawrence and I have been a few times and I know Jessie found it absolutely fascinating.'

'Yeah, I love sharing my interest if you fancy it any time, Susan?'

'Yes, I would like that. I learned a lot just in the short time I was with Lawrence at the tower.'

'Are you free this Thursday?'

'I am.'

'Good. How about eight at the caravan? Wear decent walking shoes and a warm coat. I'll see you then.'

He walked off and Hazel tutted indulgently. 'It was silly to make up that story.'

'Yes, he should realise not much gets missed around here. Anyway, how are you keeping?'

'Just going through paperwork. It's amazing how much admin there is to do after somebody dies. It's a bit grim, to be honest, but it has to be done, so I'd better get on.'

'Of course. Well, if you fancy a coffee any time, I'm next door all morning.'

As soon as Susan had shut the door, she turned on her laptop. Looking down at the dogs, she smiled. 'I've got investigating to do. You two will have to amuse yourselves.'

Susan found the Flexee site and found the page for second-hand toys and collectibles. Scrolling down each item, she could see the name of the seller and address at the bottom. There were so many items, she wasn't sure where to start. Then she remembered the Minnie Mouse hand puppet. Maybe Jessie had put it up. She typed it in the search bar and was taken to several entries. Slowly she went through each of the sellers and found one called Jay, who lived on the Isle of Wight. Clicking on it, she was taken to another page; she was sure the seller was Jessie. Clicking on Jessie's history, she was able to see all the previous items she had sold. As Jessie had said, they were all second-hand toys and most around the twenty-pound mark. Nothing looked out of the ordinary. It all appeared straightforward.

Susan closed down the browser. Well, on the surface at least, it appeared Jessie was running a legitimate business.

* * *

After lunch, Susan set off for the nursing home to see Alice and it was with a feeling of anticipation that she drew into the car park. It would be good to talk to Alice. She had such clarity of thought, cut through a lot of the confusion that built up in Susan's head. She was also excited to find out if Alice had learned anything new. Susan was surprised to find her sitting in the armchair in her room when she arrived. As she entered the room, she saw Alice press something on her iPad and place some photographs down carefully on her table.

'Hi, what are you doing in here?'

'Oh, it's very exciting. My daughter Jo has asked me to help her write a book about our experiences of living in the village.'

Susan sat down. 'That's fantastic. You were right at the heart of village life running the shop.'

'I was, and of course I grew up in the village before that. I have seen so many changes. Jo has been busy sorting through photographs. Obviously, there aren't many of me when I was young. We didn't go round taking lots of photos in those days. What she wants me to do is to sit and talk into my iPad and record my memories. The recordings are to act as reminders. She's doing all the hard work.'

'That's so exciting. I'd love to look through the photos with you.'

'And I would love to show you. However, today we ought to concentrate on other things.' Alice placed her iPad with the photographs. 'So, tell me everything that has happened.'

Susan told her about the key but said that the police were sceptical about the relevance of its disappearance.

'I suppose there should have been mud inside. That's why we used to have doormats there.'

'It is odd, but I don't see why that has to rule out the door being used.'

'I agree. It could have still been used. Have they done the post-mortem yet?'

'Yes, they have,' said Susan. 'No sign of a fight. There's a time of death between 9.50 and 10.15, which is a helpfully narrow window. The police seem pretty convinced now that it was an accident. They pointed out that Lawrence might not have attached the binoculars properly, that the key might simply have been mislaid and that there were a number of pens in his rucksack. The smart silver one may have been lost some time ago and I was mistaken in what I thought I saw.'

'And do you agree?'

'No, and Hazel is starting to feel the same.'

'Is she? What has convinced her?'

'The missing key is the main thing for her, I think. Well, that and the pen. She believes I saw the silver pen. I'm sure I must have. I mean I'd not seen it before, and I was able to give a very good description of it.'

Alice smiled. 'Then I am sure you are right.'

Susan sighed, reassured by Alice. 'Thank you.'

Alice put her head to one side as she did. 'Good, now any other news?'

'I've just learned something hot off the press about Ross. He lied about being with Cerys the whole of the time that evening when Lawrence died.

He actually left her about twenty to ten, bought some cigarettes in the shop and then walked up the downs.'

'So, he lied to the police?'

'Yes, and of course Cerys did as well. She said she was with Ross from the time I dropped her off, until just before Jessie came home, but he'd left her before that. Ross says he just didn't want the police checking up on him, although he had nothing to hide. I'm guessing Cerys went along with it because she is besotted with Ross.'

'It could be that. I wonder why he is so reluctant to be involved with the police.'

Susan shared with her what Robert had told her about Ross.

'I see,' said Alice. 'I wonder what that involvement with the police entailed.'

'I have no idea.'

Alice sat forward. 'Barbara, my cleaner, had interesting things to share. She'd not heard much of this row between Lawrence and Fiona. She heard Lawrence saying something about a fresh start, but Fiona didn't look so happy.'

'I wonder why he thought Fiona should be moving on?'

'I can't imagine. You see, my granddaughter told me what she'd heard about this anonymous complaint. She is very friendly with the head of her school, who told her in confidence that she'd been told that the local authority had received a complaint about cheating in the SATs. They are taken by Fiona's class, but my granddaughter says she is sure Fiona would never have cheated.'

'I can't imagine it either, but it's a horrible thing to be accused of.'

'I also asked Barbara about the Thursday when she saw Cerys crying. Now, she couldn't hear anything, just saw her through the window of Lawrence's office. However, she did say Cerys was much happier when she returned to the classroom. Barbara wondered if she was planning to buy somewhere with her boyfriend, Ross, as she was asking about some new flats.'

'Unfortunately, I think the relationship means a lot more to her than it does to Ross.'

'Interesting. Now I need to tell you about Daniel and Jessie.'

Alice told her about Daniel's degree in chemistry, and how he'd ended up at theological college. 'The one thing he loved seems to have been taking part in the drama society. I believe he chose his vocation for the best possible motives, but it's not turned out quite as he hoped.'

'I tend to agree. Daniel talked to me about feeling he has played a part, and one he didn't feel very well prepared for. I wonder if going over to Shiloh is an escape from it all. I would love to know what he and Lawrence argued about. It crossed my mind it could be money; Lawrence did hint about it at the meeting.'

Alice frowned. 'I can't imagine Daniel misappropriating money. Everything for him is about doing the right thing, to the extent I should imagine it could be suffocating, stopping him experiencing new things. It could even be crippling him. No, I don't see him committing a crime for money.'

'Maybe not, but he has done something that, according to Lawrence, disturbed him,' said Susan. 'He'd mentioned to Hazel he'd been upset about something. By the way, I visited Shiloh, the prayer centre he goes to every Friday, and had a good look around.'

'How interesting. What was it like there?'

'I guess for some people it would feel very peaceful, but I found it rather claustrophobic. I don't know if that was because it was a rather bleak old building or the people there. I wouldn't find it very restful, but obviously Daniel does.' Susan told Alice everything she'd found out, adding, 'Daniel mentioned this chap Alan who goes out. I have the feeling Daniel sort of admires him.'

'What did you say his name was?'

'I think it was Alan Smithee. I did meet the woman who runs the place, Martha. She was pretty uptight, dresses years older than her age. Daniel called her a saint, but I got the impression Jessie was a lot less keen.'

Alice raised her eyebrows. 'Ah, maybe jealousy, and maybe not so stupid. Her husband does choose to go over there every Friday evening.'

'You think Daniel could be sleeping with her?'

Alice pursed her lips. 'There are many ways of being unfaithful, some more threatening to a marriage than sex.'

17

Susan looked at Alice quizzically and said, 'I'd not really thought about that but, of course, you're right. I've no idea if there is anything going on there. The main thing I did establish was that people staying could come and go as they pleased, so Daniel could have left there unobserved, if he wanted to. It would be too far to walk back to the village, but of course he had his car.'

'Good. So we've broken one alibi. We now know that Cerys and Ross were not together. Cerys couldn't have been making it up a tower with that foot – I suppose she had injured it as badly as she says?'

'You are suspicious, Alice. Yes, she ended up in A & E with X-rays, but I can check up on that. Ross walked up to the downs, but I only have his word for how long it takes to walk up there.'

'Jessie was over at the gym. Is that far?'

'Not by car, and we know she drove. She uses her membership card to get in and out. There is a record of going in but not leaving – apparently the machine was faulty and often missed recording people leaving.'

'That was convenient for Jessie. She could have left any time.'

'Yes, she could. Oh, and there is something important I learned about her...' Susan told Alice about the conviction for shoplifting.

Alice's eyes widened. 'Now, that is a surprise. It is definitely something she would want to be kept secret. Of course, it could have been a foolish mistake when she was younger, but people are not that forgiving.'

'Exactly. And what if it wasn't just in the past?' said Susan. 'I mean, why would Lawrence have been upset with her around Christmas?'

'Oh dear. I do hope she isn't still stealing.'

'When I was talking to Robert, I told him about Jessie's online business, and he wondered if that was a cover for selling things on. However, I've checked it, and it looks fine. I would like to find out more, though.'

'Yes, I think we need to know more about Jessie,' said Alice. 'I didn't get to speak to her when they came for the church service, but I did observe her. It seemed she was anxious to pacify Daniel, always on edge with him. That must be quite exhausting for a young girl like her. I should imagine she would also be very defensive of him.'

'Oh, yes. I saw it at the committee meeting. She was so angry when she thought Lawrence was attacking Daniel, but then she is a very passionate kind of person. She doesn't do anything half-heartedly.'

'No. I can't imagine she does. Now, back to the alibis. What about Fiona?'

'She was at the school,' said Susan. 'There is CCTV at both the main doors. It's hard to see how she would have got out without one of the cameras recording her. Then, of course, we need a motive. What have we got?'

'Ross was about to lose his job and Cerys was about to lose him. Ross is Fiona's stepson. It was quite a slap in the face for Lawrence to be forcing him out like that, and without even consulting her about it.'

'Yes, that's true.'

'I wonder about Cerys. She's a bit of a mystery. But, of course, if she's hurt her foot in the way she says then there's no way she could have climbed the tower and pushed Lawrence off it. I should be seeing her on Friday, actually. I received a message that she is coming in after school to arrange a time to visit with Ross. They are going to sing for us.'

'That's lovely,' said Susan, and grinned. 'Why do I have a sense of a bit of a set-up here?'

Alice smiled back. 'As if I would do something like that! However, it will be good to have a proper chat with her. I am guessing Hazel won't be working for a while, which is a pity. I'd like to talk to her too.'

'If you suspect her, she does have an alibi of sorts. She was at a Zoom meeting.'

'Oh, of course. And after all, we'd have to explain why she is raising all these questions about Lawrence's death. If she had killed him and the police are content to accept it as an accident, why make a fuss?'

'I agree,' said Susan. 'Also, she did appear to be genuinely shocked, and grief-stricken by what has happened.'

'It did cross my mind to wonder about Fiona and Lawrence, but there doesn't appear to be anything in that. Barbara was saying that everyone was waiting for some kind of romance to blossom between them, but nothing was ever detected, and I'm sure it would have been. No, I think we have to assume Lawrence was a faithful husband.'

Alice sat back. 'That's quite enough to be going on with, don't you think?'

'Yes, I quite agree.'

'Now, tell me, how is your gorgeous granddaughter?'

They talked about Zoe's visit with her family and Susan showed Alice some photos. She mentioned that she was planning to travel to Southampton the next day to buy some baby things ready for future visits, and Alice asked if she could pick her up some ladies' socks, John Lewis's own brand, with flowers or bees on for her daughter's birthday.

'It would be lovely to give her something other than just money for a change.'

Susan returned home, started to sort out a few things for the next day, checking timetables for the Red Jet, and the weather forecasts. She hadn't seen Robert since the evening they kissed on the beach. They'd swapped a few texts, but neither mentioned it and she was worried that Robert might secretly be regretting it. However, he had mentioned a few times about coming over. She sent a text and asked him if he would mind coming to look after the dogs while she went to the mainland, and he replied that would be fine. He'd see her the next day.

* * *

Robert arrived at half past seven in the morning with his dogs Dougie and Gem Gem. He was very much a morning person and looked as if he'd been up a few hours already. As Susan was on an early Red Jet, they had little time to chat but, as she left, the dogs looked very settled, ready for their day together.

As Susan drove off, she saw Cerys standing at the bus stop at the bottom of the close.

Winding down the window, Susan shouted, 'I'm going to Cowes, to the Red Jet. Do you need a lift?'

Cerys hobbled over to her. 'That would be great, thanks.'

'Hang on. I'll help you into the car.'

Susan jumped out of the car to open the passenger door. She adjusted the seat backwards to allow more room for Cerys, and Susan was particularly careful closing the door to avoid knocking the injured foot.

'Are you comfortable?'

'Brilliant. This is so much easier than the bus, although it's getting easier now; I can manage without crutches. Mind you, I'll be so glad when I'm back driving.'

Once they were moving, Susan asked Cerys where she was off to.

'Southampton University. Because I'm a newly qualified teacher, we have sessions over there occasionally. Sometimes they're on a Wednesday, sometimes a Friday. It's quite nice because I get to meet other teachers who are just starting out as well. I always feel guilty leaving the school, but Fiona insists I go.'

'It's good to get support.'

'Yes, I have a lot to learn,' said Cerys.

'And you have had a lot of extra pressure for someone so early on in their career.'

'It's not been easy, but Fiona is brilliant, despite having so much to worry about.'

'You must be relieved Ross is staying.'

'Yes, it's good, isn't it? The village needs him more than ever now.'

Susan noticed Cerys was clutching her handbag with one hand while tapping the fingers of her other hand on the buckle.

The traffic became heavier as they approached the main road to Cowes, passing the prison on one side, the hospital on the other.

'I'm glad we're travelling away from and not into Newport at this time,' said Susan, looking at the queue of traffic headed in the other direction.

At Cowes, Susan dropped Cerys at the terminal and drove off to park. She was glad she had allowed plenty of time because the Red Jet was very busy with commuters.

Susan and Cerys managed to sit together, and seemed happy to sit quietly and enjoy what was thankfully a calm crossing. At the terminal in Southampton, Cerys took an Uber up to the university while Susan took the free bus into town.

Inside John Lewis, she enjoyed walking round the baby department. She took her time taking photos of items she thought would be suitable, sending them to Zoe. She was surprised but excited and, after thanking her mum, guided her to what she thought would be best. Susan was able to buy some items on the spot, others would be delivered to the island.

Having finished the baby shopping, Susan wandered around other departments. As she was walking past the perfumes, she noticed Jessie studying an expensive-looking box. A smart shop assistant in a crisp white overall and immaculate make-up was walking towards her. She remembered Jessie telling her how she liked to come over to Southampton on Wednesdays and get away from the village.

She guessed Jessie might want to enjoy her time on her own, so Susan began to walk away. However, she was interrupted by Jessie calling her and she turned around. She saw the polite smile on the assistant's face had melted away and transformed into something closer to irritation.

'Sorry, carry on shopping,' said Susan.

'Oh, no. Just looking.' Jessie grinned at Susan. 'So, what are you doing here?'

Susan explained her mission and how she was now just enjoying wandering and browsing.

'Same here: the car boot was cancelled. This is a bit more glamorous.'

As Jessie appeared to be friendly and happy to chat, Susan said, 'Do you fancy a coffee and cake? My shout—'

'Yeah, that would be great. Thanks.'

On the escalator to the next floor, laughing, Susan said, 'I know it's sad, but I still get a thrill from going on an escalator. We don't have many on the island. When I was a child, there weren't any.'

Jessie laughed as well. 'It's why we love the island, isn't it?'

It struck Susan that she'd never seen Jessie quite so relaxed. Her eyes were lit up, and she looked younger somehow. In her trendy jeans and jacket, she fitted in much better here than in church or walking through the village.

At the café, they both chose a lemon tart and balanced them with skinny lattes. They sat down by the window. As Jessie reached over to give her a serviette, Susan could smell the perfume she'd been trying on and she realised she recognised it.

'That's a lovely perfume. Isn't it the one Lawrence gave Hazel?'

'Yeah, it's Luis Vuitton. It's just gorgeous, isn't it, but very expensive. It contains may rose, iris and cedars. I love it.'

'You really know your perfume. I haven't much of a clue. Zoe gave me some for Christmas, from Marks and Spencer, which I really like but I keep forgetting to wear it.' She sipped her coffee. 'I've not been out for coffee and cake for ages. I must get back into the habit. We have so many gorgeous places on the island.'

'That's true, but I like to escape over here. I don't usually see anyone I know.' Jessie paused. 'Look, I was a bit rough on you when you came to the vicarage with your daughter. Put it down to nerves: we are all so stressed at the moment.'

'I understand. It's okay. How do you think people in the village are coping?'

'The older residents are unsettled. I mean, if a fit middle-aged man can suddenly lose his life, it makes them feel more vulnerable. Children and their parents hate change, although Fiona is doing a brilliant job of keeping everything together. I hope someone is looking after her, though,' said Jessie.

'You're so involved in the work of the parish; you're very committed to it.'

'I try to do the right thing, look after people. It's why we're here, isn't it?'

'The village is lucky to have you,' said Susan. 'Your parents must be very proud of you.'

Jessie took a large bite of her lemon tart, looked out of the window. Eventually she replied, 'I'm not sure my parents would ever say they'd been proud of me. I was a real rebel in my teens. Mum is abroad now, a hairdresser in Portugal. Dad is with someone else, with all her kids. No one quite knows what to make of what I've done now.'

'So, how come you ended up married to a vicar?'

'I met Daniel in a café. He had come in to read and I was eking out a cup of coffee. I didn't have a job or any money then. He was in his dog collar, sat opposite me as there were no spare tables. We started to chat. He told me he was a curate at the local church and then offered to buy me coffee. It was so odd; we were so different and yet we hit it off.' Susan could see a light in Jessie's eyes at the memory. 'He invited me to a fete they were holding at the church. Well, long story short, married the curate.' Suddenly the smile disappeared, the sun went behind a cloud, and she jabbed at the cake with her fork. 'You know, I may not look like a vicar's wife, not like that Martha at the centre, but I don't care. I'm going to succeed at this.'

Susan was surprised at the fire behind her words. 'Good for you. I admire that, but you must get tired, living and working on the job.'

'Yes, of course. It puts a strain on us as individuals and as a couple.'

'I can imagine. I think Lawrence was concerned about the stress you were under. He talked to me about you the night he died.'

'Did he?'

'He told me you were unhappy about completing the DBS form. I could see why that might be a problem for some people. All kinds of things are included on them, private matters.'

Jessie sat up, alert. 'Hang on, what did Lawrence tell you?'

18

'I'm not someone who gossips. You don't need to worry.'

Jessie's eyes narrowed. She leant over the table. 'What do you know about my past?'

'I'm not going to tell anyone,' said Susan.

Jessie sat back, her head in her hands. 'I never thought he'd tell anyone. Look, it won't be long until it's wiped off my record. Daniel need never know. I was young, stupid. The reason I was sitting in that café when I met Daniel was that I was out of work. No one would take me on, and I was lost. Going to church with him gave me a new start. I'd never go back to all that but it's still hanging over me, haunting me.'

'Why on earth didn't you tell Daniel?'

'I was ashamed. And what do you think his family would have thought of it all? They weren't exactly ecstatic when he married me. I'm not their type. You know, his mother tried to persuade me to break off the engagement. I've never told Daniel—'

'Goodness, that's awful. Daniel never knew?'

'No, he worships his mother. I didn't want to cause trouble, and also he might have listened to her.' Jessie gave a crooked smile. 'There are some things it's better to keep from him.' She looked at Susan. 'Lawrence always promised he would keep it to himself. I guess it was that business last

Christmas that made him break his word.' Jessie looked up. 'Did he tell you about that as well?'

Susan shook her head. 'No, he didn't.'

Jessie sat back; her eyes narrowed. 'I know you shouldn't speak ill of the dead and all that, but, like Daniel said, Lawrence was constantly interfering in other people's lives. I think he got a kick out of it, liked to feel in control. But it was a dangerous game. People become unpredictable when they feel threatened.'

'Did you feel threatened by Lawrence?'

Jessie fiddled with the handle of her mug, avoiding Susan's eye. 'When you feel someone who knows private things about you is going to tell other people, you know they don't have your best interests at heart. They're out to hurt you and you have to do something.'

Susan sipped her coffee, tried to speak casually. 'And what do you think is an appropriate response?'

Jessie lifted her head, looked directly at Susan. 'That will depend on the level of threat. If you think it will destroy your life, your work, your marriage, then I believe you have the right to use whatever means you need to protect yourself.'

An icy stillness fell between them. Susan was aware of voices, the clatter of cutlery, but they seemed far away.

Suddenly Jessie's face broke into a wide grin, although it was hard and cold. 'Goodness, this has become a heavy conversation to be having over coffee and cake. Anyone would think the world was about to end.'

Susan took a sip of her coffee and gave a conciliatory smile. 'You're right. We have a lot to be grateful for. And, of course, we have the concerts and fundraising to look forward to now: one step closer to the community centre.'

'You're right. I suppose every cloud and all that. Sorry, but as awful as Lawrence's accident was, it's good that we can go ahead with all the plans for St Jude's.'

'You must be relieved Ross is staying.'

Jessie looked down. 'Of course, I wouldn't know how to raise the money without him. He's a good man. He doesn't have to do all this extra work. We're lucky to have him.' Jessie looked at her large watch. 'I'd better be making a move. I need some new leggings for the gym, work off some of that cake.'

'You go every Friday?'

'Yeah, it's great. You could come sometime if you like?'

Susan was surprised at the invitation. 'I've never been to a gym. I've no idea what you do in one.'

'I'll show you. Come on Friday after choir.'

'I've got some old leggings from a yoga class. Would they be okay? Don't I need to do an induction or something?'

Jessie laughed. 'I've a friend there. He'll show you the ropes.'

'My daughter is always nagging me to do more exercise, so, okay, I'll give it a go. Now, it's time I was getting back to the island,' said Susan. 'Robert is looking after the dogs for me.'

* * *

Back at home, Susan discovered that Robert had, in actual fact, spent a lot of the day helping Hazel next door.

'I'm sorry. I hadn't expected that to happen,' said Susan.

'It's okay. I was out in the garden with the dogs. I could see she was struggling with her lawn mower, so I offered to do the lawn for her. When I finished, she said I could bring the dogs over and she gave me some lunch.'

'Goodness, you've been in there all day?'

'To be honest, I think she was glad of the company. She talked to me about Lawrence, had a bit of a cry and is obviously grieving. She told me how much you've helped and supported her.'

'I'm glad. I can't imagine what she's been going through.'

'She has quite a few questions, doesn't she? I guess, listening to her, I can see that she does have some valid concerns, particularly about the missing key and the pen.'

Susan appreciated that Robert was conceding that there were questions to be answered.

'Yes, it's odd. Alice agrees with me.'

'I'm going to have to meet this Alice one day. I suppose she has a lot of time sitting around at the home to come up with all kinds of strange theories.'

Susan pursed her lips. 'Alice is a really bright woman, and she speaks a lot of sense. She was right about Colette, and I believe she's dead right here.'

Robert grinned. 'Point taken. Now, I should call these dogs and get on home.'

'Do you want to stay for something to eat?'

'I ought to get back. My son is phoning. He's having problems at work.'

They both stood up and glanced around awkwardly, the unspoken conversation about the kiss hanging in the air. It was Robert who spoke up first.

'I hope you weren't angry with me about what happened on the beach,' he said. He was fiddling with the neck of his T-shirt in an embarrassed way.

'Of course not. No. It was, well, it was nice.' Susan felt herself blushing, and looked down.

'That's all right, then,' said Robert, the relief in his voice palpable. 'I know what you said about us being friends, and I wouldn't want to spoil that.'

She looked up and smiled. 'And neither would I. And, um, I was thinking. I know I have talked about my concerns about getting involved, but I know how much you still miss Carol.'

'Yes, thank you. I don't like to talk about it, really. It's not like the first year, but I still get days when it feels so incredibly sad that Carol is not with me any more. And I did feel a bit guilty after we kissed on the beach. That's the first time I have kissed another woman since Carol died.'

'I hadn't realised.'

He smiled. 'It was fine, I'm glad it happened. And now I must get these dogs and be on my way.'

Susan thanked him for all he'd done. As he walked over to the car, he gave her a cheery wave goodbye.

Alone in the house, Susan felt herself relax. Nothing was sorted but they were still friends and that was a relief. She grabbed a frozen lasagne, put it in the microwave, and poured herself a glass of wine.

She took these to the table where her laptop was open and she had already logged in. She read an article on the pages of her women's charity about the cutting of funding for a women's refuge and drafted a letter to her MP.

As she settled back with her knitting, she received a message from Ross checking that she still wanted to go for a walk the following evening and asking her to sort out the music as choir would be restarting that week. Susan reread the texts and started to make her way to bed. She hadn't really thought about this walk with Ross, but should she really be going out at night-time with someone she had on a list of suspects?

She wanted to go: she knew it was an opportunity to talk to Ross, get to know him better. Maybe as a precaution she should let someone know she was going and make sure Ross knew that as well? Yes, she would do that.

Susan lay in bed, read for a while, then switched off the light. She had no idea what time it was, but she was disturbed by the dogs barking. Reluctantly, she went downstairs. The curtains were all drawn and the house was in darkness. She settled the dogs, listened, heard nothing, and returned to bed.

The next morning, Susan headed downstairs and straight to the back door to let in some fresh air. It was going to be a lovely day. Wrapping her dressing gown around herself, she strode into the garden followed by Rocco and Libs, but pulled up short.

Over one window, a few words had been sprayed:

F*** Off. No one wants you here.

Susan gasped, shocked. She heard Hazel's patio door open. She called out, 'Hazel! Come here.'

Hazel was round in a flash, pushing her way through the side gate.

'Oh, no. Susan, that's awful. You have to tell the police this time.'

Susan nodded and Hazel, who was clutching her phone, rang the police. They said they would send someone out later.

Susan doubted somehow that anyone would come. Hazel hadn't heard anything in the night, and although she offered to stay, Susan decided to take a photo and then get out with the dogs.

She ran upstairs and dressed. She was desperate to get out of the house.

They walked through the village, but she found herself avoiding eye contact with anyone. She suddenly felt a stranger, unwanted here.

After a brisk walk around the park, she made her way home.

As she walked past St Jude's, she looked over and saw Fiona run to the school, lean against the door and take a drink from her water bottle. She looked exhausted. Fiona waved to her, and Susan crossed the road.

'Morning, Susan,' said Fiona. 'How are you this morning?'

Susan couldn't face talking about the incident at home and instead said, 'You look tired. Have you been for a run?'

'Only a wee one. It helps sometimes. Life just got even more stressful.'

'Is this to do with the anonymous complaint?'

'How? Who told ye?' Fiona demanded in that way she had that made Susan feel like a young child caught out by a parent.

'Actually, Lawrence mentioned it to me the night he died. He'd only just found out about it. I know you told me you didn't see Lawrence that night, but I'm sure he said he talked to you.'

Fiona screwed up her eyes. 'We did talk. I panicked when you asked me if I'd seen him. Of course, there was no reason why I would have needed to tell you about the complaint. Anyway, everyone will know soon. By next week when the officials from the local authority arrive, I guess everyone will know. I'll tell ye, but please don't spread it around. The complainant said that on the Wednesday of the tests, when Lawrence invigilated, he cheated.'

'Lawrence, he was taking your class?'

'I'd had to go home unwell. The complainant specifically said the cheating happened that day.'

'Is anyone taking it seriously?'

'I am hoping that the governors and I can persuade them that this is just some vindictive scandalmonger. They know Lawrence's reputation. He would never have done something like that. The awful thing is he usually sits in with me during the tests, to protect me from just this sort of accusation, but there was no one free to be with him when I went home. I regret putting Lawrence in that position now.'

'I'm so sorry.'

'I despair. As if I haven't got enough to cope with. Now I'll have all the speculations around this to sort out.' Fiona looked up at the oak tree. 'You know how we all wonder how gossip gets around this village? You can never find the source of the rumours, can you? Well, my theory is the source is this old tree. I think it stores all its sees and hears in its leaves. As the tree drops its leaves, the secrets are released and whispered on the breeze to passers-by. Those people in turn pass on the secrets, having no idea where they heard them in the first place.'

Susan smiled. 'That's very poetic. Maybe you could be right.'

'Maybe I am! Right, I'd better be off. Bye, Susan.'

Susan made her way home, moved by her conversation with Fiona. She had sounded so let down and so exhausted. As she walked up the close, she found herself reluctant to go inside. She didn't want to see that message again. However, she had no choice: she had to go in.

She was surprised when a uniformed officer arrived mid-morning. She thanked him for coming so soon.

'Actually, I had to come and talk to your neighbour and thought I'd pop in. Do show me what has happened.'

Even as she showed him, she couldn't help but feel it was rather trivial. However, the officer was polite, took notes and said to let them know if there was any more trouble.

Clearly nothing more was to be done, but Susan appreciated the kind words.

She was glad to be able to clean the window and tried to occupy herself in the house for the rest of the morning. She did notice Daniel arrive at Hazel's at one point. A few hours later, she received a text from Hazel, asking her to go and see her.

19

Hazel answered the door, clutching a tissue, tears in her eyes. Susan followed Hazel into the house, noticing a glass of wine on the table.

'I know it's early,' sniffed Hazel. 'Would you like one?'

'Um, not at the moment, thanks. What's happened?'

'The police came round,' said Hazel. 'The coroner has released the body. We can hold Lawrence's funeral now.'

'I see. Well. That's a good thing, isn't it? It's hard waiting for the funeral.'

Hazel began to refill the glass, but her hand was shaking.

Susan moved and sat next to her. So many words rushed to mind and yet none of them were right and so she just sat, her arm gently around Hazel's shoulders.

'I'm sorry,' gulped Hazel. 'Daniel has been helping. He came to the funeral directors' with me. He's very good, very understanding, but it all felt so unreal. Funerals are not something Lawrence and I ever talked about.'

She wandered over to the cabinet containing all Lawrence's awards.

'I need to find a photo for the front of the order of service and I wondered about this one of him with this cup. It's only small but it was for a project he set up involving families with children learning to read and he was very proud of it.'

Susan looked at the various photos and for a moment she was

distracted by the group photograph of the staff at the school in Cardiff where Lawrence had first worked. However, she realised Hazel was waiting for her reaction to the photo she'd chosen and turned back to look at it more closely. Lawrence was smiling, he looked so confident and happy. 'I think that would be perfect.'

They returned to the table and Hazel picked up a piece of paper on which there was a list of songs and hymns. 'I put this together with Daniel, but to be honest, Lawrence never liked hymns that much. Oh, and I talked to Daniel about whether we should involve the school.'

'What did he say?'

'He said to maybe have something at the school, a time of remembrance in assembly.' They heard a ringtone, and Hazel went over to her handbag. 'Oh, God, it's a text on my work phone.' She took a mobile from her handbag. 'I'd better answer this.' She quickly typed a reply and then put the phone away. 'It was just a quick question. I told them to phone me if there was anything. I'm going to have to get back soon.'

'You can't rush this.'

'No, but it would be good to be back in some kind of routine. Anyway, the funeral. We're holding it over a lunchtime so that some staff can come. It's next Wednesday. It's so strange. Usually I open the church for funerals, attend if I can, make sure it's all laid out properly, and now I'm doing it for Lawrence.'

'Will there be a lot of people coming over?'

'Neither of us have much family, just some cousins. There are people who worked with him in Cardiff, and Bristol. I've let the heads know. I have no idea if any of them will come. It's very difficult for teachers. They can't take leave whenever they want to.'

'All you can do is invite people.'

'Yes. I thought I'd hold the wake back here. My sister will be coming over and she'll help me organise it.'

'That's good.'

'Yes. I appreciate her coming over. I do worry about the funeral, though. It's a kind of rite of passage, after which everyone is meant to move on. But I can't. Nothing is sorted, is it? The police may be satisfied but I'm not. I...' said Hazel, despair in her voice. She burst into tears.

'I'm so sorry.' Susan hesitated, then said, 'Um, I was talking to Fiona this morning; she told me about some anonymous complaint. Actually, Lawrence had mentioned it to me as well.'

'Yes, the police have talked to me about that. They found the email from the local authority to Lawrence about it. An anonymous complainer saying that Lawrence invigilated the SATs tests on the Wednesday and cheated.'

'Fiona said he would never have cheated.'

'Of course not. The police took note that he'd been told about this the night he died, that he might have been so upset that it led him to take his own life.'

'I remember Lawrence referring to it in vague terms. He did seem a bit upset but he said everything would work out.'

'Exactly. That's what Lawrence always believed. It all sounds a lot of nonsense anyway. Fiona will be able to put them right. Now, have you learned anything new?'

Susan told Hazel about her visit to Shiloh, and that she was going for a walk with Ross later.

Hazel frowned. 'You'll be careful, won't you? Nothing feels safe at the moment, does it?'

'I agree,' said Susan. 'I'll make sure I have my phone with me.'

Hazel forced a smile. 'I don't suppose I'd be much help, but make sure you phone me if you're worried.'

Susan left Hazel, and took the dogs out for an early walk before it was time to go to meet Ross.

It was becoming dusk as she left the house, having arranged with Ross to meet him at the caravan at about half eight. As she approached, she saw him walking towards her.

'Hi. Sorry, I went to see Cerys. I just need to pick up a few things, then we can go.'

She followed him down the side of Fiona's house. The caravan was at the bottom of a large garden on a paved area.

'It's really handy that Fiona has this. It stops me getting in her way. She was given it by a neighbour who was moving and didn't want it any more. She thought it might come in handy for some friends of hers in Scotland who have been to stay. Their kids used to like sleeping down here. I'm sure it's not roadworthy any more, but it is cosy enough inside.'

At the side of the caravan was a rusty barbeque, which made the place look a bit run-down.

Ross reached down and took a Yale key from under a rock. 'Not very secure, but anyone breaking in would be most disappointed. Still, I lock the caravan when I'm not here, just in case.'

'Surely you lock yourself in at night?'

'Well, I never used to, but Cerys is nervous down here. Right, come on in. Welcome to my palace.'

Susan knew her house was untidy but the chaos in the caravan was on another level. Every surface was covered in used mugs, piles of music, an unopened bottle of whisky, some pretty heavy-duty ashtrays, and various articles of clothing. There was a small hob for cooking, and some shelves of tinned food, packets of rice and beans. Ross went down to the far end and pulled back a curtain that divided the main body of the caravan from his sleeping area.

He grabbed a torch which was next to his bed, and then collected a camera and binoculars.

'Right, I think I'm all set.'

Susan glanced at the bottle of whisky. 'I see you are a good Scotsman who likes a wee dram.'

Ross laughed. 'That was a present from the parents of a child I'm teaching. Against all the odds, they passed their exam. I didn't have the heart to tell them I can't stand the stuff. I keep it a secret. I mean I'd never be able to go back to my home town again, would I? Right, let's go.'

Happy he had all he needed, he locked the caravan, replaced the Yale key under the rock, and they set off. Head held high, he walked with the air of a man in a hurry, and Susan had to quicken her steps to keep up. Once past the shop, they crossed the road, and started up a side road. It was darker now with fewer street lights. They reached a junction where the main road joined theirs.

'That's Dave's house over there,' said Ross, pointing to a small bungalow. 'I called for him the last two weeks, but tonight he's meeting us up the top at the Jubilee car park. I think he wanted to start early.'

Past this point, the road became steeper. There were no lights now, and tall hedges lined their way.

Susan was rapidly becoming out of breath, stumbled slightly and finally asked Ross if he could slow down.

'God, I'm sorry. I hate this bit. It takes a good twenty minutes from here to the car park, and I just want to get there. I get so excited when I come out at this time. I didn't get up here at all last week. I just love night-time walking.' He paused. 'It's amazing to be out in this after London. I'm so glad I moved here.'

'It's quite a contrast to London, isn't it, but you must miss the concerts and the musical life up there?'

'I do, but I needed to come to a place of peace and healing.'

'You had a hard time?' Susan waited; she was finally going to find out what Ross's dealing with the police had been.

'I was teaching at this private school, and I started a relationship with another teacher. One night we went out for a drink and one of the men in the bar came and started chatting her up. Naturally, I didn't like it and told him to back off. Later that night, the man was attacked in the park, and I was a suspect...' He hesitated, his voice was shaking now.

'But why did they suspect you?'

'Because of this set-to in the pub. I admit I came on quite strong, told the man to leave her alone, but I was just trying to protect my partner. I certainly didn't go out of the pub and beat him up. The trouble was, though, I had no alibi. I'd been so steamed up by it all, I'd gone for a long walk on my own. The police went on and on trying to make me admit I'd jumped this man, but I hadn't. Anyway, eventually they saw there was no evidence to tie me to the attack and they dropped it. I was very shaken up, though. The police asked so many questions. They treated me like some over-possessive boyfriend, someone who couldn't control his temper, who went off walking the streets on his own. It was awful.'

'What happened to your girlfriend?'

'Our relationship finished, not surprisingly, and it was for the best,' said Ross. 'I decided to leave my job and get away from London. It never suited me. When Fiona told me there was a job going here, I was so pleased.'

'It was a big decision to move.'

'I know, but I'm so glad I did. I love the island and have settled well. The job is interesting, and I enjoy the whole community side of it. What Jessie hopes to do with this community centre is brilliant.'

'And, of course, you now have Cerys.'

'I do, although she's very young, but yes, she is very sweet.'

They didn't seem the most romantic of words. Susan wondered if after all Lawrence had been right about how committed Ross was to his relationship with Cerys.

'You nearly lost it all, though,' she commented.

'I did, and of course I'd have survived. But I was angry with Lawrence. He didn't seem to see what he was taking away from the village, and it would have broken Jessie's heart. We have so much planned. I know it's awful what happened to him, but the way people talk about him now, it's as if the man was some kind of saint, and we all know that's not true.'

'What do you mean?'

'He was all about his career. You could see that.' Ross looked up at the skies, breathing in their beauty. 'At least out here, none of those things matters. There is nothing like night walking to put your worries behind you.'

'You really love it out here, don't you?'

'For me, when the sun goes down, the magic begins. As a musician it's particularly exciting. Your sense of hearing really comes into its own. The day is noisy and chaotic. The night runs on its own time, the clocks slow. Animals, birds, stars, all that has been hidden during the day, come out. But what do most people do? They close their curtains, turn on their lights. They miss it all.'

'A lot of people are frightened of the dark,' said Susan.

'That's because they've been taught to fear it. We need to relearn, make peace with the night.' He grinned. 'I'm winning Cerys over slowly. I have some brilliant places to take her this summer.'

They finally reached the downs. It was pitch-black up there, but they could see the glimmer of a red torch.

20

'That's Dave,' said Ross.

As Susan approached, she saw Dave was in camouflage jacket, trousers and hat.

Ross laughed. 'He doesn't half scare people at night.'

Dave shrugged, then using the red-beamed torches they made their way up a gravel path, then veered off down a side path into woodland.

'Thank God it's dry tonight,' said Dave. 'The week before last the heavens opened as soon as we arrived at the car park. Now, I think we are best off down here. I came up last night, heard a long-eared owl, we might catch him again.'

They found a place to sit, and Susan saw that Dave and Ross both had their phones and cameras at the ready.

At first it all just seemed quiet, and Susan was starting to feel the cold. However, soon she heard a bird call, 'Ke-wick.'

'That's a female tawny owl,' whispered Ross.

He held up his phone and began recording the sound. Soon a male called in response, 'Hoooouh.' Again, Ross and Dave were recording the sounds on their phones.

'I must have recorded this hundreds of times,' said Ross, 'but every time I hear something slightly different.'

Suddenly, they had a new sound, one eerie hoot after another. 'That's a long-eared owl. It's wonderful, isn't it?' whispered Dave.

Susan forgot the cold, even forgot the darkness. There was rustling under the leaves, in the bush and in the trees, noises that usually scared her. However, Ross and Dave interpreted them to her as if interpreting another language and the fear left her.

'Oh, by the way, I've bought some of that feed for the corncrakes, thought you'd like some,' said Dave.

Ross looked confused initially but then smiled. 'Oh, thanks. That's great.'

Dave handed him a small, carefully wrapped package, which Ross pushed into the pocket of his black coat. He then took out some notes and paid Dave.

'If you get any decent recordings, let me know,' continued Dave.

After a while, Ross suggested they go back up onto the downs. It was just as they were walking through the gate that Susan caught sight of an owl gliding silently in front of her, its white heart-shaped face ghostly, and it let out a long, harsh scream, which seemed to go on and on.

'A barn owl,' she said. 'I've only ever seen them on television.'

'We are so lucky here on the island. We have little owls, nightjars.'

They walked back down the path and into the car park and then they said goodnight.

Ross and Susan walked back in silence. Susan found herself listening in a way she had never done before at night-time. She wasn't listening for threatening footsteps or wild animals that were going to leap out and attack her, but for owls, badgers, foxes and hedgehogs. She was almost sorry when they were back in the village, back amongst the street lights.

They walked past the site where the new houses and flats were being built.

'The village is growing,' said Susan.

'It's a shame, and they're not adding anything to the village, are they? The old houses have so much more character. I'd never want to live in a new build. I want somewhere with history, a past.'

Susan remembered Cerys's excitement about the new flats. Whatever her plans, Susan couldn't see Ross buying one with her.

It came time for them to go their separate ways. The evening had been a revelation, and despite all her worries before, she was glad she'd been. She felt that that evening she had discovered a new world.

* * *

Cerys visited Alice at the nursing home the next day at lunchtime. She explained that she had made the arrangements to come and sing one Sunday afternoon.

'That's wonderful, my dear. We shall all so look forward to it.'

'You must know I teach your great-grandson, Jacob. What a lovely little boy he is.'

'Thank you. I'm biased, of course, but yes, he is.'

'Very bright. I love asking him his opinion on all kinds of things. He always has something interesting to say.' Cerys looked around. 'It seems very cosy here.'

'It is, and the staff are exceedingly kind. And so, how are you settling on the island?'

'Really well, thanks. It's a long way from Swansea, and I know it's not an obvious place for a single twenty-three-year-old to go, but I love it. I knew about the beaches, of course, but I hadn't expected the island to have such a strong sense of identity. I hadn't realised how living on an island would affect people so much. That stretch of water makes such a difference. I like being separate from the mainland but it's a bit of a pain when you want to go over there. I have to go over for courses sometimes, and it seems to take ages.'

'Yes. Visitors see the boats and ferries as exciting and part of their holiday experience, and they are,' said Alice. 'But it's different when you wait in the rain for one, or just miss one home and end up a few hours late. Still, I'd never want a bridge. The water keeps the island special.'

'I can see that. It makes me smile when children talk about the mainland. One even called it the "other island". But still, there are plenty of people back home who think the same way.'

'I'm glad you're feeling settled. It must have been difficult for you when Lawrence had that terrible accident,' said Alice.

'It was such a shock. He was so loved by the children and parents.'

'Of course, and a very dedicated teacher. He had done so well in his career.'

Cerys interrupted her. 'It is easier for men, though.'

Alice was surprised at the sudden swerve in the conversation.

Cerys continued. 'Lawrence and I had a bit of an argument about it on a school trip two weeks ago. We took the children to Carisbrooke Castle for the day and he came to help out. We sat next to each other on the coach, and he started to tell me he felt he'd succeeded as a result of sheer hard work. He didn't seem to want to acknowledge having been helped in some degree by being a man. So often women like my mam were held back by having families and other commitments.' Alice could see her nervously fiddling with her pendants.

'Yes, you have a point there – but Lawrence didn't agree?'

'Not really.'

'I suppose there are women like Fiona who have been successful.'

'She's not a head yet, though, is she?' Cerys took a deep breath. 'I'm sorry, I was very worked up about it. He was a very good head, and I've been very happy here.'

'You have your friendship with Ross, of course—'

Alice saw the sideways look Cerys gave her and was aware again of the questions she could ask as an older lady. People expected her to be a bit nosy – it was very useful.

'Yes, I do. Ross and I have music in common. I love going around singing with him and of course he's been great for the village.'

'I look forward to meeting him.'

'He can look a bit grumpy and untidy but he's kind and we get on well. I think he's a bit wary of anything too serious, but he'll come round.' Cerys hesitated. 'Sorry, here I go again, rabbiting on. I love it here. Really, I do.'

'And how do you like living in the vicarage?'

'It's fine. Of course, I'd like my own place sometime, but Jessie has been great, really friendly. I'm glad I'm living with them at the moment. I wouldn't want to be on my own at night. Nothing's been the same since the night Lawrence died. We're all so frightened.'

Alice saw the fear in the young woman's eyes. 'You're scared?'

'Um, yes, you know, you're always watching your back.' She blinked. 'Anyway, I'm sure things will get back to normal soon.' She forced her lips into an even bigger smile. 'Enough of me, tell me about you and your life. Have you always lived on the island?'

Alice chatted about her life in the village and the shop, and was aware of Cerys's hands slowly unclenching, of the smile relaxing.

Eventually Cerys said, 'Well, I guess I ought to make a move. It's been very nice to meet you, Alice, and thank you for listening to me. It was so interesting hearing about your life in the village. It would be great to bring some of my children to chat to you. Could they come and interview you?'

'Of course. I'd enjoy that.'

* * *

Early that evening, Susan started to get ready to go to choir. She was surprised at how nervous she felt. She was sure Ross was right when he said that they needed to get back to normal but was also aware of how diffi-cult some people might find it. She collected the music folders, sorted them out and left the house.

As she approached St Jude's, Susan was also thinking about her visit to the gym later with Jessie and knew she was quietly dreading it. She had none of the fancy outfits she knew people would be wearing. She was unfit, and was sure she'd be a few decades older than most of the people there.

Once inside the church, she sensed a subdued atmosphere. One young girl let out a loud laugh and it echoed around the church, leaving people looking irritated, so that she lowered her voice.

Over to one side she saw Ross and Hazel deep in conversation. Hazel was handing Ross a piece of paper and they continued talking. Susan was reading though her music when she heard a quiet sob that bounced off the stone walls. Glancing over at Ross and Hazel, she could see that Hazel was clearly becoming very distressed and Ross was awkwardly trying to comfort her. She then saw Fiona approach them, put her arm gently around Hazel's shoulders. They sat together quietly while Ross prepared for the rehearsal.

Susan realised Cerys had come to sit next to her. 'How are you? How's the foot?'

'Still hurting.' Her voice was flat. There was no sparkle in her eyes.

'Are you okay?'

'You know how it is. School is a nightmare. I never thought I'd dread going to work—'

'It must have been difficult for everyone losing Lawrence.'

'That's awful, of course, but there are other things now. Has Fiona said anything to you?'

'Well, yes—'

'So, you do know. It seems to me to be getting blown all out of proportion. It's not like there is any proof, just some grumpy parent, and yet Fiona is taking it so seriously. I'm scared she might even think of leaving. I owe her so much. She has looked after me. I couldn't bear to see her go.'

'Let's hope it doesn't come to that.'

'I hope not. She is so together, she makes me feel safe.' Cerys turned to Susan. 'I saw Alice, your friend, at the nursing home. Ross and I are going to sing there some time.'

'What a lovely thing to do. I hope you and Alice had a good chat?'

'We did, but I talked too much. I was rabbiting on, and then I realised she was listening. She's all there, isn't she, even though she is so old? I can see why Jacob is so with it. Bright family.'

Susan saw Hazel approaching her. She looked very pale and anxious, her hands clenched together.

At that moment, Ross called them all together.

'Thank you. Now, I'd better explain where we stand. I'm to remain in post for another year, after which my job will be reappraised. It means we can carry on with our plans for the fundraiser. I'm very grateful to Fiona and the school governors for making this happen. Before we start, I want to mention that Hazel has asked us all to sing at Lawrence's funeral that is due to be held on Wednesday. I'm going to hold a special rehearsal on Tuesday evening at half past six in here. The songs Hazel has chosen are all ones we know.' He held up the piece of paper Hazel had given him.

Susan's heart went out to Hazel. No wonder she'd been so distressed.

Ross continued. 'But we want to be as well-rehearsed as we can be.' He paused and took another breath. 'I know a lot of you are still in shock over Lawrence's death. Singing and music can be very healing, and I hope it will help you. I know we will all want to support Hazel as much as we can. It's very brave of her to come out this evening and I'm sure we will all want to look after her. Now, let's start on the rehearsal. We'll begin with our warm-up exercises.'

There was something comforting about being back in the routine. The choir's voices slowly relaxed and the first piece went well. They turned to the piece in which Hazel had been going to sing her solo.

'We're not going to sing this tonight,' explained Ross. 'In fact, if Hazel finds the pressure too much, we can always make the solo a duet.' He glanced over to Hazel, and she gave a brief nod.

Hazel's eyes were bright with tears. It struck Susan how hard even being in St Jude's that evening must be for her. She looked totally bereft. Everyone, everything, here must remind her of Lawrence.

'Right,' continued Ross. 'So, we'll leave that for this evening. Cerys and Hazel, could you find a time so I can go through that with you? Now, let's move on.'

As they sang the next song, Hazel sat very quietly, silently mouthing the words, but she wasn't singing. Susan understood that at times of great distress it was as if the vocal cords knitted together. It made singing painful, if not impossible, and she felt very sorry for Hazel.

Susan scanned the choir. Daniel sat very still but on the edge of his pew, as if waiting to go, Susan assumed, to Shiloh, his prayer centre. It struck her afresh what an odd thing that was to do every week. Was he really that desperate to get away? Jessie was more fidgety than ever, moving seats and music, getting up to get a glass of water for someone, picking up dropped pieces of music for the children.

She noticed Cerys's hands were shaking. Susan assumed the business at school was very much on her mind.

Ross was lost in his music as soon as they started to sing. It was as if nothing else mattered, nothing else had happened. It was an escape Susan envied.

At the end of the rehearsal, Ross asked for the choir committee members to stay behind for a quick chat.

'We'll sit down here,' Ross said, pointing to a space in front of the small wooden door that led to the tower. 'Grab yourselves a chair.' Daniel and

Jessie placed their chairs as far away from the door as they could, and others followed suit, so they ended up in a cramped circle.

Susan realised this was the first time since Lawrence's death that they had all been together. The atmosphere was thick with tension; no one looked at each other. They all sat hunched, fiddling with bracelets, scratching hands or fists clenched.

'Thank you, I'll be quick. As you know, Lawrence always led these meetings. We never officially appointed anyone but, if you are agreeable, I will chair the meetings for the time being.'

'That sounds very sensible,' said Fiona. 'Ye'll be preparing us for the fundraiser, ye have a record of any engagements we'll be undertaking.' She scanned the group, a slight challenge in her eyes. 'We all agree?'

They nodded, or flickered a smile. No one spoke.

'I know this is hard,' Ross continued. 'But I really believe this choir can be a tool for good in the village, to help us all heal and move on.'

No one responded. Susan found the atmosphere confusing. Of course, it was going to be difficult. She would expect sadness, for people to be subdued. However, there was something else. Maybe stress or anger? She wasn't sure.

'I just need to run through a few dates,' continued Ross.

Most people grabbed their phones. Susan realised only she and Daniel were using paper and pen.

Ross began giving them the details they needed, but Susan became distracted by watching Daniel write. He was left-handed, as Lawrence had been. His ring caught the light. But it was the pen he was using that made her gasp – how had he got hold of that pen?

21

'Daniel, that's Lawrence's pen.' Susan's voice rang out, too loud, accusatory.

Hazel gasped. Daniel blinked in confusion. 'Isn't it yours, Jessie?'

Jessie frowned. 'No, of course not. I remember Lawrence using it. It's a very expensive pen. I've never had one like it. Where did you find it?'

'I'm pretty sure it was on the hall table. It didn't seem anything special.'

'That is a Cartier pen,' explained Hazel.

'I'd no idea.' Daniel's astonishment seemed genuine.

'How long have you had it?'

'A few days. Not long. Sorry, I hadn't realised. Do have it back.' He passed it to Hazel, who held it lightly, as if it was burning her fingertips.

'That pen was in Lawrence's rucksack the night he died,' explained Susan. 'Hazel has been concerned about its disappearance.' No one responded and so she asked a question. 'How on earth did it end up in the vicarage?'

'I have no idea. It was lying next to my diary and keys on the hall table. I assumed you'd left it there for me, Jessie. You know I'm always losing my pens,' said Daniel.

Jessie shook her head. For once, she seemed lost for words.

'Was it you, then?' Daniel asked Cerys.

Cerys was very red. 'No. I've never seen it before.'

'I'm glad to be able to return it,' said Daniel. 'I'm sorry I've no explanation about how it came to be with us.'

Ross coughed. 'Let's go back to the dates. We need to get on.'

The meeting ended and everyone quickly began to stack the chairs before leaving.

Susan noticed Hazel was hanging back. She was standing as still as the marble angel on the memorial stone nearby.

'Are you okay?' she asked Hazel, reaching out to grab her arm, frightened she was about to faint.

'I don't understand. How did he have Lawrence's pen? Jessie recognised the pen but denies seeing it at the vicarage, and Cerys say she's never seen it before.'

'I've no idea. You should tell the police it's turned up. It's been a difficult evening. Let's get out of here.'

She put her arm around Hazel, aware she was leaning heavily against Susan.

As they walked, she felt Hazel slowly pull herself away and by the time they were at the front door, she was looking surer of herself.

'I'm sorry, it's a shock. Lawrence often went to the vicarage. I suppose he could have used the pen there and left it, but I could swear I saw him using it the night he died. Maybe we were both wrong and Lawrence didn't have the pen that night. I don't know. I'm so confused.' Hazel looked around, still in a daze. 'Will this place ever feel the same again?'

'It will take time,' said Susan.

'I'm not sure the ghosts will ever leave. Everyone felt it. Everyone was scared. You could tell. That's not how people should feel in a house of prayer, is it?'

Outside, Hazel locked up the church. Ross and Cerys were standing away from the main path, deep in conversation. Cerys was crying, Ross comforting her.

'Poor Cerys,' said Hazel. 'She's very sensitive, isn't she? What an emotional evening it's been.' She gave a flicker of a smile. 'A glass of wine when I get home, I think.'

Before Susan could answer, she heard someone call her name.

'Susan, ready for the gym then?' called Jessie.

'Just a minute.' Susan turned to Hazel. 'Would you like to come to my house, have a drink with me? I can go to the gym any time.'

'Oh, no, really. To be honest, it would be good to be on my own. But thank you. You go to the gym.'

'If you're sure? What will you do about the pen?'

'I shall tell the police. They can come and collect it if they want to. It might simply prove their point that I made a mistake.'

'You believe that?'

'I'm not sure yet. I need to go home and think about it.'

Reassured, Susan turned to Jessie and held up her bag for life with her gym things in. 'I'm as ready as I ever shall be.'

Jessie said she'd drive them, and it didn't take long. Susan tried to make conversation, hoping to find out more about the appearance of the pen, but Jessie seemed preoccupied, and her answers were so perfunctory that Susan gave up.

At the gym, Jessie seemed slightly more relaxed. She introduced Susan to her friend, Phil. He gave Susan a tour of the gym and started to explain how the machines worked.

'I think I'll stick with the treadmill for tonight,' said Susan. 'Could you show me how to set that up at a nice gentle pace?'

Susan set to walking on the machine. She was nervous, but Jessie's friend was reassuring and gave her a very gentle programme to start with.

She was aware that everyone else was putting a great deal more effort into it than she was and at one point even found herself watching the TV and not moving at all. An hour seemed more than enough time to have spent there, so she told Jessie she would go and get a drink while Jessie carried on. Jessie, however, seemed happy to finish and, after a quick drink, they left.

As they were getting in the car, Susan was wondering why Jessie had arrived so late back to the village the night Lawrence died, nearer half past ten, if she usually finished her workout at nine.

As they were approaching the village of Castleford, Susan expected

Jessie to continue through the village, but she signalled, and turned left up a darker country road.

'We're going via Gatcombe?' Susan asked, checking, as it would take a lot longer that way.

'Oh, sorry, what on earth am I doing?' Jessie said, laughing.

Susan noticed they were passing the prayer centre. 'That's Shiloh. Isn't that where Daniel goes?'

'It is. We ought to pop in and see him. Only joking. Let's get on home, we'll go the scenic route tonight.'

Back in Bishopstone, Jessie parked close to the vicarage and, to Susan's surprise, Jessie invited her in for a drink. The inside of the vicarage seemed darker and more Gothic at night. They walked along the hallway, and it was a relief to reach the kitchen.

'This place is like a mausoleum, but the parish has no money to pay for decorating. The last vicar did at least manage to persuade them to do the kitchen. I think they were scared of his wife, and she got them to put in new appliances as well as a decent floor covering.'

On the back door of the kitchen there were rows of coat pegs. Jessie hung her own up.

Susan saw a pile of weights in one corner with a stand.

'I take those out onto the patio to exercise when it's dry,' said Jessie. She knelt and rubbed a dent in the floor covering close to them. 'Oh, no. When did that happen? I've been trying to look after this floor.' She looked up. 'Sorry, have a seat. Oh, hang on. Let's take that cushion off. It's covered in cat hair. The joys of having a Maine Coon. There are long ginger hairs everywhere.' Jessie picked up the cushion and threw it onto another chair. 'Now, let's have a glass of wine. I bought a really nice Merlot on offer this week.'

She clearly assumed that Susan was drinking and poured two glasses.

Jessie took a long sip, topped up her glass and sat down. She was very upright, there was nothing relaxed about her, and Susan had a feeling this was not going to be a casual chat.

'Last time we talked in here, you told me you were trying to help Hazel answer some questions about Lawrence's death,' began Jessie. 'I heard the way you talked about the pen earlier. You haven't given up digging, have you?'

'I'm only trying to help Hazel.'

Jessie flicked her hair and stared directly at Susan. 'No, it's more than that. This is personal. Why? You hardly knew Lawrence.'

Susan took a sip of her wine, and carefully placed the glass on the table. 'I care about truth, and I don't believe we have found out the full facts about how Lawrence died.'

'So, you don't think the police have investigated his death properly?'

'They haven't answered all the questions.'

'But there are bound to be some things that can't be explained. They are the experts. They know what matters and what doesn't. To be honest, Susan, I'm not sure why you feel qualified to be investigating this at all.'

'I know I don't have their expertise, but I promised Hazel to see if I could help her find some answers and we have grounds for suspecting some people may be hiding things.'

'And those people are supposed to be your friends,' said Jessie. 'How can you possibly suspect one of us of being involved in Lawrence's death? All this talk about the missing key – it shows you are suspecting someone who was at that choir committee meeting.'

Susan was suddenly aware of how quiet the house was. The kitchen had lost its initial cosy feel. The ticking of the clock filled the room. There were no curtains covering the long patio doors, no lights in the garden. It was just an endless expanse of black out there.

'I know and I'm sorry,' Susan replied, and she took a longer drink of her wine.

Jessie glared. 'You really suspect one of us of murder?'

Susan swallowed hard. She wanted to deny it, anything other than admit that was the case. However, taking a deep breath, she said, 'I admit that has crossed my mind. I'm sorry, it's not a nice thing to own up to but, as you said, logically that key has to have been taken by someone in our group and there has to be a reason why they took it.'

'You realise you are probably completely wrong? This is a tight-knit community. We stick together. You could find yourselves ostracised if you're not careful, and all for nothing.'

Susan felt herself push back the fear that had been creeping up. 'I realise that, but it's a chance I have to take.'

Jessie raised an eyebrow. 'You've got guts, I'll give you that, but I don't see how you can find out things the police can't.'

'I chat, I listen. One of the biggest difficulties is working out which lies matter and which ones I can ignore.'

'Who is telling lies?'

'Everyone.'

22

Susan hesitated and then said, 'I mean, you have lied this evening. Pretending to take a wrong turning. That wasn't a mistake, was it? That was habit. I don't believe you spend over two hours every Friday evening at the gym. I believe you go there for a short time and then move on to the prayer centre. You sit and you watch. Am I right?'

Jessie crossed her arms, raised an eyebrow. 'Okay, yes, I do go to Shiloh sometimes. I'm human. I'm well aware it's weird that Daniel goes over there every Friday. I can't help wondering if he is making an excuse to get away from me for the night. As it is, he sleeps in the spare room a lot now, saying he is reading or praying and doesn't want to disturb me.'

Susan didn't speak but instead she sipped her wine.

Jessie refilled her glass and continued. 'I just want to know what is going on...'

Susan could hear the hurt and bewilderment in Jessie's voice and said gently, 'So, when you watch the centre, are you thinking he might be sneaking off somewhere?'

'I suppose so.'

'But you can't watch the centre all night.'

'No, and to be honest it's pretty boring. I tend to check my online sites, do some work. But I have reason to think he goes out about nine-ish. I found a receipt for the local pub in his pocket. It had the time and the date. He went for a meal one Friday at nine. I wanted to see if he made a habit of it.'

Susan frowned. That was odd. Martha said Daniel never left the building.

'Have you asked Daniel about it?'

'Oh, no,' Jessie replied, her eyes wide. 'That would mean me telling him I'd been searching in his pockets. He'd be very upset by that.' Jessie put down her glass with a clatter. 'The main point is, Susan, I have never seen him leave the prayer centre. Furthermore, and this is for your notebook or wherever you jot down your thoughts about us all, I was there at the time they say Lawrence died.'

As she spoke, Jessie was tapping a long fingernail on the table so forcibly that Susan was waiting for it to break.

Jessie continued. 'Daniel didn't leave Shiloh. I know his car was there the whole time. I saw it was there when I arrived, and it was still there when I left. I was over there until the rain started. I didn't miss anything. I've heard Lawrence died before the rain started and I categorically know Daniel was over at Shiloh.'

Jessie sat back and crossed her arms. Susan felt that Jessie had completed a mission, and that mission had been to make it very clear to Susan that Daniel was at the centre during the time Lawrence died. She was trying too hard. It made her sound defensive, guilty even, but wouldn't anyone respond like that if they felt they might be accused of murder?

Susan took a deep breath. 'Thank you for speaking so frankly to me. As a matter of interest, what do you believe happened the night Lawrence died?'

Jessie paused. 'I think Lawrence's death was an accident and Hazel needs to accept that or she will be stuck in a state of denial. I've seen it before, people fighting hospitals and organisations after someone has died. A few, of course, are right, but for so many that anger and the need to blame someone consumes them and they never move on.'

Susan listened to the measured words. They were wise, considered. She was impressed with the insight of this young woman. 'I hear you, Jessie, and I agree with a lot of what you are saying. However, Hazel is asking valid questions and they are not going to disappear because we stop talking about them.' She stood up. 'I'd better get back to the dogs. Thank you for the wine.'

As Jessie let her out of the front door, Susan saw the path lit up.

'Those lights are a good idea,' she said.

'Yes, although we had a few stolen. They're only on spikes. Still, it's better than nothing. It's so dark out here. I wouldn't want anyone to fall. Accidents happen so easily.' Susan glanced back, but Jessie simply smiled and added, 'Right, see you at the fete on Saturday.'

Susan pushed open the gate and crossed the road, past the school and then started to walk past the pub garden. She could see couples sitting out in the garden. To her astonishment, she realised one was Robert and Fiona. They were laughing, and so engrossed in their conversation they didn't see her walking past.

Susan spotted an empty bottle of wine on their table and a second, which had been opened. It seemed so unlike Robert, who she knew wouldn't usually drink when he was driving. Then the thought crossed her mind that he might have no intention of driving home that evening. She felt her stomach tighten.

She walked quickly past and was glad to get home. After greeting the dogs, she turned on the TV, picked up her knitting, and tried to occupy herself. She immediately dropped two stiches and, annoyed with herself, threw the knitting back in its bag.

* * *

The next day was the school fete. However, before Susan went down to help, she wanted to visit Alice at the nursing home.

Alice was delighted with the socks Susan had bought for her and thanked her.

'Oh, guess who I met while I was over on the mainland?' said Susan, and she told Alice all about her encounter with Jessie.

'It was clever the way you got her to talk about the shoplifting without mentioning Robert.'

'She just assumed Lawrence had told me and I didn't put her right. The main thing is I am sure her shoplifting days are behind her but, of course, we still have no idea what it was that upset Lawrence at Christmas. However, on a slightly different tack, I did find out something else about Jessie last night. Believe it or not, I went with her to the gym.'

'You have been seeing a lot of her.'

'I know, but it's useful. Anyway, she invited me to go to the gym with her and I agreed.' Susan laughed. 'Don't ask me what I got up to there, but it was a chance to spend more time with Jessie. While she was driving us back, something interesting happened.'

Susan told Alice about the detour by the prayer centre and their conversation later.

'Jessie sounds very worried. What do you think is going on? Is it this Martha, do you think?'

Susan smiled. 'You've a good memory, and yes, that did cross my mind. Jessie had found this receipt for the pub. I reckon she was worried about Daniel leaving the centre. Maybe he was taking Martha out for a meal?'

'That is possible, of course. Remind me, did you say Daniel seemed to admire someone called Alan who also stayed at Shiloh – said he went out for a drink, that kind of thing?'

'Um, yes. Why do you mention it?'

'I was simply wondering if it might be Alan who Daniel is sneaking out to meet.'

Susan stared. 'Of course, yes. It could be.'

'And if that is more than just friendship, well, if Jessie is concerned—'

'You think Daniel is gay and that's what Lawrence found out?' exclaimed Susan.

'It has to be possible.'

'Goodness, that had never crossed my mind.'

Alice put her head to one side. 'This man, his name is Alan Smithee, isn't it?'

'Yes, that's right.'

'Mmm – I must google it. Now, tell me more about this pen turning up.'

Susan told Alice all about Daniel and the pen at choir practice.

'But he had no idea how special the pen was or that it had belonged to Lawrence?'

'No, he looked genuinely confused by the whole thing. He'd just picked up what he thought was any old pen off the hall table.'

'But if Daniel had taken it from Lawrence, that was a pretty audacious but clever way of disowning it.'

'It's hard to imagine someone like Daniel having the nerve to do that,' said Susan.

'That's true of the Daniel we see, but we know he is hiding secrets. Who knows what he's capable of? However, if he's telling the truth, then it would suggest that either Jessie or Cerys had brought the pen into the vicarage.'

'Jessie admitted to recognising it, but Cerys said she'd never seen it before. I suppose the hallway is very accessible, and a lot of people come and go in the vicarage.' Susan frowned. 'I find this business of the pen quite confusing. Why remove from the scene of a crime an object that is going to conclusively link you to it?'

'It is odd,' said Alice. 'It could have been taken for sentimental reasons, I suppose, but, of course, it was a useful item to plant on someone if needed.'

'It was also very valuable.'

'Of course, but then all the talk about it might have scared the person and they possibly decided to just leave it around, disown it.'

'Yes, it could have happened that way. Oh, by the way, I went for a walk with Ross on Thursday,' said Susan. 'We went up the downs at night, met his friend Dave, the man he says he met the night Lawrence died.'

'Ah, that was good. Tell me, did the times work out? Does his alibi stand up?'

Susan blinked. 'Of course. I hadn't thought about that. Let me see. He showed me where Dave's house was, about twenty minutes from the car park. He said he'd called in for Dave the week before, and they'd walked up together. That takes about twenty minutes. Now, Dave spoke about arriving just as it started to rain, that was ten past ten. That means, adding the time it took Ross to walk from the village to Dave's – gosh, that means we know Ross was out walking at the time of Lawrence's death, 9.50 p.m. to 10.15 p.m.' Susan paused and caught her breath. 'Ross has an alibi!'

'Well done. That's good news.'

'Brilliant. Now, what can you tell me about your chat with Cerys?'

'It was very interesting,' said Alice. 'She sat here in her flowered dress with her long blonde hair, all sweetness and light, my mum would have said, and yet I soon realised there is far more to her than first appeared. She seemed to become very agitated when she talked about a row she had with Lawrence on a school trip.' Alice described the argument to Susan. 'What I found particularly interesting was the passion with which she spoke. This was not an academic discussion about inequality: this was personal. She is only twenty-three and yet she takes life very seriously. She talked about feeling scared, watching her back, which I didn't quite understand. I also found her pendants particularly interesting, both of them. I looked a few things up, including some interesting Welsh names.' Alice looked at Susan as if she was meant to pick something up.

Susan paused. 'The pendants. Yes, there was something about them that seemed odd, but I couldn't put my finger on it.' She looked questioningly at Alice but only received a thoughtful expression in response. 'You're being unusually cryptic. I'm not sure what I am meant to be working out,' Susan said.

'I'm sorry, it's only an idea that I have. I don't want to put it in your head as I could be wrong. But if I'm right, then everything we know about this case will be turned upside down.'

23

Susan returned home to walk the dogs and have some lunch before heading to the fete. The sun was brilliant, the sky a clear cornflower blue, the trees still: a perfect day for the fete.

She arrived at the school to find it buzzing with activity. Every inch of the school building, field and car park seemed to be in use. Cheerful music was playing out of speakers, there were stalls selling cakes, jam and crafts, as well as hooplas, raffles, and children's games. On the field was a fire engine for children to visit and donkey rides at the far end. Inside the school, the hall was set out with tables and chairs and people were busy in the kitchen getting ready for the onslaught for teas, coffees and cake. It gave every appearance of some kind of rural idyll, but Susan knew that was an illusion. Not only did she have suspicions around Lawrence's death, but also there were the eggs thrown at her house, that awful message telling her she wasn't wanted here. It was highly likely that whoever had done those things was here.

Susan waved over to Fiona, who was busy spraying some last-minute signs. Susan guessed the business of the day was taking her mind off the pressures of the meeting with the local authority. It was good to see the village coming together.

Susan had signed up to do the white elephant stall. It was one of the few stalls she enjoyed working on at events like this. She kept prices low, and her main aim was to sell out by the end of the day.

Fiona approached Susan with a bottle of water. 'Everyone should have a drink, keep hydrated. It's a warm day,' she said as she patted the water bottle on her belt.

The school gates were opened, and the crowds swooped in. Susan's stall was busy with children clutching their pocket money, and parents tried to dissuade them from buying back toys they had donated or large soft toys they had no room for.

Susan was just explaining to a woman why she didn't have time to count the 5,000 pieces of the jigsaw but was sure it would be complete when she noticed Jessie rummaging among the toys. She was nervous about approaching Jessie after their last conversation but, putting on a fixed smile, she forced herself to speak.

'Are you looking for something?' she asked Jessie. 'If it's for a family you visit or something, I only want a small contribution, a few pence would do.'

'Oh, no, I'm just looking for anything I might be able to sell online.' Jessie looked around and Susan was relieved that Jessie appeared, at least, to have put the previous encounter behind them. 'If I find anything worthwhile, I'll give you more, not less. Ah, now that I can sell.' Jessie picked out a stuffed toy from *Sesame Street*.

'We're selling that for 50p,' said Susan.

'You need me on here. All the cuddly toys look the same and most aren't worth anything. But I've seen one of these online, for something like £20. This is in good condition. Yes, I could sell it. Tell you what, I'll give you £5 and see how I get on. If I make loads, I'll contribute to school funds.'

Susan smiled. 'That's great. Thank you.'

'I hope you have time to go round the rest of the fete. I heard they'd put up those photos of the staff as babies – it was a game we played at the Christmas party. It's good fun trying to guess who is who. To be honest, it was the type of clothes that gave it away for me, as much as the photos themselves.'

Jessie smiled and then left Susan to rejoin Daniel, who was talking to one of the parents.

As much as Susan enjoyed the stall, she was relieved when a parent offered to give her a break to go and look around the fete for herself and get a drink. The first thing she did was buy tickets for the tombola and, of course, won the tin of red kidney beans, not the bottle of gin. She tried to guess the name of a frightening-looking stuffed octopus which she sincerely hoped she didn't win.

Susan wandered over to a look at a board titled 'Guess the baby', which sported an array of baby and toddler photographs. At the top was a touching tribute to Lawrence, with two photos, one of him as a baby and one as an adult. It was amazing to see the likeness between Lawrence at one year old and fifty-five years old. There was the same confident smile, facing the world, blond hair and blue eyes. Susan remembered Jamari, seeing that smile, the likeness of Zoe and herself in that tiny baby, and marvelled at nature.

Below were the photographs of various members of staff. As Jessie had said, it was the fashions and the style of photography that gave the game away and she easily picked out Cerys and Fiona.

Fiona was sitting on a rug with a Fisher-Price telephone and activity centre. A TV that was laughably small was in the corner of the room, the wallpaper brightly coloured, a hangover from the previous century. Fiona herself was wearing a dress and hand-knitted cardigan, her hair clipped back in a plastic slide. However, even back then she looked eager to be getting up and going.

Cerys's photo was of her a little older. She was sitting in front of a birthday cake with four candles on it, waiting to blow them out. Under her arm she was holding a baby Annabel doll tight. She was wearing denim dungarees and a jumper, sitting up at a pine table in a cream-painted room. In the corner was a Christmas tree, with lights on. It all looked so cosy, but Susan wondered if she was living with foster parents by then or still with her mother. Whatever her situation, Cerys was smiling at the photographer. It crossed Susan's mind that it was possible that, even at that age, Cerys had learned to plaster on a smile for the world.

Susan wandered off, but she couldn't get the photos out of her head. She returned and looked through them again, starting with those of Lawrence at the top, and working her way down. Her mind returned to Hazel choosing the photograph for the funeral. She remembered the day she helped Cerys at the school, and Alice talking about her visit from Cerys. She had definitely been hinting at something. What was it? She'd mentioned Cerys being scared, the pendants, that row between Lawrence and Cerys. What had she meant?

However, the harder Susan tried to think, the more muddled she became. In the end, she went inside to get a cup of tea and a beautifully decorated cupcake. She decided to get out into the sunshine and walked across the playground. She knew there was a wooden bench hidden around the end of the school building and headed towards it.

However, she was just approaching the edge of the school when she heard raised voices.

'You have to understand, this is nothing to do with you now.'

'But I want to help—'

'No. You must keep away. I mean it, if you don't...' Jessie paused, looked over, and saw Susan.

Ross had his hands resting on Jessie's shoulders. She shrugged him off, and forced her face into a false smile.

'Oh, hi, we were just having a rather heated chat about Ross trying to take over the song I am organising with some of the kids. He's a control freak.'

Ross took longer to recover, and it took a few seconds for him to speak. 'Susan, hi, um, good to see you. Now, I'd better get back to the fete. I'm meant to be helping out on the raffle.'

'Yes, I expect Daniel will be wondering where I am,' said Jessie, looking down the playground. 'In fact, here he comes now.' Waving to him, she rushed towards him. Ross gave Susan a quick smile and began to make his way towards the school.

Susan went over to the wooden bench she'd been looking for and sat down, thinking. What had she stumbled on? It certainly hadn't been a discussion about a children's song. It had been intimate, something much more significant.

She turned and saw Robert walking towards her.

She felt her face flushing as she remembered seeing Robert with Fiona at the pub. She'd told herself many times that it probably meant nothing and, even if it did, it shouldn't matter to her. However, as she looked over at him now, she knew that for some reason it did.

'Hi, I thought I'd find you hiding away,' Robert said, and moved to sit next to her.

'I didn't realise you were coming,' Susan mumbled, not able to meet his eye.

'Fiona asked me to.'

'Oh, right. Um, I saw you with her the other night at the pub.' Susan had blurted the words out before she could stop herself.

He grinned. 'Nothing is secret in a village, is it? Why didn't you come and have a drink?'

'I didn't like to interrupt. You looked very cosy.'

Robert threw back his head and laughed loudly. 'Oh, really, Susan, we weren't on a date or anything. She sent me a text, asked me over for a drink. She's had a very rough time, you know.'

Susan squirmed but couldn't resist adding, 'I was surprised to see you drinking wine. You wouldn't normally when you're driving.'

Again, he laughed. 'God, you never stop playing detective, do you? I didn't drink, by the way, and I was quite able to drive myself home.'

'Okay, well, how did you find Fiona?'

'Pretty down, actually. She's putting on a good act today, but she's going through a lot.'

Susan glanced around to check they couldn't be overheard. 'I know about the complaint. Fiona told me. It must be a worry for her. Oh, word is out that I'm investigating Lawrence's death. Jessie seems to have worked it out. She saw how I reacted to Lawrence's pen turning up at choir practice. I haven't told you about that yet, have I? A few things have happened.'

Susan told Robert about Daniel and the pen, going to the gym, the journey home via the prayer centre, followed by the conversation back at the vicarage.

'It's interesting about Jessie being on to you.'

'Yes, and talking of Jessie, I just stumbled upon something a bit worrying.' Susan told him about the scene she had just witnessed between Jessie and Ross.

'Jessie said they were arguing about organising a song. It's just the sort of thing people do row about, you know.'

'I don't think it was that. Ross looked very upset, and he had his hands on her shoulders when I arrived.'

'It's probably nothing. It sounds as if you are winding enough people up as it is. Keep out of that. That means it's quite likely the others have caught on, watch your back,' said Robert.

'I'll be fine.'

'Just don't go walking down dark alleys with any of them.'

Susan laughed and then told him about her walk with Ross.

'Oh, really, Susan, that was a risk. If I had to put my money on any of them, it would be him.'

She explained that in actual fact Ross was the only one she knew with an apparently cast-iron alibi, adding, 'It was actually very interesting. I know now how to record a badger on my phone, something I had no idea how to do before the walk.' Susan finished her tea. 'Right, back to my stall. That mother will be cursing me. Have a good time. Oh, by the way, Hazel has arranged the funeral. It will be on Wednesday, over here in St Jude's at twelve.'

'I shall come.' Robert stood up and Susan had a sudden panic he was going to kiss her goodbye. Aware of the parents and children nearby, she made a quick getaway.

When she returned to her stall, she was disappointed to find a lot of the stock still there. The parent, meaning well, had repriced some of the items, doubling the price, thinking she would make more money. Susan simply thanked her, but when she had left quickly declared a sale on and was pleased that by the end of the fete, she only had a few items left.

'Ye've done well,' said Fiona, coming to collect the money and noticing the empty table.

'I've done a few of these in my time. I really don't see the point of packing up loads of the same stuff year after year. Get shot of it and start again next time is my motto.'

Fiona smiled. 'Quite right. Now, I wonder if ye could do me a wee favour. Put those few things in the wee box, take them to the old storeroom and while ye're there, bring back a few more empties. Here are the keys, this is the one ye need.'

'I don't think I know where the storeroom is.'

'Oh, sorry, of course not. It's down past the staffroom. You'll see an old wooden door. It was where we used to keep the sports equipment. It led straight on to the playground, which was quite handy. Anyway, that was a few years ago now.'

Susan bundled up the remains of her table and headed to the storeroom.

It was well hidden away. She had no idea it existed. As she opened it, a musty smell of old paper and wood greeted her. She put on the light, neatly stacked her own box, and then looked around for any empty ones. It was a small, narrow room and she pushed past some old Christmas decorations to reach the far end, where she thought she saw some boxes. Nothing had prepared her for what she would find.

24

What Susan found at the back of the storeroom was a locked door, which she realised must lead on to the playground. Glancing down at the bunch of keys that Fiona had given her, Susan picked out the one most likely to fit and pushed it in the lock. To her amazement, the door opened easily, and she found herself looking out on to a high metal fence that ran along one side of the school. Looking down, she saw it led straight to the side of the front of the building. She realised immediately that this was a way in and out of the school unobserved by CCTV.

Susan looked down and saw old cigarette butts, a few tins and a broken bottle. She wondered if teenagers hung around here at night.

'What ye doing?'

Susan turned to see Fiona and quickly went back into the storeroom. Fiona seemed taller, more threatening than usual. 'Oh, sorry, I was simply curious,' Susan stammered.

'Why did ye open that door?'

'I, um, was just wondering where it led.' This sounded weak, even to Susan.

Fiona screwed up her eyes. 'Jessie told me we were all under suspicion.'

'It's not like that.'

'I believe it is. I'm not sure why ye're sticking your nose in. Ye've only lived in the village a wee while.'

Susan stepped back, her heart racing. 'Hazel is worried about how Lawrence died. The church key went missing, his pen as well. She is worried someone else went up the tower after I left Lawrence.'

'And so you suspect that one of us, his closest friends, went and killed Lawrence?'

'I'm just trying to help.'

Fiona walked towards her, pushed her to one side, and pulled the door closed. Susan handed her the keys and Fiona locked the door. The room suddenly seemed very dark, quiet; they were alone.

'I know what you're thinking, and aye, there are nae cameras or alarms on this door, but it is never used. I dinnae go creeping out of here the evening Lawrence died. That's enough, we need to get back to clearing up the fete.'

Fiona stormed out. Susan quickly followed and was glad to be back in the playground. She breathed deeply and realised Fiona was raising her voice to address them all.

'Thank ye all for helping today. I know in the circumstances it was extremely hard, but we have brought our village together, given it heart and hope, so thank ye all. This evening I will be in the pub at eight. If you pop in, there will be a wee dram on me waiting for ye.'

There was a mumble of thanks followed by a self-conscious hand clap and slowly everyone went back to work.

When she returned home, Susan felt in need of escaping the village. She put the dogs in the car and drove them over to Newtown Woods.

Keeping the dogs on the lead, she walked them through the woods, taking in the sounds of the blackbird singing, the bees on the carpet of wildflowers, the buzzard high above. She caught a brief magical glimpse of a hare and saw brightly coloured butterflies resting on the bushes.

She wandered through the still, shaded woodland until she reached the breathtaking beauty of the estuary. At first, she needed to adjust to the brightness of the sun out here and then she was able to take in the spectacle of white waterbirds flying in formation along the horizon, the cacophony of geese, the ducks chattering, the oystercatchers searching for food in the wet mud.

Susan decided to venture out to the bird hide. Once there, she was excited to see seals on the bank opposite, basking in the early-evening sunlight.

She thought about her altercation with Fiona. Of course, Fiona was under a lot of stress, but her violent reaction had shocked Susan. Was it guilt that made her say those things? Had she in fact escaped through that door to go over to St Jude's and kill Lawrence? Of course, she would have had to steal the church key beforehand, but it was possible.

The main question was: why? What motive did Fiona have for killing Lawrence? Everyone talked about how devoted she was to him, but had that worn thin over time? This business of Lawrence wanting her to leave, what was that based on? Was it something to do with this complaint? Whatever the motive, Susan now knew Fiona had the means to get to the church.

Eventually it was time to leave, but she returned home refreshed.

She was settling down to a glass of wine in the garden when she heard someone call her over the fence.

Susan walked down the garden to where she could speak to Hazel.

'I was wondering if you fancy going down to the pub to meet up with everyone?' Hazel asked.

'I'm not sure—'

'Please come. I don't want to go on my own.'

Reluctantly, Susan agreed and they walked down to the pub together. As they made their way, Susan told Hazel about her conversation with Jessie the night before.

'I understand why Jessie is upset,' said Hazel. 'It's horrible to think someone suspects you of something so terrible, but she has to understand there are things that need explaining, and if she is innocent then she has nothing to worry about.'

'I suppose not, but you can see why it's hard to not be quite that objective about it.'

Hazel frowned in concern. 'I should never have asked you to do this.

Here you are trying to settle into your new home, and I've asked you to do something that has the potential to make you enemies, not friends.'

Susan shook her head. 'If it means we get to the truth about what happened to Lawrence, then I don't mind. I wasn't saying I regret this at all. I just want you to be aware that the deeper we go, the more difficult it could become.'

'That doesn't put me off. Thank you for the warning, though.'

They arrived to find Fiona sitting with Daniel and Jessie, Cerys and Ross, at a long pub table. Seeing them, Fiona jumped up, avoided eye contact with Susan but, speaking to Hazel, said, 'Let me get ye both a drink. In fact, I'll get a bottle. Sit down.'

Susan and Hazel joined the table. She glanced around. No one was chatting. Daniel was fiddling with his glass. Jessie was scrolling on her phone. Cerys and Ross sat silently, side by side. Hazel looked over at Susan and gave a nervous smile.

They all seemed relieved when Fiona returned with two bottles of wine and set them down on the table. She poured glasses for Hazel, Susan and herself, and offered the bottle to Cerys and Jessie, who were also drinking wine.

Fiona started the conversation, talking easily about how well the fete had gone, and slowly people relaxed.

Suddenly, Hazel tapped the side of her glass.

'I wanted to thank you for the support you have given me since losing Lawrence.' She paused and took a sip of her drink. 'I have a few questions about Lawrence's death. I expect you will know about the missing side door key by now. The only explanation I can come up with is that someone intended to use it to go up the tower to speak to Lawrence secretly.'

Fiona scowled. 'That's a bit of a leap, Hazel. Ye need to check again, look around for the old key. I'm sure it's somewhere safe.'

'It's not in my house. And in any case, there are other questions. Why would Lawrence have gone to the edge of the tower and looked over in that way when he was scared of heights? Why weren't his binoculars attached to the harness when he fell? How come his pen has suddenly appeared when I was sure he had it with him the night he died?'

Daniel coughed and spoke slowly. 'Lawrence's death was sudden and a terrible shock. It's only natural to have questions, but we have to accept that unfortunately some of them will never be answered.'

'That may be the case, but I'm not ready to let it go yet and I've asked Susan to help me,' said Hazel. 'If any of you know anything about what happened that evening that you haven't told the police, please come and tell me. I have to know. I can't move on with my life until I know exactly what happened.'

Daniel sat forward, fiddling with his pint glass on the table, directing his words to it rather than the group. 'I'm sure if any of us knew anything, we would have told the police by now.'

'I'm sorry,' said Hazel more quietly. 'But I can't let it go.'

Fiona turned on Susan. 'This is your fault, feeding her these ridiculous ideas.'

As she had been earlier, Susan was struck by the level of aggression Fiona was showing her.

However, she took a deep breath and tried to speak calmly. She turned to Fiona. 'Hazel is my neighbour, and she has asked for my help. I've not put ideas into Hazel's head. She has explained the things she's worried about, but the one thing she didn't mention is her gut instinct that something here is very wrong. I share that and have a feeling some of you do too. There was no mistaking the atmosphere at the meeting after choir last night.'

Ross took a noisy slip from his pint then slammed his glass on the table and spoke. 'Susan's got a point. Don't tell me no one is keeping secrets here. It's time to be open with each other. I have admitted to one lie. I wasn't with Cerys at the time Lawrence died. In fact, I had an interesting walk from the vicarage, through the village, before I went on up the downs. It's amazing what you see at night, and not just among the wildlife. So, how about someone else owning up to a lie? It's quite liberating.'

No one met his eye. Nobody spoke.

He looked over at Susan. 'It's up to you then to keep digging.'

Susan blinked, surprised at his words. 'You think I should?'

'Of course. I mean, who knows what you might find? I know I'm pretty surprised at who I see walking around at night – even the night Lawrence died. You never know who might be around.'

The group was far more subdued now. As soon as they had finished their drinks, everyone seemed relieved to have a reason to leave. Hazel and Susan walked back to their houses together.

Susan decided on an early night. However, once in bed, she was annoyed to find that she couldn't sleep. She tried reading, listening to the radio, making herself a drink, but nothing seemed to work.

It was two in the morning when she finally pulled on her jeans, old jumper and coat and went and took the dogs out for a walk. They were excited and she was relieved to be out in the fresh air. She remembered her walk with Ross. He was right, there was something incredibly special about being out here in the darkness.

The moon had disappeared behind clouds now and there was a slight drizzle of rain. It felt cold on her face but soothing. She went on to the main road and only the glimmer of a street light led the way to St Jude's, which was in darkness apart from that stream of light going down one side of the tower.

Susan realised the rain was getting heavier, and was about to turn back, when she had a feeling something was wrong, what was it? What could she smell?

Susan looked up the road, was that smoke in the air? She hurried towards it until she was outside Fiona's house and heard the crackle of fire.

25

Susan rushed down the side of Fiona's house, tied the dogs securely to a tree at the top of the garden and ran towards the caravan. She could see flames inside and ran to the door, but it was locked. She remembered the Yale key, lifted the stone, and opened the door, then climbed up the steps, shouting, trying to make her voice heard over the fire and smoke alarm. Suddenly Ross appeared, pulling back the curtain, and stood there, his eyes wide in terror.

'You have to get out now,' she shouted.

But the flames started to creep higher. The heat pushed her back out of the caravan. She ran to the other end, saw Ross crawl out of a window at the back and collapse on the ground. Fearing an explosion, she dragged him as far up the garden as she could, pulled out her phone, hands trembling, and dialled 999.

Once that was done, Susan collapsed into tears. Terrified, she looked back up at the house, which was in darkness. Was Fiona at the school?

She looked down at Ross, who, even though he was breathing, appeared to be unconscious.

Suddenly she heard screams from the top of the garden and looked up to see Fiona staggering out of the house. 'Oh my God, Ross.'

Susan shouted to her, and she ran over to Susan and Ross. 'Is he—'

'He's breathing.'

Fiona slumped next to Ross, touched his face. 'I'm so sorry.'

Susan looked down at Fiona. The last few times they'd talked Fiona had been so angry, so assertive, but now she looked broken, and Susan felt a rush of compassion. She reached out and put her arm around her.

Suddenly the night air was full of the sounds and lights of the emergency vehicles. Susan felt as if she was in some kind of nightmare, watching the caravan fire being tackled and paramedics approaching her and Ross. While some attended to Ross, one came over to speak to her. 'It's okay, everything is under control now. We're here to look after you. You don't have to be frightened,' said the paramedic, gently comforting her before saying more firmly, 'We need to get you to the hospital.'

'I have to sort out Rocco and Libs. Wait.' She tried to stand up, but her legs were wobbly, and she was finding it hard to breath. She looked up the garden and, close to where she'd secured the dogs, she saw some people from the village standing in a group watching on. Seeing Tracy from the shop, Susan staggered up to her.

'Tracy, they want me to go to the hospital,' she stammered. 'I'm worried about the dogs.'

'Of course. Don't worry about them.' Tracy approached the dogs and fussed them. 'They'll be safe with me.'

'Thank you so much.' Susan bent over, coughing, and stroked their heads. 'Be good for Tracy. I'll be back soon.'

'They'll be no trouble,' said Tracy. 'I've some nice cooked sausages in the fridge. Don't worry: they'll be spoiled rotten.'

The dogs seemed to understand. Tracy untied the leads, and they went with her, only occasionally looking back at Susan.

The paramedic had caught up with her now. 'Come on, please, we need to get you checked out.'

At the hospital, Susan was taken straight to a ward and a nurse came to settle her in. He was quietly competent, and she felt herself relax, allowing herself to be cared for.

The nurse asked her if she had a relative or friend they could contact. Taking out her phone, she found Robert's number, gave it to the nurse who sent a short text to him.

After seeing a doctor, she lay down on the pillow. She found herself occasionally shaking. Every time she closed her eyes she saw the flames, felt the heat and saw Ross staring at her.

Suddenly she heard a familiar voice. 'What have you been up to now?'

She turned to see Robert, who smiled, but his eyes were creased with concern. It was only then that the tears started to fall down her cheek and soak into the pillow.

Robert pulled up a chair, laid his strong hand on hers. 'Hey, it's okay. You're safe now.'

'How is Ross?'

'He's going to be fine. The burns are mainly to the top of his arm. He was incredibly lucky. You saved him from very severe burns, probably saved his life.'

Susan began to sob harder. 'I was so scared.'

'I know, but you were very brave. Now, you need to rest, close your eyes. I'm here. I'm not going anywhere.'

And so slowly she started to drift off to sleep. She couldn't escape the scenes in her head: the fire, the smell, but when it became too dark, she felt for Robert's hand and knew she was safe.

Susan was woken by the sound of people chatting and greeting each other. A new shift was coming on, and nurses who had looked so energetic when she'd arrived now looked pale and exhausted as they handed over to the day staff.

Robert had fallen asleep, his head resting on the covers by her leg, but he was still holding her hand. Slowly he looked up and blinked. 'Good morning.'

Susan smiled. 'You stayed all night.'

'How are you feeling?'

'Better than you. You look shattered. Please go home now.'

'First, let me check when you're going to be leaving.'

Robert staggered down the ward, and she saw him speaking to a nurse.

When he returned, he said, 'It sounds like you just need to be seen by the doctor when he does his rounds and then they will let you go home.'

They were brought a cup of tea and Susan sat up as Robert explained. 'After I received your text, I phoned Fiona. She told me everything.'

'It was awful. I've never been so close to a fire before. Do the police know anything about how the fire started?'

Robert shook his head before going on to explain that the caravan was now being treated as a crime scene. A friend had told Robert that initially it looked like the fire could have been started by a cigarette, but it was early days.

Susan nodded. 'I'm so scared, Robert. What if someone set fire to the caravan on purpose?'

'You think it was arson? But why?'

'Ross had said some difficult things at the pub earlier that evening, telling me to carry on with the investigation into Lawrence's death and even hinting he'd seen someone out that night.'

'I see. Gosh, it was a pretty desperate thing to do. We'll know more soon.'

Susan smiled. 'You look done in. What time did you get to the hospital?'

'It was about four in the morning.' He grinned. 'God, I'm knackered. Could you have your next emergency at a more reasonable time?'

'I hope there won't be another time,' she said, smiling.

Robert stood up. 'You're looking brighter. I'll go home, have a shower and something to eat. Give me a ring when they say you can go, and I'll come and run you home.'

'That's really kind, but it's a bit of a way to Ventnor.'

'That will teach you to move all this way.' He laughed, too loud, too hearty, as always, and people on the ward glanced round. For once, Susan didn't care.

Later that morning, Robert collected her from the hospital and drove her home.

She was glad to get in, shower and put her smoky clothes in the wash, and then said to Robert, 'I have to go over and pick up Rocco and Libs.'

'I can do that for you.'

'What about Gem Gem and Dougie? Are they okay?'

'I left them with a neighbour who just adores them both, but I'll get back to them later.'

There was a knock at the door and Susan saw that it was Hazel.

'Oh, you poor thing.'

Robert smiled. 'She's doing fine. I'm just going to go over and get the dogs. I'll leave you two to chat.'

Hazel sat next to her. She was very calming. Susan heard the church bells ringing in the distance, and realised it was the first time she'd heard them here in the village since she'd arrived. Of course, the tower was open, the steps mended.

'It's good to hear them again, isn't it?' said Hazel. 'Daniel told me to take the morning off. He's not expecting many at St Jude's today. This evening they're going to open for an hour for people to go in to have a time of prayer and meditation.'

'That sounds a good idea.'

'The bells make it feel like the village is getting back to normal,' said Hazel, but then pulled at her sleeve. 'But it isn't, is it? Nothing is as it was before.'

At that moment, Susan heard barking outside the house and went to the front door.

Rocco and Libs went mad, pulling on the leads, trying to get to her. She leant down and gave him both big cuddles. 'Oh, I've missed you both.'

'And they've missed you,' said Robert, 'although they've been spoilt rotten, particularly by Tracy's husband. He's loopy about them. I shouldn't think they'll need to eat for a month. When I got to Tracy's they were both lying next to empty dishes after finishing a bowl of beef stew Tracy happened to have in the fridge. I'm not sure how they're going to go back to kibble after the feast they've been having.'

Susan grinned. 'I don't care. I'm just relieved they were happy.'

Hazel had stood up. 'I'll leave you to it, Susan, but I'm only next door, so just give me a shout if there's anything at all I can do.' And with this she quietly left.

As Susan went to the kitchen, she heard Robert's phone ping a text.

'Any news?' she asked.

'They still believe a cigarette started the fire, and that Ross had been drinking. They found a half-drunk bottle of whisky.'

'So, are they saying he started the fire accidentally?'

'They're not sure, still looking into it.'

Susan sat back in the chair and both the dogs snuggled up next to her.

She glanced out of the window to see the sun was shining. 'Listen, I know this sounds odd, but I'd really love to come over to Ventnor and have a walk along the beach there with you. Would that be okay? I can drive myself.'

'Are you sure you feel up to driving?'

'I'm fine. I need to get out now.'

Robert smiled. 'Okay, but I'm going to follow you. Any problems, pull in and I'll sort things out.'

They drove down to the Military Road along the coast. The sun glistened on the sea, and Susan opened her window so she could hear the crashing of the waves, and the gulls, and crows above. On such a beautiful Sunday morning, the road was quite busy. Cars were top-heavy with surfboards and packed with children and parents, with the mountain of stuff they needed for a day at the beach.

Finally, they turned inland, drove through the picturesque village of Whitwell, and down into Ventnor. It was Susan's first visit since moving house and it was as if she had two homes now. She'd lived in Ventnor for nearly forty years and had so many memories here.

They went by Robert's house. He popped into his neighbour's, picked up Gem Gem and Dougie, and then they all went together to the beach.

The breeze was warm on her face, and she closed her eyes to breathe in deeply. Dougie managed to find an old plastic ball which he came running back with. Rocco, Libs and Gem Gem sniffed amongst the seaweed and dug holes.

The events of the night before slowly faded. The stench of the smoke started to drift away.

'Thank you. This is just wonderful,' she said to Robert. 'I don't know how to thank you for looking after me.'

'You can start by taking me up to that café for a large coffee and a sandwich. It's nearly lunchtime.'

Susan laughed. 'Some people are easily pleased.'

As they were drinking their coffee, Robert received a text, and as he read it his face darkened.

'What is it? What's happened?'

26

Robert looked up, his face grave. 'That was another message from my friend on the police force. They've found that key, the one to the side door of St Jude's, stuffed under a sofa in the caravan.'

'Ross had the key?'

'Yes. They confirmed it's the original for the side door with Daniel or Hazel. They are now questioning Ross about the night Lawrence died.'

'They're suggesting Ross killed Lawrence?'

'They're not openly saying that.'

'But it can't have been. Ross has an alibi. He was walking with his friend Dave.'

Susan looked out over the sea and suddenly it seemed less blue; the wisps of clouds were spreading.

'I need to get back to the village,' she said.

'I understand.' Robert reached forward and squeezed her hand. 'Look after yourself now.'

Susan returned home and, later that evening, hearing the church bells, she decided to make her way to St Jude's.

As she left her house, she saw Hazel out the front of her house gardening and approached her.

Hazel wiped her muddy hands on her trousers and stood up.

'I'm going down to the church, would you like to come with me?' asked Susan.

'I'd rather stay here, thank you. I expect you've heard by now. They found that old church key in the caravan after the fire. They showed it to me and it's definitely the old side door key. It's all bit much to take in. I can't believe Ross would do such a thing.'

'Oh, but he can't have killed Lawrence...' Susan explained about Ross's alibi. 'But then, why did he have that key?'

Hazel raised her hand. 'I can't even think about it. It's why I don't want to go to the church this evening. I don't know if it's common knowledge yet, but I can't face the gossip.'

'That's fair enough. I'll leave you to your garden. If you want to chat, you know where I am.'

Susan left Hazel and made her way down through the close into the village and entered St Jude's, but her mind was racing.

Daniel had arranged the seating in the church for a time of silent thought and meditation. There was no music, no one conducting a service. No one was loudly greeting each other. There were no forced smiles, no eye contact.

Individuals were dotted around, sitting alone in pews. Daniel sat at the front with his back to them, and the early-evening sun shone through the stained-glass window, reflections of yellows, blues and reds dancing aimlessly on the cold stone floor.

No one spoke, no one moved. It was as if they all sat united in shock. Outside were the brash sounds of cars driving past, youngsters shouting greetings at each other, but inside St Jude's it was silent, a sanctuary.

Susan wondered if anyone there knew about the discovery of the old key.

Daniel stood and, without turning round, he picked up a long taper and lit a candle, his hand shaking. Susan watched him. Her gaze was drawn to the flame flickering. She imagined the warmth reaching out to her, held her hand up to shield her face and looked away.

Jessie sat alone to one side of the church. She sat very still, staring ahead of her, her face very pale, the only sign of emotion being the tears silently falling unchecked down her cheek.

Susan became aware of the sound of short, gulping sobs, and turned to see Cerys, her head in her hands, her body shaking. She was wearing her trademark flowered dress, her hair tied in a ponytail with a matching ribbon, clutching her pendants: the white flower with 'MAM' engraved on it and the fancy cross. She looked very young and fragile, and Susan remembered that photograph of the toddler in her dungarees. How much hurt had she been hiding behind that dimpled smile?

Her mind went back to all those questions she had had that day at the fete, and the conversation with Alice about the pendants. Both were interesting, Alice had said. What was it about Welsh names?

And as Susan watched that beam of light streaming through the window, it was as if it shone into her mind: she could see clearly, understand what all these things meant. She was glad to be sitting somewhere quiet. It was so much to take in, but yes, she was sure she was right.

Suddenly, she needed to get out of the church, to be out there in the sunshine, but she wasn't going to go home. No, she had to talk to Cerys.

As quietly as she could, she picked up her things and walked down the aisle, but aware her footsteps still echoed around the church. Once outside, she felt she could breathe more easily. Looking for somewhere to sit and catch her breath, she walked around the side of the church to the spot where Lawrence had fallen and sat on the bench that she'd sat on with Hazel that night. The flowers in the pots were now in bloom and she smiled as she looked down at the red geraniums, the flamenco dancers of the plant world. But she was distracted by a glint of lights in the pot. Leaning over, she realised it was no tiny mammal but two small solar lights, similar to the kind Daniel and Jessie had on their pathway.

It seemed odd they should be there. Looking up, she saw they were directly below where Lawrence had fallen and suddenly an idea came to her: yes, it had to be possible. She was about to make her way back, but before she did, she took out her phone and googled a website about haemophilia. It confirmed something that had been on her mind. She then searched for one more thing, looking through a list of beautiful Welsh names and their meaning. Yes.

Still deep in thought, she started to make her way back to the entrance to the church. As she hoped, Susan caught Cerys as she was leaving. Their eyes met and Cerys approached her. Susan saw Cerys wiping away tears from her face, but her voice was calm as she spoke. 'I wanted to thank you; you saved Ross's life.'

'How is he?'

'I visited with Fiona this afternoon. He's sitting up. The main worry was his arm, but I think it will be okay. Have you heard about the old side door key being found in his caravan?'

'I have.'

'The police came to talk to Ross. He had no idea how the old key got there. He's so disorganised. There will be some simple explanation. I told him not to worry.'

'He has an alibi,' said Susan. 'There has to be some explanation. How are you? You've been under a lot of stress.'

They started to walk on the pathway that led to the vicarage gate. Cerys looked around as if to check they were alone. 'I might as well tell you. It will soon be common knowledge. I was the person who sent in the anonymous complaint to the school.'

Susan blinked, surprised at first. However, she quickly assimilated it into her new understanding of Cerys and realised it made sense.

'It was a stupid thing to do,' continued Cerys. 'I was sulking after a poor teacher's assessment done by Lawrence.'

Susan paused, looked directly at Cerys. 'That's not the real reason you sent it, is it?'

Cerys stepped back and screwed up her eyes. 'What do you mean?'

'The real reason why you made that complaint was that you were angry after an argument you had with Lawrence on a school trip about how much harder it is for a woman to get on in her career than a man.'

'I don't know how you know about that or why you think a small differ-ence of opinion like that would make me do something so drastic.'

'But it wasn't a minor disagreement,' said Susan. 'It was far more personal than that. You had watched your mother, a teacher, struggle. She'd lost everything, even you at one point to foster parents because life became too much for her. And then you had to listen to Lawrence saying he got where he was through sheer hard work, denying all the advantages he had.'

'I suppose I was angry about that.'

'You were furious because your mother struggled all her life, while your father had left and gone on to have a highly successful career. Everything had worked out for him. The real root of the problem is in the identity of your mother and, of course, your father.'

'What the hell?' Cerys's eyes were wide with fear now. Susan could see her hand reaching towards the gate. She was ready to run away, but appeared to change her mind.

'I know who they are. I know who you are,' continued Susan. 'I was pointed in the right direction by Alice at the nursing home and have now worked it out for myself.'

Cerys stepped back, very pale. She started to wind the chiffon scarf around her finger but this time it was tighter and tighter: the end of her finger was turning white.

'I know your mother was Blodwen, a teacher in the school in Cardiff, a close friend of Hazel. I saw her photo at Hazel's, but it took me a while to realise that the photograph I'd caught a glimpse of in your purse was the same person. Once I did, I knew there had to be a very special connection between you both. And, of course, there was the white flower pendant you wear. Blodwen was wearing that in Hazel's photo. I should have immediately recognised it when I saw you were wearing it, although of course it looks a bit different now you have had it engraved.'

Cerys gasped. 'You worked that out?'

'Not on my own. Alice at the nursing home got there before me. She worked out Blodwen was your mother, and now she and I also know the identity of your father.'

Cerys stood very still and waited.

27

'You know who my father is?' Cerys asked, her voice shaking.

'I do,' said Susan. 'I realise now why Alice told me both your pendants were important. The one with the complex cross design is, of course, a medical alert. I've just checked online that women can inherit haemophilia from their father. I read they can become carriers of it, sometimes even have some symptoms, or bleeding problems. I'm guessing that is why you wear the pendant.'

Cerys was white now, frozen, hardly breathing. Scared Cerys was going to faint, Susan gently took her by the elbow, pushed open the gate into the vicarage garden and led her to a small seat.

'There were other clues,' continued Susan. 'I saw those photos at the school fete. You have your father's smile, as well as his blond hair and blue eyes.'

Cerys nodded. She seemed calmer now. 'I've been waiting for people to comment on it. When those photos first went up in the game at the Christmas party, I was shocked at how alike we were. I thought everyone would see it, but not even Lawrence did.'

'Did that hurt?'

Cerys's eyes filled with tears. 'Yes, I could see it never crossed his mind but then, I suppose, why would it?'

'Did you always know who your father was?'

'No. Mam only told me when she was very ill. Until then I had no idea. I told her then that I'd like to meet Lawrence, but she insisted I never try to find him or tell him who I was.'

'I see, but you came.'

'I couldn't resist. I was desperate to find out what kind of person he was. I told myself I would never betray Mam and let Lawrence or Hazel know who I was. Anyway, it was easy enough to track down his school. Then last summer I saw they were advertising for a teacher. I had trained like Mam, so I applied and got the job. I was so nervous when I came. I did wonder if Lawrence would be alerted, as I'd had to state I was a carrier of haemophilia on my application forms, but he never even mentioned it to me. I didn't wear the white flower pendant at first, but then we had the Christmas party. I wore it and, of course, the photos were put up. Hazel asked me a few questions about the flower pendant. I wondered how much she was working out. Hazel didn't say any more for a while. She invited me to lunches and was very friendly, then one Sunday we went for a walk, just her and me. She told me she thought she recognised the flower pendant and told me she'd casually asked Lawrence about my medical alert pendant and discovered I was a carrier of haemophilia. She also commented on the likeness between Lawrence and me in the photos. I broke down and confessed.'

'What did Hazel say?' asked Susan.

'She was amazing, kind, very understanding. As I said, she'd worked it out herself really. The seed was planted when she saw the white flower pendant. Although she tried to dismiss the idea of me being Lawrence's child, the longer she thought about it, the more she saw it was possible. Her own relationship with Lawrence had been such a whirlwind, they'd got married within weeks of going out. Hazel knew that Lawrence had been in a relationship with Mam just before she and Lawrence had got together, and realised timewise it was possible that Mam had been in the early stages of pregnancy when she and Lawrence broke up.'

'Hazel must have wondered why your mother never told Lawrence about the pregnancy.'

'She did ask me. I explained Mam had not wanted to cause problems for them and, in any case, her relationship with Lawrence was over. She wanted to raise me on her own. Hazel understood that. She was sorry we'd had such a hard time though.'

'Hazel seems to have been incredibly accepting of all this—'

'I know. I thought she might hate me or something, but she was adamant none of this was my fault. She wasn't angry with anyone. It had all happened before Lawrence and she got married.'

'And so how did Hazel feel things stood now?'

'She believed we should tell Lawrence. We talked about ways of doing that and decided that she would tell him in the summer, when he would be less stressed and we could spend some time together.'

'If you were waiting for the summer holidays, did it mean Lawrence never knew about you?'

'No, it's seeming like a miracle now. He found out the day before he died. I lost my purse in school on the Thursday and the receptionist gave it to him. He looked inside and saw the photograph of Mam holding me. He'd known I was a carrier of haemophilia from my records, but it was the photo in my purse that made him realise who I was. We talked after school on the Thursday before he died. It was very emotional. I'm so glad we did. At least he knew I existed.' Cerys smiled sadly. 'Hazel was pleased when I told her. She was worried he'd died never knowing about me.'

'She didn't know?'

'No, she was away that night and Lawrence asked me not to say anything until he had broached it with Hazel. I think he was going to find the right time that weekend. It was hard not to say anything when I took those books around to Hazel, but I respected his wishes and never said anything. So sad to think they never had time to talk to each other about it, though.'

'It must have been a huge shock for Lawrence.'

'It was, but he was excited. He was also absolutely riddled with guilt for all me and Mam had been through. He was angry about some things, though. He was upset I'd spoken to Hazel before him, and that Mam had never contacted him. He hated that we'd struggled, that I'd been in a foster home.' She paused, looked away. The sweet innocence had melted away now, and she looked older than her years.

'I'm so sorry. It's been a long, difficult road for you, hasn't it?'

Cerys nodded. 'You hope it will all be happy families meeting your real dad, but it's a lot more complicated than that. I thought I'd feel relieved and kind of complete when he finally knew who I was. I did, in some ways, but I also had this anger raging around inside. It was so hard to process it all,' she sighed. 'I nearly told Fiona, actually. The night Lawrence died, I rang her up. I was desperate to talk to someone, but then I backed out. I knew Lawrence didn't want me to tell anyone.'

'It was very hard to handle all this on your own,' said Susan.

'It was, I felt very alone.' She sighed. 'Still, it's not a secret any more, is it? If you've worked it out, others will. I have a lot to talk to Fiona about tonight.'

'I'm sure people will be understanding. And, who knows, maybe it will be easier now it's out in the open.'

Cerys gave a sad smile. 'I hope so. I've not liked the feeling of deceiving people. I guess it will give everyone something new to gossip about.' A little abruptly, Cerys moved on. 'Right, I have people I need to see.' She stood up and then slowly walked away.

Susan walked home through the village. Cerys's story seemed complicated and sad. She saw Tracy putting stock away for the evening, waved but didn't go to chat. She needed time to think. For the same reason, she walked straight past Hazel's house.

Susan let herself into the house, sat on the sofa and cuddled the dogs. 'Thank God I've got you two. When everything else seems to just go crazy, you are there waiting for me, always loving, always ready to listen to me.' She smiled as their tails wagged frantically. 'Come on, let's get you both a treat.'

Susan went to bed but stood for a while, staring out of her bedroom window. The darkness enveloped the village, a blanket covering all its secrets. How would Cerys be feeling? Would there be a sense of relief that everyone would finally know her secret? Susan doubted it somehow. She got into bed.

It was one of those fitful nights when she was relieved to see dawn break. However, just as she was planning a long walk with the dogs, she heard an urgent knock at the door.

Susan's heart raced as she ran downstairs to answer.

'I'm sorry to come so early,' said Hazel. 'I needed to talk to someone.'

'That's okay. Come in. I'll make us coffee.'

Hazel followed her into the kitchen, and they took their drinks to sit outside in the early-morning sunshine.

'I wanted to talk to you about Cerys,' said Hazel. 'She came to see me late last night. She told me about being the source of the complaint against Lawrence. I was surprised. I hadn't expected that.' Hazel paused. 'She also told me how you'd worked out that she is Lawrence's daughter.'

Susan sipped her coffee. Rocco and Libs came and sat at her feet in hope of a biscuit.

'So, you've known since April?'

'Well, I'd more or less worked it all out before that, but you know about the photos and the pendants,' said Hazel.

'I do.'

'I felt sorry for Blodwen, to be honest. She'd been a good friend to me. However, she did have a lot of issues. She was very unpredictable. I appreciate she was trying to protect our marriage, but I think there was more to it than that. When she was with Lawrence, they had a very turbulent relationship. She had great highs and lows. She told Cerys she loved Lawrence, and I am happy to let that be, but I'm not sure she hadn't grown to hate him. She said some pretty nasty things to me about him, but fortunately I didn't believe her. I don't think she wanted a life with him.'

'Cerys has really appreciated how kind you have been to her.'

Hazel's face softened. 'I know some people might find it hard to accept her, but the way I see it, none of this was her fault, no one was really to blame. Cerys has had a hard life. If for any reason I'd wanted children I am guessing discovering Lawrence had fathered a child may have hurt a lot more, but not having children had been a choice.'

'You really never wanted children?'

'No, I never had and with the way things were with Lawrence, it wouldn't have been straightforward. He was haemophiliac. He'd suggested genetic counselling or adoption, but I had never been one for having a family and Lawrence was quite happy with that decision as well. I know a lot of people don't understand, but it was honestly how we felt, and we had a very full and happy marriage.'

'So, do you feel as if you and Cerys have become good friends?'

'We have. We both love music, read the same books, and I have so enjoyed her coming round for meals and walks. We've organised a little weekend break for her birthday in December.'

'Would you have been happy for her to have a relationship with Lawrence?'

'Of course. She had lost her mother and I'm sorry she didn't have any time with him as a dad.'

Susan let out a long breath she'd not realised she was holding in. 'You sound so calm and logical about it all.'

'I'm not a robot. I did have a few wobbles, but honestly, this is how I feel,' said Hazel. 'When I heard about Lawrence, one of my first thoughts was that he died not knowing he had a daughter. But Cerys told me last night that he had discovered the truth the day before he died. They'd talked after school on the Thursday.'

'Lawrence didn't talk to you that evening?'

'I was over on the mainland watching *Mary Poppins*. We didn't speak properly at all on that Friday. Cerys told me he'd asked her not to say anything because he'd wanted to talk to me properly himself over the weekend, but of course we never had that time.' Her eyes filled with tears. 'You always think you are going to have more time, don't you?'

'I'm so sorry.'

'It's okay. I'm glad it's going to be out in the open. I don't want it to be seen as some dirty secret. I want Cerys to be proud of her dad. I hope people will be kind and not gossip too much.'

'People will understand. Cerys is liked and respected.'

'Yes, she is,' said Hazel.

'And what about you?'

'I hope no one feels sorry for me or blames Lawrence. I could do without all that. If anyone says anything to you, could you please tell them I'm fine about it all?'

'Of course.'

It was late that evening when Susan took Rocco and Libs out for their walk. She found herself walking in the direction of Fiona's. For some reason, she needed to reassure herself that the fire had gone, that the village was safe.

'Good evening, Susan.' The voice behind her startled her.

28

'Fiona,' Susan stammered. 'Just coming back from work?'

'From the hospital.' Fiona stared down at the house. 'Part of me dreads going back home. I keep looking out the windows—'

'How is Ross? How is his arm?'

'It could have been much worse. Ye saved his life.'

Susan looked down. She didn't want to hear that. Partly because it took her back to the accident, partly because she didn't feel she deserved it. She'd acted on instinct, that was all, and maybe if something had been even slightly different, she would have run away. She'd rather not think about it.

'I expect you've heard about that business with the key they found in the caravan,' said Fiona. 'The accusation by the police is absurd. How could anyone imagine Ross would kill someone? It's madness.'

'He has an alibi. He can prove that he was walking with his friend Dave when Lawrence died.'

'I hadna realised—'

'Yes, you're not to worry. I can't explain why he had the key, though—'

'Oh, Ross has nae idea how it got there. He's so disorganised. He could have picked it up weeks ago, or someone could have put it in there and he'd never have noticed. He's convinced, though, that he started the fire accidentally. I always worried about him smoking in there.'

Susan cast her mind back to her visit to the caravan. 'I remember seeing the ashtray. It looked pretty heavy-duty.'

'I know, but then, if he'd been drinking – they found that half-drunk bottle of whisky...'

Susan frowned. 'Oh, yes, but I remember Ross telling me he didn't like whisky. That's odd.'

Fiona's eyes widened in alarm. 'He's never confessed that to me. Now I think about it, whenever I've offered him a Scotch he's made an excuse – I'd never dreamed he didn't like it.'

'I'm sure that's what he said. And if that's the case, he's not going to drink half a bottle.'

'Maybe he was desperate for a drink and didn't have anything else in. If Ross says he started the fire, we have to believe him.'

Susan picked up something close to panic in Fiona's voice, turned to her, and spoke gently. 'I can understand why Ross would rather believe that than imagine someone had come and purposely set fire to the caravan.'

'No one is suggesting that.'

Fiona looked over at the path that led down the side of house.

'Would you mind coming down to the garden with me?'

Susan blinked. This was a very different Fiona from the person who had confronted her both at the fete and the pub. 'Of course,' she agreed.

What they found when they reached the garden shocked her. As soon as they entered, the garden was flooded with light.

'Wow!'

'I'd been thinking for a while I needed some lighting back here. I was speaking to a dad first thing in school, and he offered to come and set all this up for me. I met him here at lunchtime and by the end of school it was all set up.'

Susan turned to Fiona, saw her eyes scanning the garden.

'It's certainly very bright.' Despite trying to avert her eyes, Susan found herself staring down at the fire-damaged caravan. She could feel the heat, smell the smoke, feel her legs giving way.

'Sorry, I shouldn't have brought you here. Are you all right?' asked Fiona.

'Yes, it just takes time, doesn't it... to forget?'

'It's going to have to be taken away,' said Fiona, following her gaze. 'I've suggested Ross move in with me. It will be strange. We never lived together, you see. He left home for university when I married his father.'

They walked around the garden.

'I understand you know everything about Cerys,' said Fiona. 'She came to see me first thing this morning before school. It was a lot to take in.'

'I'm sure.'

'I'd wondered if something was up when she rang me late on that Friday evening when Lawrence died. It was such an odd conversation, and there was obviously something she wasn't telling me. I remember she finished the call quite abruptly. I thought maybe she'd lost signal because of the rain. Now I realise how much she had on her mind. I can see the situation is complicated but, I'll be honest, I dinnae understand why she had to send in that complaint.'

'She's young, and she has been storing up a lot of anger,' said Susan. 'I feel sorry for her. What do you think will happen to her now?'

'I managed to talk to the head of governors and one of the inspectors from the local authority today. I've explained things as best I can. They can see that the complaint was in no way based on fact, so now the main concern is how Cerys is to be handled.'

'Will she be able to keep her job?'

'Yes, I'm quite sure she will. The circumstances were exceptional, and I personally don't want any further action to be taken. I'm hopeful it will be put to one side.'

'I'm glad for her.'

'Yes, so am I,' said Fiona. 'As for the whole story about Lawrence being her father, well, that is something else for us all to get our heads around. I am shocked, so heaven knows how Hazel is feeling. I'm glad Lawrence knew he'd had a daughter and that she was following in his footsteps. It's just sad he never had time to enjoy that relationship.'

'It's going to cause quite a stir in the village.'

'It will. I feel sorry for Hazel. I hope people don't become too intrusive. And as for Cerys, well, it won't be easy, but I will support her the best I can.' Fiona looked down the garden. 'Thank you for coming with me. It's not like me to be nervous. I'm sure I'll be back to my usual self very soon. Let's go back to the front door.'

After they'd said goodnight, Susan made her way back on to the high street, thinking about Fiona. She was clearly very upset, but then who could blame her after such a traumatic event? However, she was also very scared of something. Why else have all those lights put up? Did she really believe that fire had been started accidentally? Was it possible she knew who had started it or even been involved herself? Had she gone down to plant the key on Ross, and started the fire accidentally? Or, even worse, gone down to silence Ross by starting the fire? Susan knew now she had the means to have got to Lawrence and possibly a motive connected to the complaint. Fiona's first word on coming down the garden that night had been 'sorry'. Susan had assumed she was sorry about Ross, but what if she had been saying she was sorry to have caused an accident or sorry that in a fit of panic she had tried to kill her stepson?

Susan paused for the dogs to sniff the lamp post, and was suddenly aware of rustling in the hedges, the darkness surrounding the pools of light from the lamp posts. Anyone could be hidden there, anyone could be watching her, following her. She'd always felt so safe walking around the village at night, but that feeling had gone.

* * *

The next day, Susan was on her laptop when she received a text from Hazel. She sounded in a panic, saying she'd been told something important, and she needed to talk to Susan.

Susan quickly shut down her laptop and hurried next door.

Hazel rushed her inside and they sat down.

'Firstly, I have news about the old church key they found in Ross's caravan. The police checked it in the side door of the church. It doesn't work.'

Susan gasped. 'But it has to—'

'No. It turns out it's just too old and rusty. They could hardly get it in the lock, let alone turn it. You do see what this means, don't you?'

Susan nodded. 'I suppose it shows that the side door key couldn't have been used to get in the church the night Lawrence died.'

'Exactly. That key was probably the most important reason for us suspecting someone went up to see Lawrence and may have been involved in his death. Knowing the key doesn't work means no one went up there. They couldn't have unless Lawrence let them in. In any case, Lawrence was alive and well when they left; we know he let them out of the church and locked up again because he had the key.'

Susan sat down, stunned. Had she been wrong all this time?

Hazel continued, her eyes full of tears. 'The police were here earlier. They brought back Lawrence's rucksack and his binoculars.' She walked over to a table where the rucksack was sitting and picked up a bracelet, smiling sadly. 'This was his medical alert. He hated wearing it, but I insisted.' She touched it tenderly and placed it gently back on the table. 'They told me that Ross has now been ruled out of their enquiries. They've checked his story of walking up to meet his friend and the timings corroborate his story.'

Susan shook her head. 'I still don't get it. Why would the key you showed me end up in Ross's caravan?'

'I was thinking about that. Maybe someone had thought of going to see Lawrence and taken the key. They may have gone there, found the key didn't work and given up, or changed their mind and not gone at all. Hearing us going on about a missing key, they might have hidden it in Ross's caravan to try to implicate him.'

'I suppose you could be right.'

'I'm sure I am. And you see, Susan, I've come to a decision. I want to stop looking into Lawrence's death now. The missing key was the main reason for us to suspect someone had been with Lawrence, and we know now it was never used. I've had enough. For my own well-being, I need to accept what happened. I have to accept I've lost Lawrence and nothing I can do will bring him back.'

Susan could see the strain on Hazel's face, the dark circles under her eyes, how pale she was. She looked exhausted.

Hazel moved over to sit next to Susan and took her hand. 'I know it's not easy. You desperately want to tie up all the ends, but we'll never do that. Who knows why Lawrence went to the edge of the tower? There could be all kinds of explanations.'

'You really want to stop?'

'Yes, particularly now everyone knows about Cerys. That's enough now. I must look after her. I'm so grateful to you for all the support you gave me. I desperately needed someone to take me seriously, and you did that. But now we have the funeral to say goodbye to Lawrence, and that must be the end. I may even move away from the village, start again somewhere new.'

Susan nodded. 'I see. Well, I respect that, Hazel.'

Hazel smiled. 'Thank you. You have been a true friend.'

Susan thanked her before inviting Hazel to Jamari's celebration that was planned for that Saturday.

'Thank you. I'd love to come. Would you like to borrow some of these small tables and chairs? Some of these came from Fiona, I can hold on to them a bit longer. I'm sure she won't mind. Also, I have plenty of glasses. We were always holding staff dos, we've ended up with far too many.'

'That's brilliant, thank you. Can I come and collect them on Friday?'

'Of course, and thank you, Susan, for everything.'

As Susan returned to her house, she tried to unravel her thoughts. She'd agreed to end the investigation. Hazel clearly wanted to stop, and she had good reason to.

Susan let herself into the house and sat on the floor stroking the dogs, still mulling things over. Surely this was for the best? She could start to settle properly into the village, become part of the community.

'Come on, you two, let's get out for a walk.'

She took the dogs down to the beach. It was a beautiful day and yet only a few young families were down there. Susan found there were times when only the sound of the sea could calm her mind. The unique thing about living on a small island was that the sea was never far away. The ancient cliffs, the fossils among the rocks, the rolling waves that had been coming in and out for thousands of years, had a permanency about them that comforted her. They gave her a sense of place in a history so much bigger than herself. They put life in perspective.

As Susan walked, she churned over Hazel's decision. The key turning out not to work was certainly a bit of a bombshell. And yet it had been taken. Someone had stolen it from Hazel's drawer. Who had done that? It could have been Ross, but then he hadn't been to the church. She knew that. So maybe someone had taken the key, found it didn't work, maybe shouted up to Lawrence after all – but still they'd have been stuck with the key. Maybe with all the suspicion going around they had decided to plant it in Ross's caravan.

Susan sighed. It was all so complicated, because of course even if someone had shouted up, Lawrence had to have let them out of the church... maybe she'd been wrong all along.

Her mind went to the pen. Why wouldn't anyone own up to putting it on the table in the vicarage? There were still all those issues with Daniel and Jessie, and then the fire. It was odd about the whisky. She knew Ross didn't like it, but had someone who didn't know that put it there to suggest Ross had been drinking? Susan shuddered. The fire scared Fiona and it frightened her.

Susan had only just arrived back at her house when she was surprised to receive a visit from Ross. He was carrying a big bunch of flowers and some chocolates.

29

'Come in. How lovely to see you,' Susan said to Ross as she led him into the sitting room. They sat on the sofa.

'Sorry, these are just from the hospital shop,' he said, holding out the flowers. 'I bought them before getting in a taxi.'

'They're lovely. Thank you.' Susan took them into the kitchen and then returned to Ross, saying, 'You should have phoned me. I could have come and picked you up.'

'You've done more than enough.'

'I'm glad to see you're out. How are you feeling?'

'Rough, but glad to be home. Hospitals don't suit me. I just wanted to thank you for everything.'

'I only did what anybody else would have done,' said Susan. 'I'm glad you are safe now. How is your arm?'

'Painful, but it could have been a great deal worse. Fortunately, all the damage is at the top half of my arm so I'm still able to play. I'll be there at the funeral rehearsal this evening, and of course at the funeral itself. I insisted they let me home for that. Now tell me, how are you?'

Susan appreciated his concern and explained that she was fine, although still a little shaken.

'I suppose I'm still in shock too. The fire was very scary and there was a point when I really didn't think I was going to get out alive.' Ross shuddered. 'It was a terrible experience. It really frightened Fiona too – have you seen all those lights she's had put up?'

'I have, and so you're going to live with her now?'

'Yes,' he said and, after a hesitation, continued, 'I owe Fiona so much. Let's face it, she hardly knew me, and she owed me nothing. But she still got me this job, gave me the caravan to stay in and now she's offering me a home with her. She's gone way beyond what she needed to, and I appreciate that. She's a good woman. And look at the way she's handled this complaint business with Cerys.'

'How do you feel knowing Lawrence was Cerys's father?' asked Susan.

'I feel relieved to know the truth. I just wish she'd told me.'

'She's been holding on to that secret for a long time now. Only Hazel knew. It won't be easy as everyone in the village learns the truth. It's good she has you to stand by her.'

'Of course, and Fiona has already been brilliant.'

'So, do you know if they have got any further with the investigation of the fire?'

'The police were playing with the idea of arson, that someone might have thrown a cigarette among the papers on purpose,' said Ross. 'I said that was ridiculous. I'd been drinking, and I must have made a mistake. It was all my fault, I'm sure of it.'

'I was confused by that. They said it was whisky, but you don't like it, do you?'

His eyebrows shot up. 'You've got a good memory.'

'So how come there was a half-drunk bottle in the caravan?'

'Um, I must have given some to a visitor. I'd been drinking something else. It doesn't matter. The point is, I started the fire, not anyone else. Good God, why would anyone want to set fire to my caravan? It's madness.'

'I can understand why it's a frightening thought, but surely if someone had been involved, you'd want them caught?'

'No one was involved. This will never happen again.' The words shot out like bullets, but there was fear in his eyes.

Susan felt the tension in the air and spoke as calmly as she could. 'I see, so what about the old church door key? Fiona told me you had no idea how it got there.'

'Oh, I must have picked it up sometime and forgotten. I just want to forget the whole thing. It's time we put Lawrence's death and now this fire behind us. After the funeral tomorrow, we can all move on.'

Susan frowned. 'When we were all together in the pub the night of the fire, you told me you thought I should keep digging around into Lawrence's death. Have you changed your mind?'

'I was just winding people up that night. This needs to be dropped now,' Ross said, giving a short laugh.

'So, you didn't mean it when you gave strong hints about seeing someone out and about the night Lawrence died?'

Suddenly he became grave. 'I was a fool. Seriously, Susan, you need to stop this now. It's dangerous to go meddling in other people's business. You don't know how they're going to react.' Ross stood up. 'Thank you, Susan, for everything. I heard from your daughter, Zoe, about the celebration on Saturday. Cerys and I will be coming along to sing.'

Susan heard an owl close by and she looked around in confusion.

Ross laughed. 'That's my ringtone, sorry. Look, I'd better answer this, so I'll be off now. Nice to chat.'

And with that, he was gone.

Susan slumped down onto the sofa. She had a horrible feeling she'd just been warned off by Ross, but she couldn't think why. He had an alibi and the key had turned out to be insignificant. If he had any suspicion that someone had caused the fire, why not encourage the police to investigate?

She paused. There was, of course, the possibility that he was covering for someone. But who, and why protect someone who had tried to kill him?

She had so many questions. With a sense of relief, she realised she was due to see Alice that afternoon. She desperately needed her insight and sense of perspective. She would help her work out what to do.

* * *

Alice sat tucked up in her usual chair with her iPad, doing a crossword. Seeing Susan, she put it on the small table next to her and greeted Susan with a concerned smile. 'My dear, how lovely to see you. I've been very worried about you. Tracy told me about the fire.'

Susan slumped into the chair next to her. 'It was awful, Alice, really frightening.'

'Tracy told me you saved Ross's life.'

'I did what anyone would have done, but he was lucky I was out.'

'It was a strange time for you to be walking the streets...'

Susan gave a slight smile. 'You're the only person to pick up on that. I couldn't sleep. It had been a very stressful day at the fete and then at the pub. I had to clear my head.'

'Ross was very fortunate then. Tell me, what happened when you saw the fire?'

Susan went through the events of the evening up to the time she left the hospital.

'Do the police know how the fire started?'

'Ross is insisting he started the fire accidentally, smoking while drinking. The police had their doubts but now they are rather taken up with the finding of the key in the caravan after the fire.'

'The key?' asked Alice.

'They found that key to the side door of the church in Ross's caravan. At first it looked like Ross might be accused of killing Lawrence, but then of course he has an alibi. They tried out the key and discovered it didn't work in any case. The problem is, Alice, the key was our main reason for suspecting there had been foul play. Also, the pen we thought was missing has turned up, and the police are thinking it was never used by Lawrence that night, that I made a mistake. Hazel thinks I should stop investigating now.' She paused, took a deep breath and added, 'Not only is there the key business but I am guessing you have heard the news about Cerys? You guessed that before me, didn't you?'

'It was Cerys' pendants that got me thinking. I noticed she touched them a lot. They were important to her,' said Alice. 'I felt sure I'd seen the floral one before, but couldn't think where. However, I had a sense that the fact it was a white flower was significant in some way. So, I went online and searched around. I found that the origin of the Welsh name of Blodwen is "white flower". Then everything started to fall into place. I remembered the photograph Hazel had shown me of her friend, and the pendant Blodwen had been wearing – the enamel glazing made it look antique, kind of medieval. I admired it and Hazel told me it had been a present from her to Blodwen.'

'Of course, I remember Hazel telling me about them exchanging gifts when they were in some kind of medieval opera. Blodwen had given her a bracelet of copper leaves,' said Susan. 'How did you connect the pendant to Cerys?'

'Well,' continued Alice, 'the pendant was so unique, it seemed unlikely that Cerys should just happen to have an identical one. It made me wonder if it was possible that Cerys had got hers from Blodwen. But how, and why? Then I thought of the engraving Cerys had added: "MAM".'

'And that led you to suspect the relationship between them—'

'Exactly. As for the medical alert pendant, well, another resident here wears one, and Hazel told me about Lawrence's blood disorder. Then, of course, there was Cerys's age, twenty-three. Well, it all started to add up.'

'You were dead right. You were also correct about there being a personal element to that row Cerys had with Lawrence. In fact, it bit so deeply that Cerys made up that complaint about Lawrence.'

'Ah, so it was her.'

'It was. She is very upset about it all now and was very worried that Fiona was going to get into trouble. Fortunately, I think Fiona is being very understanding about the whole thing,' said Susan.

'That's a relief for her. So, tell me, how is Hazel with all this? Did Lawrence ever have an idea?'

'Well, Hazel was the one to guess first. She saw the pendants, and eventually asked Cerys. Lawrence was much slower, and only figured it out the day before he died, from a photo he found in Cerys's purse.'

Susan went on to tell Alice the whole story. When she'd finished, Alice smiled. 'Well, I'm glad things are good between Hazel and Cerys. They can look after each other now through a very difficult period of their lives and it sounds as if Cerys will be staying at the school?'

'Yes, she's been very lucky Fiona has defended her.'

Alice sat back. 'So much has happened since I last saw you. How are you feeling about everything now?'

'To be honest, Alice, I'm not sure what to do next. Hazel wants me to stop the investigation, and yet I still have so many questions. I know the finding of the key could mark the end, but we can't get away from the fact it was taken on that Friday night. I was thinking what if someone took it so that they could go up to see Lawrence, got there, found it didn't work and then shouted up to ask Lawrence to let them in? I know we don't like that idea, but they might have been lucky and shouted up when no one was around.'

Alice nodded. 'Yes, of course, it has to be possible.'

Susan sighed. 'But Lawrence had to let them out of the church as he had the key on him when they found his body.' She paused a moment, and then frowned.

'What's up?' asked Alice. 'What have you thought of?'

Susan looked at Alice. 'I've just remembered something. When I visited Hazel earlier, she told me the police had returned Lawrence's rucksack. Now, on the night Lawrence died, Hazel had reminded Lawrence to keep the keys safe in the rucksack. He made some joke about it, but he was very conscientious. I remember when he was letting me out of the church, he left the rucksack on a chair, open. I'm sure that was to remind him to put the keys back in there. It would have been really odd for him not to put the keys back in there, so why were they found in his pocket?'

'It seems unlikely.'

'Exactly. What if this person had shouted up, been let in, killed Lawrence, then let themselves out, ran round to the body and put the key in his pocket?' Susan sat forward. 'It's possible, isn't it?'

Alice nodded. 'I agree.'

Susan sat forward. 'If this is possible, I really can't give up on the investigation, Alice. I've still so many questions and, in any case, if one of this group killed Lawrence, they're a dangerous person. They can't be allowed to get away with it.'

'You're right. I quite agree.'

'Thank you. I'm not going to involve Hazel any more, but I need to continue. You know this fire worries me, Alice.'

'You said Ross is insisting he caused it?'

'I know, but I have a feeling he may be covering for someone.'

'But why would he cover for someone who tried to kill him?'

'It has to be someone close to him. Maybe he thought they started the fire by accident somehow.'

'It's possible, I suppose. If he is covering up, then I would guess maybe Cerys as she's his partner now.'

'It could be, or maybe Fiona. He was telling me how much he owed her. And there is one other person I have discovered he is close to—'

'Who is that?'

Susan told Alice about finding Ross and Jessie together at the fete and that, despite what Ross said by way of explanation, she was convinced they had some kind of relationship.

Alice pursed her lips. 'If Lawrence had found out, it may be the reason he was upset with Jessie.'

'That's what I was thinking. I'm guessing. I could be wrong that the relationship is in the past, and maybe Ross is wanting it to continue. I don't know, because of course he is with Cerys now. Maybe they're just close friends now. I think Jessie wants her marriage to work, and I can't help but feel sorry for her.'

'Yes, I can see it's been difficult. Going back to the fire, this was on Saturday night. Now I am guessing most of the people in this group would have been in bed alone, and could have sneaked out, but wouldn't Daniel have noticed if Jessie had gone?'

'She did tell me he sleeps in the spare room a lot—'

'I see.' Alice sighed. 'I agree Ross might have persuaded himself that someone started this fire by accident but, I'm sorry, to me, if someone else is involved, it seems more likely to have been a deliberate act, and that would be very worrying. This person is dangerous.'

Susan shuddered. 'You're right. We can't get away from the possibility that someone tried to silence Ross, because they are the person who killed Lawrence and they're scared he saw them in the village that night. Oh, I need to tell you what I found out at the fete about Fiona.'

Susan told Alice about the discovery of the back door in the old storeroom.

'Fiona was very upset with me, told me she knew I was asking questions about Lawrence's death. Of course, this means she could have got out of the school, bypassing the CCTV, and gone to the bell tower.'

'She could have. I know everyone talks about how devoted Fiona was to Lawrence,' said Alice, 'but we know their last conversation was an argument and that talk about a fresh start for Fiona.'

'I know. Something was very wrong there. We've been saying Lawrence wanted Fiona to leave because of the complaint, but when you think about it, he was the one at risk, not her. So why did he want her to leave the school? She was upset by the idea. I saw that when I mentioned it to her. What had been going on between them?'

'There is more to find out there, I'm sure,' said Alice. 'I can't see why Ross would want to cover for Daniel, but that doesn't exclude him from this fire. Have you found out any more about Daniel and what he'd been up to?'

'Not really. He's a bit elusive, you know. Hard to get to know. I need to go to that pub and try to meet this chap Alan, I think.'

'I did google Alan Smithee, by the way.'

Susan smiled. 'You never cease to amaze me, Alice. So, tell me – what did you find out?'

'Oh, something and nothing,' Alice replied mysteriously, 'but I do think it's important to go and meet him.' She smiled. 'Maybe we need a break from all this murder. I wonder, would you get us both a coffee from the trolley, and I think we deserve a biscuit as well.'

When Susan returned, she carefully placed Alice's cup on the small table that she pulled in front of herself, and they sat quietly drinking and chatting. As she was showing Alice some of the latest photos of Jamari, she invited Alice to the celebration on Saturday. 'I do hope you can come. It's in the afternoon, so I could come and collect you and bring you back. It's not really a christening, more a kind of blessing, and it will be in my garden.'

'Now that sounds very pleasant. Thank you so much for inviting me.' Alice smiled. 'Tell me, are any of the people from the choir committee coming to the celebration?'

'Actually, most of them will be there. I've invited Hazel, who's providing glasses and chairs. Cerys and Ross are singing, and of course Daniel and Jessie will be taking part in the celebration. That only leaves Fiona. I must have a word with her soon.'

'Well, that's great. It will be good to be out in the real world.' Alice smiled. Her eyes twinkled in anticipation.

Much later that evening, Susan took Rocco and Libs out for their final walk. Susan remembered the small patch of woodland and decided to go there, inspired by her night walk with Ross. She turned off down the road that led to the park, kept going until she reached a small patch of woodland on her left. It had a gravel path and she started walking through, listening for owls, but it seemed incredibly quiet in there.

She approached the pond, keeping Rocco and Libs on the lead. The whole area was floodlit by the moon. It was so beautiful. Susan walked to the edge and sat on a log in front of a large bush.

The dogs sniffed contentedly at the bottom of the trees. Susan remembered Robert's warnings about going down dark alleys alone. They seemed so ridiculous here. Everything was so calm and peaceful.

Suddenly she heard a twig break behind her. She turned. She couldn't see anyone, but she could feel their presence. Long fingers of fear grabbed her. She couldn't breathe. She couldn't move. Then the person spoke.

'Get out of this village. Next time, it won't be eggs or words on a window. Remember Lawrence, remember Ross,' a menacing, raspy voice hissed. It wasn't like anything she had heard before.

Rocco and Libs were staring at the bush now. Susan heard footsteps and then silence. She knew it was easy to get out of the woodland, on to the pavements. Quickly, she went round the other side of the bush, and saw there was a narrow, overgrown pathway out on to the pavement. Taking the dogs with her, she clambered out, and looked around. There were street lights further up the road, but there was no one to be seen.

Breathing hard and fast, she quickly walked up the road and made her way home.

Inside, she slammed the door. Rocco and Libs had picked up on her mood. They were excited and started to bark.

'It's okay, we're home safe now,' she assured them.

She put on all the lights downstairs, poured herself a glass of wine and sat down.

The loud banging of a car door startled her, and she spilt her drink. She heard somebody ringing the bell at Hazel's and went to look out of the window.

It was Hazel's sister arriving, carrying heavy supermarket bags of shopping. Hazel said her sister would be organising the wake and she looked like a woman who had things in hand.

Susan's thoughts returned to the woods. Should she phone the police? She knew she couldn't. No, it would sound ridiculous. But she knew it had happened. She had heard that voice. Someone had been in those woods with her. She tried to conjure up the voice. She should know who it was, but they'd disguised their voice well. No, she couldn't even tell if it was male or female. 'Remember Lawrence, remember Ross.' They'd said those words. This wasn't some prank, this was serious.

30

Susan opened the curtains the next morning and saw a fine drizzle of rain. The sky was white and grey. She'd slept badly, wondering what she was going to do about the things that had happened in the woods the night before.

The words of warning were terrifying, and yet she knew she had no intention of being pushed out of the village. She was sure this was to do with her investigation into Lawrence's death. Shutting her eyes, she tried to hear that voice again. It was fainter, but there was one thing now she remembered. What she'd heard was fear: this person may have scared her, but they themselves were frightened. They were desperate, and that meant she was getting closer.

Robert would be coming later for Lawrence's funeral. Should she tell him? On balance, she thought not. He would want her to stop, to leave things alone, and she knew she couldn't do that. No, she would keep this to herself for now.

Robert arrived with Gem Gem and Dougie, who greeted Rocco and Libs enthusiastically. Susan opened the back door, and they all tore outside, barking madly. The windows and doors next door were all open and she could hear the frantic activity of a vacuum cleaner crashing around in the kitchen.

'I've brought my suit,' said Robert. 'I'll wait till the last minute to change, otherwise it'll have dog hairs all over it. What time do we need to go over?'

'Well, the funeral is at one, so I need to be there by about twenty to one. As we've got a bit of time, shall we take the dogs down to Brook Beach, give them a good run?'

'That's a good idea. We can take my car if you like.'

The beach was deserted on a day like this. Susan was wrapped up in her old parka and Robert wore his massive waterproof. The dogs didn't care about the weather. Gem Gem, as always, kept away from the sea. Dougie managed to find an old plastic box which he was immensely proud of, while Rocco and Libs dug holes, sending sand flying into the air.

The sea was rough. Snowy white foam was tossed into the air. Gulls, noisier than ever, were screeching overhead. They walked towards Compton, and as they did so Susan told Robert about Hazel's feelings now the key had been found.

'She wants to stop investigating now, but I'm not so sure.'

'Why doesn't that surprise me? Why do you need to continue?'

'It was talking to Alice that made me rethink.' She saw Robert grimace. 'And don't groan like that. Alice is not the needy old lady you imagine. You'll meet her on Saturday. You are coming, aren't you?'

He laughed. 'I haven't received a formal invitation but, yes, I'd love to come. I'll leave the dogs with my neighbour. It could get a bit hectic with four of them. Did you say Steve will be coming over?'

Susan felt that familiar punch in the stomach that still happened every time her ex-husband's name was mentioned. 'I'm afraid so. Of course, he should be there, but it makes it all so much more stressful. Hester, his partner, is coming as well.'

'I'll be interested to meet her, and to see Steve again. It's years since I last saw him. It's odd, he was so wonderful as our GP, so caring with my wife Carol, but now I see him as the man who was cruel to you.'

'I wouldn't say cruel—'

'I don't know how else you would describe suddenly telling your wife you were leaving her after forty years of marriage. He treated you badly, Susan.'

'At the end of the day, he wanted to go and, if he'd stopped loving me, it was best he did. We need to make things work now for Zoe, Fay and Jamari. I really want Saturday to be a celebration. I don't want any rows.'

'Well, it'll be the first family do I've been to without one if it is.' Robert grinned, but became more serious. 'Right, so back to the business with Lawrence. Why do you feel the need to carry on investigating? I can't see why now you know the side key wasn't used.'

Susan nearly mentioned the voice in the woods but decided against it. Instead, she explained her other concerns, and the way she felt someone could have found a way to be up the tower with Lawrence.

'So, you've found a way of someone getting up there, and we know, in the right circumstances, anyone could have pushed him, but you still haven't really come up with a motive.'

'No, but I know some people are lying and I'd like to understand why.' Susan paused, looked up at Robert. 'What is your gut feeling about Lawrence's death?'

Robert paused, picked up a pebble and rubbed it between his thumb and fingers. 'I know you think I'm biased about the police, but they deal with accidental deaths a lot. I know they're busy, but if they seriously thought there was something up, they would throw everything at it. Look at the way they responded to the key being found at Ross's caravan. They didn't try to duck away from that. They immediately reopened the investigation, were prepared to say they could have got it wrong.'

'I can see that,' said Susan. 'What they can't know, however, is the hidden motives. They don't get to feel the fear in the atmosphere, the stress everyone is under. There is something wrong here and I don't want to live in a community containing someone who has killed once and possibly attempted to kill again.'

'Of course not. So, you don't think Ross's fire was an accident?'

'No, I don't think so.'

'To be fair, the police officer I spoke to said he was uneasy about the fire as well. Ross may be disorganised, but he wasn't that drunk. Ross is insistent it was an accident, though. Either he's hiding something, or he is covering for someone.'

'If the police suspect that, why aren't they doing more?' asked Susan.

'Because there's no evidence. Ross is now insisting he could have dropped a cigarette, he was drunk. He's saying anything to make them back off. There are no obvious signs of a break-in, they can see clearly where the fire was started. There were no additional accelerants that would usually indicate arson.'

'I see.'

'But I don't like it if there is something up. I don't want you involved.'

'Someone has to keep digging.'

'But why does it have to be you?'

Susan bit her lip. 'I may not have known Lawrence that well, but I really don't see why, if someone killed him, they should get away with it. How can I live in a community knowing someone there may be a killer and I've not done everything I could to find them? I need to know what happened. It's who I am. I can't ignore things.'

Robert smiled. 'I am coming to understand that, and I admire it. I just don't want you to get hurt.'

He reached out and touched her hair. The lightness and yet intimacy of his touch made her heart race. She looked deep into his eyes. 'Thank you,' she said quietly.

He took his hand away but stayed looking at her. It was as if all her senses were heightened as she smelled the salt air, felt the warm wind caressing her face.

She knew they were a whisper away from kissing but, as wonderful as that might be, she knew that it would be different to the last time. It would be saying that the last kiss had not been a one-off, they were moving into something more serious. As much as part of her longed for that, she knew she wasn't ready.

She took a step back. Robert gave a slight nod and smile and stepped back too.

They continued their walk, and finally Susan was calm enough to speak. 'I suppose we ought to get back, sort out these dogs and make ourselves respectable.'

By the time they got back to the car, they were all very windblown, sandy and wet.

Back at the house, Robert washed the dogs' paws under Susan's outside tap while she found the old towels to dry them. It was at moments like this that she envied people who just went out for wet walks without dogs, who could just get inside, take their coat off, sit down and make a hot drink.

They fed the dogs and gave them a final dry. Content, the dogs flopped onto the carpet and rested.

'Good, that's them done then,' said Robert, smiling. 'Now we'd better get ourselves sorted out.'

They went upstairs, showered and changed, Robert using the spare bedroom. There was something very companionable about getting ready together and Susan realised it was something she missed.

She put on some black trousers, but the best she could find to keep with the sombre dress code was a dark blue top with tiny pink flowers on it. She wore her pearl necklace, and even put on some lipstick, then went downstairs.

Robert wore a suit well, and Susan could feel herself blushing when she noticed how handsome he looked.

'Will I do?' he asked.

'You look very smart,' Susan said.

'Well, you look gorgeous.' Susan grinned but looked away. It was a long time since anybody had commented on her appearance.

Thankfully, the rain had stopped now. As they left the house, despite the short distance, she saw a funeral car arrive to take Hazel to St Jude's. Hazel had told her the same car would wait and take them on for a private cremation.

The church was comfortably full. Susan left Robert to go to the vestry to join the other choir members. There was an awkward air, as if nobody knew quite what to say. Fiona came running in at the last moment, out of breath, and gulped water from her water bottle. She still had a tracksuit and belt on, but she had chosen a black one with very little writing on, clearly her concession to the occasion.

Susan heard a bell tolling, mournful and sobering. They quietly settled in the choir stalls. Ross was playing the organ, and even in such sad circumstances you could appreciate the beauty of the music.

At the front of the church, Hazel and Cerys sat with Hazel's sister and her husband. At the front of the church stood the coffin with beautiful white roses arranged on top. Susan was aware of the importance of the gesture Hazel was making by asking Cerys to sit with her. It was a very public acknowledgement by Hazel of Cerys's place in the family and she noticed they sat very close together.

Daniel stood up. Ross stopped playing. Silence fell. The funeral service was short, dignified and deeply moving. It was at occasions such as this that Daniel was most at home in his role. His sincerity was a comfort.

After the service, Hazel, her sister and Cerys were taken to the crematorium with Daniel and Jessie.

Fiona returned to school and Robert headed back to Ventnor with Gem Gem and Dougie.

Susan spent a few minutes with Rocco and Libs, giving them a run in the garden and their lunch. She heard the sound of Hazel and her sister returning and took herself next door.

Cerys had decided to go home but Hazel's sister was in the kitchen sorting out food. Most people were hungry by now and tucked in with more enthusiasm than usual at a wake.

Susan chatted to a few people. She noticed a number of people making their way out into the garden, and she joined them. She enjoyed walking around looking at the neatly laid-out beds and blossoming cottage garden plants. She must ask Hazel for some tips.

Susan was looking out over the fields when Hazel's sister came to join her, carrying a plate loaded with sandwiches and crisps.

'I'm Rowan,' she said, adding with a half-smile, 'Mother named us after trees.'

Rowan held herself with a confidence Hazel lacked. Her appearance was smart, expensive, functional rather than fashionable. Susan could imagine Rowan having the shift dress she was wearing in several colours, taking one out each morning to wear with a neutral tailored jacket.

'I'm guessing you must be Susan. I just want to thank you for looking after Hazel.'

'It's been a terrible shock for you all.'

'Yes. Hazel has always been so dependent on Lawrence, so it's a big change for her.'

Susan heard a loud guffaw of laughter from Rowan's husband, who was talking to a guest. Rowan shot him a disapproving glare. He grinned, but lowered his voice.

'It's not easy living on an island, is it?' continued Rowan. 'The need to always be getting ferries and boats would drive me mad. Trying to get over here the day after Lawrence died was a nightmare, so much was booked up.'

'It can be difficult, so it was good of you to come so quickly. I understand you have family and a business to run.'

Rowan took a bite of her sandwich, swallowing it quickly. 'I wanted to be here. I would have stayed longer but I know I wear Hazel out. We love each other, obviously, but drive each other mad at the same time. It's the way it can be with sisters.' She took another large bite of her sandwich, then, glancing over at Hazel, who was talking quietly to a guest, she said, 'Of course, she has all this business with Cerys to handle as well.'

'She seems to be coping very well. She has been very kind to Cerys.'

'Yes, I admire that. Hazel told me the day after Lawrence died. She hadn't mentioned it before. It must have been a huge shock for her. She was worried that Lawrence had never known about Cerys but since then she's found out they spoke the day before he died, and Hazel is pleased about that. I thought it was very good of Hazel to ask Cerys to sit with us at the funeral, sends a good message to the village. Cerys seems a very pleasant, bright kind of girl.' Rowan looked down at Susan's hands. 'Oh, you don't have anything to eat—'

'I'm fine, thank you.'

'Well, don't go hungry. I brought far too much.' She quickly scanned the guests in the garden to check everything was going smoothly. 'It's a shame Hazel never had children of her own. They would be here now to look after her, wouldn't they? But still, she never wanted them. Her choice.'

'Do you think Hazel will stay on the island?'

'I hope not,' Rowan answered quickly and then gave an apologetic smile. 'Sorry, no offence, but it makes it a lot more difficult to visit her. But she seems to like it here. She told me she's enjoying the choir, and now she's church warden, so she's been getting involved with the village. Still, I'd love her to come back to the mainland.' Susan watched as Rowan ate another sandwich. The food on her plate seemed to be disappearing fast, and yet she'd hardly stopped talking.

'You sound a busy person. Hazel was telling me how successful you've been in your job, and I hear you act as well?'

'Oh, only amateur stuff, but it's good fun,' said Rowan. 'I keep telling Hazel to join an amateur dramatic society, it would suit her.'

'Acting? But she's quite shy.'

'Hazel is like a lot of shy people. Put her on stage and she blossoms. It's the one-to-one contact that's difficult for her. My guess would be your vicar is like that.'

Susan grinned. 'You're right, he's just like that. I have to say Hazel has a fabulous voice. She certainly seems to lose her nerves when singing.'

'Gosh, yes, she really should have gone into it professionally.' Rowan looked over at Susan's house. 'So, you've not been here long? Hazel tells me you're an islander, though, so did you know the village well before you moved?'

Susan told Rowan about her background, about her roots being here and the years she spent in Ventnor.

'It's not easy starting again, is it?' said Rowan. 'My husband always says I'd be fine without him, and to be fair I am out a lot, but he's my rock, my foundation. I would be lost without him.' She grinned, adding, 'Don't tell him that.'

Susan left soon after and had a quiet afternoon at home. It wasn't much later when she heard the remainder of the guests leave and then the sound of the vacuum cleaner started.

* * *

Susan returned the next day to Hazel's to collect the glasses and furniture ready for Saturday.

As Hazel let her in and led her to the garden, Susan was impressed at how tidy everything was.

'Oh, that was Rowan, she went through the place like a whirlwind after everyone left.'

'I enjoyed chatting to her.'

'Yes, she's quite something. Now, let's sort out what you need.'

When they had finished, Susan thanked Hazel for her help and realised that she had to face the rest of the day sorting out the house alone.

For days she'd been pushing to the back of her mind the fact that Steve and Hester would be coming here, to her home. She was desperate for it not to dominate the day. This was a special day for Zoe, Fay and Jamari.

However, as hard as she tried, the thought of them visiting plagued her. This house was more personal to her than anywhere else she'd lived, and the thought of them coming in here was worrying her.

The more she thought about it, the more she realised that it was actually Steve she was most worried about. What would he think of her new home? What would he think of the new life she was building for herself? She told herself it shouldn't matter now, but she knew that was nonsense. It mattered a great deal.

31

Susan was up early the next day. She took Rocco and Libs out before she set about decorating the garden with banners and lanterns.

Susan had ordered the bread, cakes and pastries from the village shop, where the owner, Tracy, had kindly offered to have Rocco and Libs for the day. Her husband would be taking their own dog up on the downs and would happily take them with him.

She arrived home just as Zoe, Fay and Jamari arrived mid-morning. It was wonderful to see them and to focus again on Jamari. She'd changed even since Susan had last seen her, her eyes that bit brighter and more alert. She even gave Susan the gift worth a purse of gold, a smile.

Fay carried the bags in.

'Are you okay to take them up to your room?' asked Susan. 'I thought you could make a home for yourselves up there, somewhere to escape to, and of course Jamari will need her sleeps.'

'Brilliant,' said Fay. 'I'll just go and put the cake somewhere safe.'

'Wait till you see Jamari's celebration babygrow: it's fab. Fay embroidered it; she's so clever.' Zoe looked adoringly at Fay, who blushed.

'Now, use your room to retreat to anytime you want,' said Susan. 'At least the sun is out, we can definitely use the garden.'

They had lunch in the garden, then Susan went up to get changed. She pulled out her comfortable empire-line jersey dress, brushed her hair, popped on a bit of lipstick.

She could hear Fay and Zoe getting ready in their room, chatting away to Jamari, and smiled. They were such wonderful parents: what a lucky little girl she was.

She heard a commanding knock at the door and caught her breath; she knew who that was.

As she opened the door, the first person Susan saw was Hester, standing in front of Steve. She was wearing a tight flowered dress, her curly blonde hair a shade lighter than the last time they'd met.

Hester was loud, flirtatious, loved clothes and spending money, and was quite unlike most of Steve's fellow doctors. However, Susan could appreciate that after a lifetime of being seriously committed to his work, Hester's love of the good life, of travel and anything new and exotic, must have seemed exciting and the complete change he felt he needed.

Hester wrapped Susan in her arms. 'Susan, how wonderful to see you again. Look at your gorgeous home: it's so quaint.'

'Thank you, come inside.'

'Good to see you, Susan.' Steve didn't attempt to hug her, for which she was grateful. The familiar frozen smile, the way he flicked each of the fingers on his right hand, spoke volumes about how nervous he was.

As they entered the main room, Zoe and Fay came down with Jamari. Zoe was right. Susan was impressed with Jamari's outfit, which was very bright, covered in rainbows and stars. She looked gorgeous.

Hester blinked. 'I might have guessed there would be no white christening gown.'

'That's because it's not a christening,' said Fay. Susan was surprised at the uncharacteristic sharpness from Fay.

Steve stepped forward. 'She looks perfect.' Jamari rewarded him with her best smile. Babies and children always loved Steve. Susan believed it was because behind that slightly hesitant manner, they recognised a stability and caring that made them feel safe.

Susan noticed Alice being helped out of a car outside and hurried to greet her. Although Susan had offered to collect Alice, one of the staff had volunteered to bring her and suggested that she phone when she was ready to return.

'You made it. Brilliant,' said Susan.

Alice stood very upright, although her hands clutched her Zimmer frame. She was wearing a white lace blouse with a pink cardigan and a navy skirt, and a delicate pink wrap had been carefully arranged around her shoulders and pinned in place.

'You look gorgeous,' said Susan.

'Thank you. My daughter bought me this blouse, and this wrap was from my granddaughter.' Alice looked up at the cottage. 'I'm glad you bought this house. I remember the family who were here when I was in the village. They were so happy.'

Susan guided Alice through the house and settled her in a comfortable seat in the garden.

Next to arrive were people from the village: Daniel and Jessie, but also Ross and Cerys, ready to sing, followed by Fiona and Hazel. Zoe's friends came in a group of four: loud, dressed up, carrying presents and bottles of Prosecco. They greeted Zoe and Fay with enthusiasm and cooed over Jamari. It was good to see Zoe back with her friends, laughing and joking.

Finally, Robert arrived. Susan smiled over at him, and he gave her his usual bear hug. As he did, however, she saw Steve watching and pulled away.

Everyone had arrived now. In the garden, each table had chairs around it, and people had settled into small groups. She noticed Steve and Hester were sitting with Fiona and Hazel. They seemed to be chatting happily. She was also pleased to see Fay and Zoe were sitting with Alice. As they were the focus of attention, it meant Alice was in the centre of the activity, which she was clearly enjoying.

The sun shone even brighter and soon Daniel stood in front of them and invited Zoe and Fay to join him so the ceremony could begin.

It started with a short poem, followed by Cerys and Ross singing a few songs, including Susan's favourite, 'You Are My Sunshine'. Susan and Steve each made short speeches. Daniel said a few concluding words.

Zoe turned to their guests. 'That's the end of the ceremony. Thank you so much, everyone. We'll cut the cake, then please dig into the buffet laid out in the kitchen.'

32

Susan saw Hazel and Fiona sitting together at a table. They had a bottle of wine, and Fiona was filling Hazel's glass. Fiona caught Susan's eye, gave her a friendly smile. Susan was grateful to her for looking after Hazel so well.

She turned and realised Hester was approaching her with Steve.

'It's gone well,' said Steve.

'Yes, nothing like any christening service I've been to, but as Zoe said, that's not what this is,' added Hester.

'Robert's here, then,' said Steve. 'I wasn't sure you'd keep in touch once you moved over here. It's quite a trek from Ventnor.'

'We still walk the dogs together and he's helped me moving in.'

'I love your house. It suits you. Quite a change from our place,' said Steve.

'I know, but it's cosy and it made me do a lot of clearing out.'

'Did you chuck out anything of Steve's?' Hester demanded.

Susan blinked, surprised at the sudden attack. 'Steve knows everything I disposed of. I sent a list to his solicitor, but he said he'd taken everything he wanted. I've put a few boxes in the garage, Steve, for you to look through. It's mainly books I wasn't sure what to do with.'

'You never told me about this list,' said Hester. 'We have to furnish the new place. I should have seen it.'

'You're buying a new place?' asked Susan.

'We don't need my flat on the island now,' said Hester. 'We've been renting a flat in Chichester and want to buy there now. We've friends there and, of course, the sailing crowd. We don't have anything to bring us back to the island now.'

Susan glanced at Steve. He was very quiet.

'You were having a good chat with Hazel and Fiona,' said Susan, trying to change the subject.

'Yes. Hazel was bringing me up to date on the state of GP practices on the island. The perennial problem of getting people to come here to work seems to be getting worse, not better, which means the doctors who are here are working longer and harder. I feel quite guilty that I've abandoned them all.'

'We both worked very hard while we were here. We deserve this retirement,' said Hester. She turned to Steve and, somewhat coldly, said, 'We should mingle.'

'I'll go back to our table,' said Steve firmly. Susan noticed that Cerys and Ross were saying goodbye to Zoe and Fay. It was only when Susan drew closer that she noticed something she'd missed earlier.

'You've lost your boot!' she said to Cerys.

Cerys grinned. 'They told me this morning it could come off. I'm just bandaged up now, but I'm so much more mobile. I was lucky it didn't need plaster. They said it's just a matter of time now, but no more crutches or boot: bliss. No driving quite yet, though.'

'That's brilliant, and thank you so much for your singing.'

Gradually, more people came over to thank Susan and say their farewells as the party was breaking up.

Hazel seemed a bit tipsy. 'You're a bad influence on me,' she joked with Fiona. 'When did we start a second bottle?' She smiled slightly glassy eyes at Susan. 'There's no rush for anything. We can sort the glasses out in a few days. Now I'm away home to get some coffee.'

'Thank you for looking after Hazel,' Susan said to Fiona. 'She doesn't find social events easy, and without Lawrence they must be even harder.'

'That's okay. She's good company, and it's something I feel I can do for Lawrence. Now, I must help Robert stack up the tables and chairs.'

Susan saw Alice and offered to run her back to the nursing home.

'You must have a lot to do,' replied Alice.

'No, come on. We've not had much time to chat.'

'That all went very well,' said Alice.

'It was a long way from a traditional christening.'

'That wouldn't have suited Zoe and Fay at all. It was a real pleasure to meet them both. Zoe reminds me of you.'

'Now I always think of her being like her dad,' said Susan. 'She has his looks.'

'True, but she has your spirit, and Jamari has your smile. What a dear little thing she is.'

'I think so, but I'm biased. You had a few chats, didn't you? How did you find Cerys?'

'I'm still worried about her.'

'She's bound to be on edge after all that's happened, wondering what people think of her.'

'Of course, but I still think she is holding something back,' said Alice.

'Did you have an opportunity to talk to Steve and Hester?'

'I did, and I've been watching them. I wouldn't be surprised if you don't go home to some fireworks this evening.'

'Why do you think that?'

'I can feel a storm brewing back there. There's a lot of strain between Hester and the rest of your family, even between her and your ex.'

'You saw that?' asked Susan.

'It was obvious. The problem is that jealousy is such an unattractive trait. It makes people behave in what appears quite a spiteful way.'

'You think Hester is jealous?'

'Oh, yes,' said Alice. 'You see, the whole occasion must have emphasised how close you are as a family, how much of an outsider she is. A wise person might sit back, wait, and slowly integrate themselves, but Hester isn't like that, is she?'

'I know there have been problems but it's not as if anyone has tried to push her out, make her feel like "the other woman".'

'No, I'm sure you've all been very kind and reasonable. That probably makes it harder. A good row sometimes clears the air.'

'I'm trying my best to keep the peace,' said Susan.

'And that is to your credit. Oh, I had a good chat with your friend Robert. I like him. He's a nice, straightforward kind of person.'

At the nursing home, Susan took Alice inside, where she was given a warm welcome by one of the carers, who offered to take Alice back to her room and settle her back in.

'Thank you so much for coming,' said Susan.

'It was very enjoyable. Thank you for asking me. Now I shall have a good rest and a nice cup of tea.'

Back home, as she opened the front door, Susan noticed an unsettling quiet in the house.

'I'm back,' she called, to no response.

She found Zoe and Fay together in the garden, with Steve sitting slightly apart.

On the table was the baby monitor. Susan guessed Jamari was up having a sleep.

'Is something wrong?' she asked lightly.

33

'It's Hester. She's stropped off,' said Zoe.

Steve was very red and was flicking his fingers madly.

'She said that Fay and I were ungrateful for the gift, that she wasn't wanted here,' continued Zoe. 'Anyway, she grabbed the car keys and she's driven off. She sent Dad a text saying she's getting on the next ferry, and he can make his own way back to the flat.'

'I'm sorry this has happened, today of all days,' said Steve. 'At least the drama happened after everyone had gone.'

'She's left you a bit stranded,' said Susan.

'Dad can come back with us,' said Zoe. A grumbling came from the monitor. Zoe and Fay glanced at each other and then both rushed inside.

'Look, I know this is a bit of a liberty,' said Steve, 'but I wonder if you'd mind if I stayed over? I would go first thing in the morning.'

Susan stared at him, unable to speak.

'I'm sorry. Is it too much to ask?'

'I thought you would want to go with Zoe and Fay.'

He thrust his head into his hands. 'I need help, Susan. I've made such a mess of things.'

Susan couldn't stop herself; he looked so miserable. 'If you need to stay, of course you can.'

Zoe came back out. 'Mum, I think we'd like to try and get the next ferry. It's two hours until the one after and Jamari is all over the place, bless her. She's had such a lovely, exciting day but she's not been in any routine.'

'Of course, love. That's fine. She's done so well, not a tear all day.'

'Are you ready, Dad?' asked Zoe.

'Your dad is staying, love, just catching his breath.'

Zoe raised her eyebrows, but her mind quickly went back to Jamari, and she picked up the monitor.

'Let me get your gifts together,' said Susan. 'You just sort yourselves out.'

In record time, they had loaded the car, said their goodbyes and Susan and Steve waved Fay, Zoe and Jamari off.

It felt very awkward when they were alone in the house.

'Look, I must go and get Rocco and Libs, so how about we take them for a walk on the beach? We could pick up a takeaway for tea?'

'That sounds great. Thank you.'

Although Steve was a naturally quiet man, he always had the look of someone on the verge of action. But today his eyes were blank in a way Susan had never seen before.

'You wait here. I won't be long.'

Susan walked quickly down to the shop, carrying a bunch of flowers she had bought for Tracy. Glancing further down the road, she could see Robert's car parked. She was surprised, having assumed he would go straight home. Shrugging, she went into the shop and was greeted with a huge smile from Tracy. The dogs had been very well behaved and just had some sausages and a sleep after a long walk on the downs.

'They're not going to want to come home,' said Susan. She held out the flowers. 'These are for you, just a little thank you.'

'They're beautiful, thank you, come on through,' said Tracy.

Both dogs were laid out asleep but as soon as she said their names, they were up, tails wagging and ready to go.

Susan returned home, picked up Steve and drove to Brook Beach. As soon as he was out of the car, Steve leaned his head back and breathed in deeply.

'That's exactly what Zoe did last time we were here.'

'You've no idea what it's like to be away from the island for any length of time.'

'You're always at sea—'

'It's not the same: this is home.'

They walked down on to the beach and let the dogs off. Susan waited for Steve to speak. After a long silence, he started to explain the problems he and Hester had been having. It seemed the decision to sell the flat on the island had not been as straightforward as it sounded. Steve had been very reluctant to let go of this final link to the island, and the friends they had in Chichester were far more Hester's 'type' than his. He was also getting worried about money. Hester had expensive taste and was treating their retirement as one long holiday, always wanting to go to the most expensive restaurants and shops.

When Susan tentatively suggested that he should be talking to Hester about all of this, not her, he said he had tried but didn't get anywhere. He had been looking at selling the boat, which was in his name, and returning to the island. Susan was shocked. She asked him how much of this he had shared with Hester. The answer appeared to be very little. She started to lose her cool.

'Oh, really, Steve. You're making the same mistakes all over again. My guess is that you've hardly spoken to Hester about your concerns. You've bottled everything up and you're going to just pull out of the relationship without a word of warning, just as you did with our marriage.'

He stopped, looking stunned. 'But we saw the end of our marriage coming. I'd been talking about getting a boat and sailing for a few years. It was clear, though, that it wasn't something you wanted to do. I showed you that article online about early retirement and you said it looked like a good idea.'

'Good God, Steve. I don't remember that at all. You mentioned a boat a few times, but you never sounded that serious. You should have been a lot clearer about what was going on.'

'I'm sorry, really I am.'

'But what about you and Hester? The least she deserves is for you to talk to her properly. Have you tried to explain your feelings about the island?'

He sighed. 'Whenever I mention the island, she thinks it is you I'm missing. In fact, she's convinced I'm still in love with you. She's very insecure about it all. It explains how she is being with Jamari, wanting to be you, I suppose.'

'That's very sad but, Steve, this is not my problem.'

On the way home they picked up fish and chips. Susan fed the dogs, put plates with their fish and chips on trays and opened a bottle of wine.

'Come on then, let's go and sit on the sofa.'

'Not at the table?'

She laughed. 'I've got into bad habits. I tend to put my tea on a tray and watch TV now in the evenings. I have discovered a whole new world of *Sewing Bee* and *Bake Off*. My parents would be horrified.'

They began to talk about their parents, then Zoe, and the foster children they had brought up together. Like Susan, Steve was still in touch with some of the children.

Much later, they walked the dogs through the village and, as they approached St Jude's, Susan began to tell Steve about Lawrence's accident and hinted at her suspicions.

'Fay told me about the business with your lodger over in Ventnor. I can understand why you did what you did.'

'You can?'

'Of course. You've always fought for the truth. The fact Colette was so on her own would have made it even more important to you.'

Susan smiled: of course he understood. 'Thank you.'

'You always did fight. I remember when you went off to Greenham. My parents thought I was mad letting you go.'

'It wasn't a matter of being allowed to go,' she said firmly.

'I told them that. I admired what you did then. I was so proud of you.'

'You never said—'

'No, and I should have.'

As they walked past the school, Susan noticed the lights for once were off. She told Steve about the hours Fiona worked.

'She's often working until the early hours in the school. I mean, I know teachers work long hours, but I've never met anyone who is actually in the building at that time.'

'I wouldn't have thought the governors would like that.'

'They don't. I think there's a problem with the insurance. She did confess to me she sometimes falls asleep.'

Steve started to flick his fingers, his face screwed up in concern.

'What's the matter?' Susan asked.

'I was concerned about the amount she was drinking at the celebration; she must have drunk nearly two bottles of wine.',

'Are you sure? She seemed fine when she left. It was Hazel who was staggering.'

'Hazel only had a few glasses, enough to make you a bit tipsy. The fact that Fiona drank a great deal more, and showed no effect, is far more worrying. It could indicate someone who routinely drinks excessively. I wonder if she is doing it at school in the nights when she stays late.'

'But why would she do that at school rather than at home? She lives alone. It would make more sense to be drinking at home,' said Susan.

'You don't know she's not drinking at home as well. She may rationalise it to herself that drinking while working is not as bad as drinking alone at home.'

'So, you think she has a serious problem with drink?'

'I can't say that from only one brief meeting. It would be interesting to know what is in the bottle attached to her belt, though.'

'Oh, that's her water bottle. She always has that with her —'

'So why, when there was a jug of water and glasses on our table, was she needing to drink her own water and why did she have that look when she took a sip?' said Steve. 'It's the same look you see on a smoker's face when they take that first drag on a cigarette.'

'I'd honestly never thought about it. I've never seen her drunk or smelled booze on her breath early in the day.'

'I could be wrong, and I'm not saying to stage an intervention or anything, but keep an eye, she might need a friend.'

'Do you think Lawrence could have suspected something like this was going on? You see, he suggested she move schools.'

'Telling her to move on wasn't going to help her.'

Susan bit her lip and thought to herself that this could have given Fiona a motive. If Lawrence had suspected she was drinking on the job and was desperate enough to ask her to move, had he also threatened to reveal her problem to the governors?

'You look preoccupied,' said Steve.

'Sorry, lots to think about. It's been a long day.'

Back at the cottage, Susan suggested they turn in for the night.

After settling the dogs, they went upstairs. Susan showed Steve to what she thought of now as Fay and Zoe's room.

She closed the curtains and turned on the bedside light.

'This is all made up; they only slept in it the one night.'

'This is great, and thank you, Susan. It's really helped being here. Heaven knows I have no right to ask favours of you. You always were kind.'

'We were married a long time and I thought of you as my best friend for most of that. As much as I might like to just be angry and forget about you, I can't.'

'I'm very sorry for hurting you. I wish now we'd been to counselling, talked about things. Who knows...' He stopped.

'But we didn't,' she said gently. 'We're divorced, Steve, and you are with Hester—'

'And you're with Robert? Don't say there's nothing between you. I've seen the way he looks at you.'

'Robert has been a very good friend to me.'

'Yes, but he'd like more. I can tell.'

'That's for me and Robert to sort out.'

'Do you ever miss me?'

'Oh, Steve, that's not fair.' Susan was close to tears. Of course she missed him, and today she'd had glimpses of why they had been happily married for so long. She had seen the old Steve she had fallen in love with.

He walked towards her and gave her the smile she was so familiar with. She didn't tremble, her heart didn't race, but she felt comfortable.

Steve gently kissed her on her forehead. 'I miss you every day.'

34

'And I miss you,' Susan replied. The statement was stark but true. She felt him draw her closer and they sat down on the bed, still wrapped in each other's arms. A tiny alarm rang in her head. She pulled away and stood up. 'I'm sorry, but I can't do this. You are still with Hester and, anyway, we can't just pretend the last three years haven't happened.'

'You said you missed me.'

'I do, of course I do. I lived with you and loved you for forty years. But I am just starting to heal from you leaving me. I mean really heal, so that I can be happy, make plans. I must protect that. I'm not throwing that away easily. I've worked too damn hard.'

Steve nodded, smiled in a way that showed he understood. His phone rang, urgent and brash.

'I expect that's Hester,' said Susan. 'Talk to her. I'll say goodnight now. There's towels and everything in the bathroom, help yourself.'

Susan went to her own room, closed the door and started to change. She didn't give herself time to think until she was in bed.

When she did, she felt warm tears on her cheeks. She could hear Steve's voice, low and soft, but couldn't make out any words until she heard, 'We'll talk again tomorrow. Goodnight.'

She listened as Steve went to the bathroom and returned to his room.

She hated the part of herself that wanted him to come in to her. Her head knew it would be all wrong, and yet she knew also how much she missed being held by him. If he was here maybe she would feel truly safe again: no more threats, no more voices in the woods.

As miserable as she felt, though, she knew that taking on this investigation had been of her own choosing. Steve would never have understood why any more than he had understood why she had gone on marches and to Greenham Common.

Susan lay back, closed her eyes, tried to remember the day. She was pleased for Zoe and Fay that it had gone so well. Snapshots from the day flashing up. Jamari in her beautiful babygrow, Zoe and Fay, such intense but loving parents, the lovely family tree Steve had given them. However, her mind inevitably returned to Steve, lying there, so close by in the next room, alone.

* * *

Sunday morning

Susan wondered if it was going to be awkward as she went down to breakfast. However, Steve, always an early riser, was up and seemed more in control.

'I'm sorry about last night,' he said as she entered the kitchen, adding, 'But I meant it. I do miss you, and I'm sorry for the way I hurt you. I hope we can get back to at least being friends.'

'That will take time. Did you speak to Hester?'

He sighed. 'I did. She wasn't too happy that I was here. I hadn't realised it would be a problem.'

'Oh, really, Steve. That was a bit naïve, even for you.'

'Honestly, until she told me last night, I had no idea how threatened she was by you. She always seems so together, so confident.' He shook his head. 'For a doctor, I'm not particularly good at reading people, am I?'

'You were incredibly good with your patients, but you flounder a bit outside your surgery. At least you and Hester have started to talk. It can't have been easy for her yesterday.'

'You're always kind, thank you.'

Susan noticed the dogs standing quietly by the back door. However, when she looked out, she saw plates with fruit cake on the tables. She needed to clear that up before the dogs went out.

'I'm just going into the garden. I won't be long,' said Susan.

She grabbed a bin bag and rushed out. It was good to be in the fresh air and keeping busy. She didn't feel up to any more intense talks that morning.

After a few minutes, she heard the house phone ring. It was bound to be a cold caller: friends usually rang her on her mobile, so she shouted to Steve to answer it and carried on collecting scraps.

Having successfully gathered everything, she went back into the house as Steve was just replacing the receiver.

'Um, that was Robert. I think you must have turned your mobile on to silent. He was just checking up on you.'

'Oh, right. Well, never mind. I'll phone him later.'

'I need to shower and then I wonder if you could run me to the catamaran over in Ryde. I'm sorry, but it would be the easiest way for me to go. Hester will be waiting to pick me up.'

Susan was pleased he was making plans to leave soon. 'Okay, I'll bring the dogs. They can have a run on the beach there.'

However, before they left, there was just time for Steve to look through the boxes in the garage.

'They are mainly old medical books. I don't need these,' he said, then he picked out a beautifully illustrated book about the night sky. 'You gave me this for a birthday, didn't you? I'd like to hold on to this. It's the only thing among all this I want to keep.' They held each other's gaze, until Susan broke the spell.

'We need to get a move on to catch the catamaran. Let's go.'

Susan was relieved that the drive over was easy. There were few cars on the road as it was still early. She loved the slow drive along the pier, leaving Ryde behind, the sea either side glistening in the morning sun. When they reached the pier head, Steve undid his seat belt, and turned to her in the car. 'Thank you for everything.'

She kept her seat belt on, tried to avoid eye contact. 'You'd better run, they're boarding.'

He stepped out of the car. Susan put the car into gear. She didn't need to sit here, watching him go.

She had tears in her eyes as she drove away, but she kept going until she found a parking space on the seafront. It was a beautiful morning, and there was a long stretch of sand where the dogs were allowed to run.

Now Steve had gone, she had time to think. She'd surprised herself at the feelings she still had for Steve but was also relieved that nothing had come of last night. It did make her wonder again how and when their marriage had gone so wrong. Had she missed something? Was there something she could have done to prevent the break-up? But she stopped herself. She'd asked herself those questions hundreds of times over the last few years and never come up with an answer.

The truth was that she hadn't missed anything. Steve had never asked to sit down and talk, never suggested there was any problem, never so much as hinted that he didn't love her any more. He hadn't told her that he was unhappy, that he'd met someone else, that he was desperate to retire and go off sailing. No, he really hadn't ever said any of those things.

And wasn't that in a way a form of lying to her? She had always trusted him, never dreamed he would lie to her, but he had hidden the truth and he knew how much that mattered to her.

Susan lifted her head, breathed in the sea air, lowered her shoulders and felt herself relax. She felt that she had at least stumbled on a deeper understanding of the breakdown of her marriage. It didn't stop the hurt, but at least she knew where some of the pain was coming from.

She thought about her confusion over Robert, her home, in fact everything about this 'fresh start'. And then she realised that idea of starting again with a clean slate was, to an extent, an illusion. She was starting a new chapter in her journey. The previous parts of the story were still there, the good and the bad. They had led to this point. But now she held the pen, she could choose how to write the next part, but she also needed time to heal, time to reset.

When Susan got back, she fed the dogs and made herself coffee. The only sounds were the birds, and distant traffic. She realised that what she had said to Steve last night was right. She *had* started to feel content and happy on her own.

* * *

It was late when she took Rocco and Libs out for their final walk. The evening was quiet and still, as she walked through the close and into the village. As she crossed the road she met Fiona, walking more slowly, head down, so unlike the Fiona she had first met.

'Evening,' said Susan. 'Late night at the school?'

'As always.'

Susan remembered her conversation with Steve: she had to say something.

'Um, could I talk to you a minute?' she asked.

Looking mystified, Fiona nodded, and they walked towards her house.

'We could go into the garden as I have the dogs,' suggested Susan.

As they walked down the side of the house, the security lights lit up the garden like a football pitch.

There were some wicker seats at the top of the garden, and they sat there.

'So, what's up?' asked Fiona briskly.

'This isn't easy, but, look, my ex-husband Steve is a doctor. He mentioned to me he was worried about how much you were drinking yesterday. I've not come to judge or anything, but I wondered if I could help.' The words tumbled out. Susan flinched, waiting for the angry denial.

Fiona took hold of the whistle that always hung around her neck and started to tap it against her chest. 'That took some nerve, didn't it?' she said quietly.

Susan waited.

'I thought I saw him clocking what I was drinking. The answer to your question is complicated. I do drink a lot. I use it as my prop when I'm stressed. I drink alone. I drink excessively. I've fallen asleep drinking. I have read about it, looked things up online. I know I'm certainly in a dangerous place with it. Whether I am a functioning alcoholic is another matter.'

Susan blinked, amazed at Fiona's insight and honesty.

'Lawrence knew, and the reason he was covering the SATs alone was because I arrived at school hung-over.' Fiona scratched her knee hard with one hand. 'I may sound as if I can talk about this quite easily, but I'm deeply ashamed and embarrassed.'

'Was there a reason you'd been drinking the night before the SATs?'

'I'd heard the news about my ex-husband's death. Ours was a short and unhappy marriage. Within months he had been unfaithful. I was devastated. Our marriage ended and I moved here. But I had loved him. To know I would never see him again was still heartbreaking. I was drinking at school the night before and was very hung-over when I went back the next day. Lawrence sent me home.'

'Had it happened before?'

'Once before. Lawrence told the staff I had a migraine. On the Friday he died, he'd come to the school after the choir committee meeting and found the complaint. We both knew he hadn't cheated, but he felt he'd been put in a difficult position because of me. He then shocked me by telling me he thought I should move schools. He knew that some nights I was drinking at school. He didn't want the governors or parents finding out and causing a scandal.'

'How did you feel?' asked Susan.

'I was terribly angry and hurt and I felt betrayed by him. Heaven knows, I stuck by him through thick and thin. I was also in denial that I needed help. I'm still devastated that it was the last time we spoke. As soon as I heard what had happened to him, I tried to block the conversation out of my mind, hence denying to you that we'd even spoken.' Fiona paused, then asked, 'What are you going to do? Are you planning to use this as a bit of juicy gossip or are you going to go to the governors?'

'I'm not planning to do anything. I came here as your friend. I think you need to get professional help, and I've a feeling you already know that.'

Fiona slumped. 'Of course I do, but I'm petrified of losing my job. It would be on my medical records. What do I do? Take time off to go into rehab? I can't think of any way of keeping this a secret in the village. At least I know Ross won't say anything.'

'Ross knows?'

'I had to tell him. When he moved in, I noticed him subtly checking drawers, watching when I was pouring a drink. I asked him if he had something to say. He looked so scared. I don't think I'm that formidable, am I?'

Susan smiled but didn't reply.

'Anyway, he told me he was worried about me. Although he seemed unconscious the night of the caravan fire, he had heard me say, "I'm sorry." What I'd meant, of course, was that if I hadn't been drinking, I'd have seen the fire start or someone going down the garden.'

Susan looked down the garden. The burnt-out wreck of the caravan was still there and for a minute she could still smell the smoke, feel the heat of the flames. She shuddered.

'He thought you tried to kill him?'

'Oh, no. He thought I'd gone down to look for drink or cigarettes as I've done it before. He guessed I'd been drinking and started the fire accidentally. He didn't want the police digging around and discovering I'd been there. Anyway, we had a good talk, and he was relieved. It did show me how worried he's been about me, though. He's already helping me, but I know it's not fair to depend on him. I shall call my GP and talk to her.'

'Good. I'm sure she will be discreet. I'm not going to tell anybody, Fiona.'

'Thank you.'

* * *

Early the next morning, Susan received a call from Steve. He thanked her for letting him stay the night. He explained that he'd had some very good chats with Hester and discussed some changes to their plans. They had decided that they would keep the flat on the island, but it would be in Steve's name and then the new place in Chichester would be in Hester's. Susan found it unnerving that Steve could be coming and going to and from the island without her knowing, but she couldn't stop him doing that anyway.

The call from Steve reminded her that she'd not spoken to Robert since he'd called. She tried phoning but her call went through to voicemail, and she left a message to say she was sorry to have missed him and she'd be in touch soon.

After this Susan decided to take the dogs a bit further afield for a change and chose Parkhurst Woods.

Once she'd settled them in the car, she drove out of the close. Standing at the bus stop she saw Cerys, and wondered if she was going over to the mainland for one of her meetings.

Susan pulled up and wound down the window. 'Are you off to the Red Jet?' she asked.

'Hopefully, but the bus is late.'

'I can give you a lift, hang on, I'll open the door for you.'

She noticed Cerys was moving a lot easier now and got into the car without difficulty. However, as she was shutting the passenger door, Susan suddenly noticed something she'd missed about Cerys. How on earth had she missed such a vital clue?

35

Susan's mind was racing as she drove along. When she had given Cerys a lift home the night of her fall, she remembered being very careful not to bump Cerys's injured foot as it was close to the gearstick. That was because Cerys had injured her right foot. Also, Susan knew she had been on Cerys's right side when she had helped her down the path to the vicarage, and she was sure Cerys had leaned heavily on Ross to avoid putting any weight on her right foot. Yes, Cerys had definitely hurt her right foot when she fell outside Hazel's house. And yet now it was her left foot that was bandaged and had been in the boot.

She tried to recall her time in the classroom with Cerys, arranging the chair to rest her foot on, watching Cerys taking the register. Yes, it had been her left foot on that tiny chair, Susan was sure of it. How on earth did that make sense?

'How is your foot healing then?'

'It's doing well; the doctor is pleased. The bandage is much easier to live with.'

'It's hard to imagine how you crushed those bones like that with a fall—'

'Yes, um, I was surprised as well.'

Susan added, as lightly as she could, 'It's strange, I can remember that evening so well. I could have sworn I was trying to avoid bumping your leg with the gearstick, but it wouldn't have been a problem if it was your left foot.'

She was expecting Cerys to gently contradict her, laugh off a mistaken memory. However, Cerys's reaction was defensive and there was anger in her voice. 'That's ridiculous, of course this is the foot I injured.'

The atmosphere in the car turned icy. Cerys stared out of the passenger window. After a time, Susan tried to ease it by changing the subject and chatting about the dogs.

Cerys seemed to unwind and asked, 'So, what are you doing over on the mainland today?'

'I'm not going there, actually. I'm taking the dogs to Parkhurst.'

'Oh, but we've passed it, I've taken you out of your way.'

'It's fine really, I'll come back another way to avoid the traffic going into Newport. Don't worry about it.'

Susan pulled in at the Red Jet terminal and went round to help Cerys out of the car. Once Cerys was standing, she looked directly at Susan. 'You don't miss much, do you? You seem motherly and innocent somehow, but you're not.'

'It's not that I want to see the worst in people. I'm just not able to ignore things that don't add up.'

Cerys sighed. 'Look, I'm going to tell you something, but I'd be grateful if you kept it to yourself. You are right that when I fell outside Hazel's, I didn't hurt my foot that badly. I was fine when Ross left me and went up the downs. I had a short call with Fiona, but then I had another fall, and this time it really hurt. And yes, it was the other foot. When Jessie came home, I was in a lot of pain and so she took me to the hospital. I just felt so stupid. I didn't want to go telling people that I had had two falls in one night, and that's all. There's no great mystery.'

Susan was about to speak when Cerys looked at the queue outside the Red Jet terminal; they were starting to board.

'I need to go,' said Cerys. 'Please believe me. It really is that simple.'

With that, Cerys strode away awkwardly. If Susan accepted Cerys's explanation, she knew it just raised even more questions.

Susan drove out of Cowes, through Porchfield and round to an alternative entrance to Parkhurst Woods. This was a special time of year to visit the woods and at this time of day, there was still a lot of early-morning bird-song. She took Rocco and Libs down into an area of ancient woodland where tall oaks and ash trees stood side by side. It was quieter over here. Most people would be at the main car park to the south.

She stopped and listened to a thrush high up in the trees, its song stunning. She caught sight of one of her favourite little birds, a long-tailed tit with its delicate pink chest. There was a flash of colour as a jay flew past. Above hovered a buzzard. The woods were alive. They rejoined the pine wood. Susan knew she stood a chance of seeing the red squirrels. She knew the signs to look out for: the gnawed cones on the forest floor, the silent movements of branches above. Then she caught sight of one. For once, she had seen the squirrel before it had seen her. It was busy putting on a death-defying display, leaping between the tiny branches.

It was good to be out in nature, to breathe, to still her mind. Her thoughts went back to a previous conversation with Jessie, and again she was faced with a problem: which lies mattered, which could she ignore?

* * *

Before Susan went out to choir that Friday evening, she tried contacting Robert again. However, she was surprised to find herself transferred to voicemail again. She left another message, this time asking him to contact her soon. After this she made her way to choir rehearsal.

There was a more relaxed atmosphere now and Ross was able to take them through the songs with little fuss. Although no one mentioned it, Susan guessed from the odd sly look in Cerys's direction that news about Lawrence being her father had spread quickly. She also saw a lot of strain on the faces of the choir committee members. Hazel, naturally, was still very pale and subdued, but Cerys, Daniel, Jessie and Fiona all looked on edge, while Ross seemed to get lost in the music.

Susan was distracted by her plans for later that evening as she was planning to go to the pub over at Castleford and attempt to meet Alan Smithee.

At the end of the rehearsal, Susan walked out of the church with Hazel and waited while she locked up. Hazel mentioned that she'd had a few phone calls and people approaching her to check she was okay after the news about Cerys.

'Of course, they just all want more gossip,' she said, laughing. 'I don't mean that nastily: they do care as well, but it's always nice to be the one with a new nugget to share. I think they have been a bit disappointed at my upbeat response. The news will soon be replaced by something else.'

As they approached their cottages, Hazel asked Susan in for a drink.

'Um, no, thanks. I'm going out,' replied Susan.

'I hope it's somewhere nice. Are you meeting up with Robert? Oops, sorry, just being nosy.'

'No. It's not Robert,' said Susan. 'I'll see you around.'

Susan checked on the dogs, let them run in the garden for a few minutes, then drove over to Castleford.

She parked in the small car park opposite Shiloh and walked down the hill, into the village to the pub.

The light was starting to fade, and the pub was busy. It suddenly seemed a long shot that she would meet this man, but she just had to hope that he came.

She bought herself a lemonade and lime with a large packet of crisps. She had a good description of Alan and knew to look out for the hat and the colourful clothes. And, of course, he would probably either be on his own or with Daniel. She should be able to pick him out.

Glancing around inside, everyone seemed to be in groups. There was no one fitting Alan's description, so Susan went outside.

There were a couple sitting opposite each other at a long table. Susan sat well to the other end, slightly turned away from them. Checking her watch, she saw it was half past eight.

Time passed, people came and went. She was starting to think this was a waste of time. Susan went to buy another drink. A young man with a name badge, Kev, served her. As he handed her the drink, she decided to take a chance.

'Um, I was hoping to meet a friend here. He comes regularly. I wonder if he's come in and I've missed him. His name is Alan. He wears a hat, colourful clothes.'

Kev laughed. 'I know who you mean. He usually sits outside, unless the heavens open like they did the other night. Then he comes inside.'

'Thanks,' Susan replied, and returned to the garden, finding a different seat.

And then she saw a man arrive. It had to be Alan: the hat, the bright shirt. She was sure it was him.

She watched him go into the pub, presumably to order a drink and food, before he came back into the garden.

She saw a family get up from a table and Alan sat straight down.

Susan panicked. How on earth was she going to approach this stranger? She hadn't planned anything she was going to say, but she couldn't let this opportunity pass.

Taking a deep breath, she picked up what remained of her drink, put the empty crisp packet in a bin and went over to the table.

Alan was bent over his drink. She coughed, and then spoke. 'Hello, are you Alan Smithee?'

As Alan looked up, Susan saw his face. She gasped.

'Daniel?'

He stared, his mouth open. 'Susan!'

'But... what?' she spluttered and slumped into the seat opposite him.

Daniel fiddled with his pint, stared down at the table. 'Lawrence was right. Someone was going to stumble on this eventually. I'm just amazed it took so long.' He gave a faint smile.

'But why? What's going on?'

Daniel took a long sip from his glass, and looked up, meeting her gaze. His voice was steady. There was no sign of the stammer.

'When I first started coming over here, it really was simply for a time to meditate and pray. One evening, by mistake, I left the centre to go for a walk without signing out. I walked down the hill, found myself looking into the garden of the pub. I watched all the people laughing, drinking, and I wanted to join them. But, of course, I had my collar on, and, anyway, that's not something I did, something I'd never do. Not me, Daniel Green.'

He took another sip of his beer.

'I started to imagine what if I wasn't me, if I was someone else. And that was the seed of the idea. It grew like some monster after that. I created another person, Alan Smithee: the name of a non-existent director, he had to be so different to me that no one would suspect.'

Daniel sat back now, speaking in a relaxed and confident way Susan had never seen before.

'I created an email account for him, so his key code would be sent every week, and the rest was quite simple. I had the two codes, so when I arrived, if no one was around, I would pick up keys and sign in for the both of us. If someone was, I would pop down when it was empty, sign in for Alan and pick up his keys. I'd go to my room with a change of clothes, and as far as everyone was concerned, Daniel Green remained in his room, making it very clear to everyone I was not to be disturbed. I was able to lock my door just in case someone tried to go in to see me. Then I'd change and become Alan. No one seemed to register that they never saw him arrive. It was easy. As soon as I put these clothes on, I'm Alan. It's wonderful. I feel so free.'

'Surely they notice Alan's room isn't used.'

'Oh, I always ruffle up the sheets.'

'But what about mealtimes?'

'Alan never went to breakfast. I signed him out first thing on a Saturday morning whatever time I was going. If things were busy, I'd just leave his keys somewhere and send an email apologising for forgetting to sign out. The worst that could happen if I got caught was that they would decide I was odd. I mean, I paid for two rooms. I wasn't committing a crime.'

He spoke in a leisurely way, but there was a hint of smugness. He was proud of what he'd done. He continued. 'I bring what I see as my outfit. I have a wig, nothing too crazy, just longer than my hair and darker. The hat is a brilliant disguise, as are the brightly coloured clothes. Initially I thought someone would be bound to recognise me, but I realised no one looked at me that closely. People started to expect to see Alan, and, over time, I've developed his backstory. I give him a slightly different accent, a bit more London.'

'You sound as if you enjoy this. Where did you get the name Alan Smithee from?'

'I got the idea from watching an old movie ages ago. A friend told me that it was an official pseudonym used by film directors who wish to disown a project. The point is, Alan Smithee doesn't exist. It's just a game.'

Susan remembered Alice saying she had looked up the name. 'Something and nothing,' she had said she had learned and now Susan understood why. Looking at Daniel grinning, she suddenly remembered Jessie and all the stress she had been under.

'It might be good for you, but what about Jessie? Don't you think she worries about you coming over here every Friday?'

'I don't see why she would.'

Susan blinked, feeling irritated by his lack of sensitivity. 'You sleep here every Friday. Any partner would wonder why they are being left every week. Don't you realise Jessie comes over here every Friday after being at the gym and sits in the car park, watching the centre?'

Daniel's eyes were wide with horror now. 'She spies on me? Why?'

Susan tutted. 'She is worried about what you're doing here. She found a receipt from the pub. I'm guessing she thought you'd been here with someone, Martha or Alan.'

Daniel was open-mouthed now. 'Why didn't she ask?'

'Because she was frightened of the answer.'

Daniel's eyes narrowed. 'I can see how all this looks to you. Poor Jessie, the neglected wife. She's not the innocent she makes out, you know.' Susan saw an angry glint in Daniel's eyes.

'What do you mean?'

'She thinks I don't know. Honestly, she must think I'm stupid. I know why she made a fuss about that DBS record.' He paused; his eyes met Susan's. Seeing her response, he said, 'I'm guessing you've worked that one out?'

'Lawrence spoke to me the night he died,' she said evasively.

'He assumed I wasn't aware, but I knew she had a criminal record. We've had to do a few of these forms, I spotted one of hers a while back now.'

'And you didn't talk to her about it? She's been so worried you would find out.'

Daniel shrugged. 'I thought it would be better for her to tell me, and in any case, I quite like knowing more than people think. It gives you a sense of power.'

Susan scowled. She didn't like the way he was talking. It seemed pretty manipulative to her.

'Don't give me that disapproving look,' Daniel snarled. 'Maybe you don't know the rest about her, about her fling with the music master...' Seeing that Susan failed to register surprise, Daniel said, 'I can see you worked that out as well. I stumbled on them in the church a few times, acting all innocent. My guess is Lawrence knew. When he found me out here, he told me there were things to talk about. Honestly, that man thought he was some kind of god. I told him to butt out, but I could see he was going to keep on sticking his nose in...'

Susan again saw that flash of anger.

Daniel continued. 'You're as bad, aren't you? Digging away. I think it's time you left. And don't you go spreading around what you've seen this evening. You're the only person alive now who knows. You need to watch your back, remember what happened to Lawrence.'

Susan stood up and walked quickly out of the pub garden. She started to make her way up the hill.

When she was about halfway up, there were no street lights. She suddenly felt very alone. There were high hedges to her right, leading into the castle fields. The other side was also all lined with hedges and bushes. There were no houses, no comforting lights from living rooms. She heard an owl, and thought of Ross and his phone, recognised it as the call of a barn owl.

A twig snapped. She stopped, listened. Was Daniel following her up the road?

She made herself walk quickly and, as she did, she dug into her bag until she found her keys.

She held them between her fingers in a way Zoe had once told her to, in case she needed a weapon in an attack. Now she knew it would be useless, she had no idea what she would do with them.

She reached her car, opened the door and got in. She frantically locked all the doors, switched on the headlights, needing light. She was grateful she'd reversed in; she started the ignition.

As she did so, she realised there was another car parked behind her. Someone was in the driver's seat, on their phone. The light lit up their face.

36

It was Jessie, sitting in her car, as she must do most Friday nights.

Susan wondered whether to speak to her, but decided it would be better to go home.

She put her foot on the accelerator, started to pull away and, as she did, she glanced in her mirror. Just for a second, she was sure her eyes met Jessie's.

Swallowing hard, she continued out of the car park. As she travelled, she tried to slow her breathing, calm herself, but she was pleased to arrive home.

Shaken, her first instinct was to ring Robert. She knew that whatever had happened, he would be straight over to reassure her.

She knew that wasn't fair, that she shouldn't keep calling on him only when she needed him, but she was scared, and she couldn't hide from that. Jessie had seen her. She knew Jessie was angry, possibly a killer. If she'd been capable of killing Lawrence, maybe even attempting to kill Ross, surely she wouldn't think twice about trying to silence her.

To take her mind off her fears, she opened her laptop. The first thing she did was google the name Alan Smithee. What she read made her smile. Alice was right: she really should have followed her example before.

And then she heard a gentle tapping at her door. She hadn't heard a vehicle. Who would come here at this time of night? The dogs pricked up their ears, but stayed in their beds. Susan walked slowly to the front door. She heard someone say her name.

Susan slowly opened the front door, but Jessie pushed her way in. Both Rocco and Libs came running over to her, excited to see a visitor.

'I'm sorry, I had to come,' stammered Jessie.

'It's okay. Sit down.'

Jessie sat back, closed her eyes. 'I'm so tired,' she sighed.

'I know, it's been so hard for you. Keeping secrets, covering up for people—'

Jessie sat up. 'You understand? Daniel and I are both innocent.'

Susan bit her lip. 'The trouble with your alibi for Daniel is that, from where you sit in your car, you can't see the car park at Shiloh. It's behind the building. Who is to say Daniel didn't drive out before you arrived, travel to Bishopstone, kill Lawrence and return after you'd left?'

Jessie sat with her mouth open. 'But no, it can't have happened. Daniel would never do something like that. I know him.'

'Do you? Daniel is a very complex person. I have a feeling you know that in your heart, and I've seen glimpses of his temper. I think you might be scared of him. Is that why you turned to Ross?'

Jessie nodded. 'I saw your face when you found us that day at the fete. I guessed you knew. It was a friendship that got out of hand. Lawrence walked in on us in the church just holding each other, but it was enough. You have to believe me. It never went further than that. I was lonely and confused. I've tried so hard to make this marriage work.'

'But you can't make Daniel love a job I sense he probably hates. One he is doing simply to please his parents.'

'But he's always talking about his need to pray and meditate.'

'He's desperate to try and fulfil this role out of a sense of duty. But he said to me that he often feels he is shouting into the dark. He also said he acts a part. In fact, this evening, I saw he literally does that every Friday.'

'What do you mean?'

Susan explained what she had seen earlier that evening.

Jessie shook her head. 'I can't believe it. That's just weird. I'm not sure I wouldn't rather he was having an affair. I don't get this at all.'

'No, I was shocked too.'

'He goes over to be someone else. No wonder Lawrence thought we needed to talk. What a mess. I feel like I don't know Daniel at all.'

'And yet this evening I discovered he knows more about you than you think. He knows about your criminal record; he knows about Ross.'

Jessie gasped, her eyes wide in fear. 'He knows about Ross? Oh, my God.'

Susan waited.

'I've been scared, you know, since that pen...' Jessie stood up. 'I have to go home.'

Susan was alarmed. 'I don't think so.'

Jessie rushed to the door. 'I'm going,' she shouted. Susan ran out into the close, but Jessie was fitter than her, and she was already out of sight.

Susan's heart was racing. What was she going to do? She saw a light on in Hazel's. She caught a glimpse of her shutting the curtains upstairs. Jessie's shouting must have disturbed her.

She looked back and saw both the dogs sitting patiently at the front door, watching her.

'It's okay. Come on. Let's go back inside.'

The first thing she did was to open her laptop, go to the Flexee site and check Jessie's history. After this, she sat back, and ran through the events at the pub earlier that evening.

She had a feeling that this volcano of an investigation was about to erupt, but when and exactly how she was not sure.

* * *

Saturday

Susan started the next day by taking the dogs on a long walk over the downs, desperately trying to clear her mind. Back home, she decided to try and get to grips with the garden. She was no gardener, but fortunately the person before her had been, and so at least she could try to maintain it. She was out weeding one of the beds when her phone rang.

It was Zoe, and she settled down for a long chat with her, including a lovely FaceTime with Jamari. Zoe, of course, was curious about Steve staying over, more concerned that her mother take care than trying to rush them back together.

After the call, Susan returned to her weeding. This time, she worked her way down one side of the garden. Sitting back, she was pleased with what she'd accomplished and was thinking about going to the garden centre to buy some new plants. She tried to remember the plants in Hazel's garden. She must have the same soil. Maybe she would get some inspiration at the nursery. She was about to go out when there was a knock at the door.

Susan looked down at Rocco and Libs. 'My goodness,' she said to them, 'what a busy morning we're having. Who is it now?' She opened the door to find Robert, looking slightly red-faced and awkward.

'Come in,' she said. 'Have you got the dogs in the car?'

'I have, but I'm not sure how long I'm going to be staying.' He still hadn't stepped inside the house.

'What's the matter, Robert? What's going on? I've left a few messages on your phone.'

'Look, I need to check about something Steve said on the phone to me. I'm not going to mess about. He told me that you were finding me a bit of a nuisance, that it was embarrassing that I kept coming over to see you.'

Susan was furious. 'How dare he! That's just not true, Robert. You should have known that. God, I'm so cross with him.'

Robert's face relaxed. 'Well, I could give him the benefit of the doubt and say he was just trying to look out for you, but to be honest, I think he was jealous.'

Susan felt herself blush. 'You could be right, but Steve and I have got a few things straight. Look, do you want to come in? We can talk properly.'

'I wouldn't want to intrude,' he said, grinning.

'Of course you're not.'

He came in, but he didn't sit down.

'Is there something else on your mind?' Susan asked.

'I've had a few chats with Fiona this week. She mentioned that Steve stayed over on Saturday night.'

Susan stared. 'How the hell... oh, I suppose it got round. Come and sit down. Right,' she said. 'Steve stayed because Hester ran out on him. He could have had a lift with Zoe, but he asked to stay. It was difficult. I admit to realising that I still have some nostalgic feelings, I mean, they don't just disappear, do they? But we didn't sleep together and when he left the next morning my main feeling was one of relief.'

'I see. Thank you for telling me. I'm sorry I asked.'

'I'm glad you did.'

Rocco and Libs were standing next to her, waiting. Robert usually meant a walk and she could see they were wondering if he had Gem Gem and Dougie with him.

'I think these two are asking for a walk. Do you fancy going up the downs? I've something important to tell you.'

37

Susan followed in her own car as Robert drove up into the car park at Mottistone Down. They led the dogs out, through the gate and started walking up the path. Susan began to tell Robert about Cerys being Lawrence's daughter and also Cerys's explanation for her injured foot.

'I'm not sure about that story about the foot, but I'm amazed about her being Lawrence's daughter.'

Susan went on to tell him about meeting Daniel at the pub. He responded, 'Mind you, I don't think you should have been doing that on your own at night.' Susan gave him a sideways look and he held up his hands. 'Okay, I'm just saying.' He coughed and added, 'By the way, I think Steve has a point about Fiona. I tried to talk to her about her drinking after the celebration, and she broke down. We talked about a lot of things, but she did mention the night Lawrence died. After the choir committee meeting, she'd spoken to Lawrence about some complaint. She had been very upset and had a drink. She thought of going home but took a call from Cerys. The call was short, but the rain had started by the time they finished, so she stayed at the school. Fiona went online, looking up sites for help with drinking problems, fell asleep, and finally went home when she woke up.'

'I feel very sorry for her. I talked to her a while as well. I hope she gets help soon.'

They sat on the bench at the top of the downs, looking at the sea in the distance.

'I can breathe here,' said Susan.

Robert reached out and placed his hand on hers. 'Listen, about you and me. What are your thoughts?'

Susan smiled. She loved how straightforward Robert was. 'I love having you as my friend and you have been so kind, looking after me through all the drama. I know I make it difficult, one minute being quite independent and then asking for help.' She gave him a shy smile and then became more serious. 'I've realised recently just how much Steve hurt me. In effect, he lied to me over and over again. He took my trust and tore it up into tiny pieces.' She swallowed hard, the words like stones in her throat, and she felt tears in her eyes.

Robert squeezed her hand. 'You put on such a good show of keeping it together, no one would ever know.'

Susan shrugged. 'What I'm trying to say, Robert, is that it's going to take a long time to put that trust back together. That's not your fault. I'm sorry, you deserve someone who can give you that.'

He smiled sadly. 'It's not your fault either. I don't want to rush anything.'

'How do you feel about more serious relationships? You said you'd felt guilty after we kissed.'

He shook his head. 'Like I said then, I still miss Carol, but I'm aware I'm also ready to start a new relationship. But I'm not desperate, if you know what I mean. I like company, I like doing things with someone, particularly you.'

Susan heard a little woof and saw Libs was busy running among the hedges. Susan was sure she'd picked up the scent of a rabbit.

'I do understand you need time,' said Robert, 'but I'm glad we can be friends.' Robert sat back. 'Look, how about we just muddle along? Our ties will be our friendship, but no commitment. I've no inclination to go off joining some online dating app but, well, we both meet people every day, don't we? Let's see how things go.'

'Thank you, yes, I'd like that.'

Suddenly his face broke into that familiar grin. 'I do have a plan B. It's rather exciting, actually.'

'Tell me about it.' She waited, dreading him telling her that he was moving to the mainland.

'I don't know if you've heard about the changes planned at Bishopstone Manor?'

'Only that someone has bought it.'

'A wealthy entrepreneur has taken it on, and she's planning to set up a restaurant and some accommodation there,' said Robert.

'That sounds exciting. How are you going to be involved?'

'She asked some friend on the island for recommendations for a handyman. They mentioned me, and she got in contact. I would be acting as a kind of caretaker for a few months as she's settling in. I've been thinking about it, and I am tempted to accept.'

'It's a fair drive every day from Ventnor, though, and what about Gem Gem and Dougie?'

'Ah, I shall be living in, and they will come with me. In fact, I have been offered a small ground-floor flat. I can stay when I want to, but I shall keep my home. I'm not totally moving in.'

'You have it all sorted, don't you?'

'Not quite. I'm worried you'll think I'm stalking you, coming over here. I'm serious. If you think it's too close, I'll turn it down.'

'It's lovely of you to ask, but of course I don't mind. It sounds exciting. And just think: when you stay over, we'll be able to go for walks on the beach some mornings, won't we?'

He smiled broadly. 'It had crossed my mind.'

Later, as Susan drove home, she had time to think over Robert's news and knew she'd really meant it when she said she was happy for him to be close by. She was glad that she wasn't going to lose his friendship.

At home, Susan sat on the chair by her dressing table, and looked at her hands. It was time she did something. She opened her jewellery box. She carefully removed her wedding and engagement rings. She moved the engagement ring to her right hand, but she took the wedding ring and placed it in the box. Her left hand suddenly felt light, empty. There were deep indentations where the rings had been, but she guessed over time they would go. Eventually there would be no trace of them.

She felt a hot tear trickle down her cheek. Before Steve left her, she had imagined the actual divorce process would be a brief, brutal execution. No one had warned her it was a long, painful journey. For her it had started the day Steve told her he was leaving. Since that day, three years ago, there had been other quietly heartbreaking days: the first Christmas, the first birthday, the day the divorce came through, clearing the house, packing up their life. And now this, taking off her ring.

She went downstairs, poured herself a glass of wine, grabbed some crackers and cheese, and sat down in front of the TV, too tired this evening even to get her knitting out.

She put on an old black-and-white film and started to get lost in it. However, at one point the young couple in the film were having a long, intense talk in the rain. Susan was momentarily distracted, wondering how anyone could be oblivious to getting so very cold and wet.

As she watched the film, her mind went back to lying in bed listening to the rain falling the night Lawrence had died. Only an hour before, she had been up the tower with Lawrence, talking about the people in the choir committee, watching Lawrence complete his last entry in that beautiful journal.

Susan could picture Lawrence up there. It was so clear. That silver pen reflecting the light. There was no doubt in her mind that was the pen he'd been using. She could even remember him using his left hand, holding the pen at a slightly awkward angle.

She looked down at her own hand, which felt naked without her wedding ring. She stared at it for a moment, and slowly she was aware of an important part of the puzzle she'd been missing all this time. She had to be sure of what the real motive for the killing was.

She glanced around the room, saw her photograph of Jamari, remembered the baby photos at the fete and that picture of Cerys with her birthday cake, sitting in front of the Christmas tree. Of course, that was another important piece of the puzzle.

These two new pieces she was sure were genuine, so the other pieces had to be made to fit around them.

She could make the pen fit. She could explain why the binoculars hadn't been attached, why Lawrence had gone to the edge of the parapet. She was, however, uneasy about the idea of the killer shouting up. If she was right, it was very unlikely this person would have done that.

All this business with the keys had been so confusing. Susan paused. Of course, they only had one person's word about that. Yes, it was possible it had been done that way.

She went through the suspects one by one. The timing of that rain was so much more important than she'd realised. She thought about Fiona. Yes, the rain affected her as well and, for that matter, Daniel.

Ross was fortunate, it had secured his alibi and Jessie also, she knew now, had been speaking the truth. When Susan had checked her history on Flexee for the night Lawrence died, she'd seen Jessie had been working in her car in the rain. There was a clear record of the transactions she had made at the time Lawrence died.

And then there was Cerys. What a complicated picture surrounded her. Her story of falling twice didn't quite sound right. She had definitely hurt her right foot slightly and then her left foot more severely, crushed bones in her foot. What would have caused that? Susan pictured Cerys in the kitchen – that new lino on the floor – of course, that could explain it. It was a good job Jessie had taken her to the hospital. Susan paused again. What was that Jessie had said about finding a dry coat for Cerys? Why did Cerys have a wet coat if she hadn't been out in the rain that night?

Susan held her breath: another puzzle piece she'd missed, and that had to fit with all the others.

She called to Rocco and Libs. 'We're only going for a short walk tonight. I've a lot to think about,' she warned them.

38

They left the house, walked out of the close and along the main road in the direction she had walked with Ross.

It started to spot with rain and it felt like there was heavier rain to come. Susan decided to head home before they all got soaked. However, as she approached, she saw that Hazel's porch light was on and she was coming out of her house in her coat.

Susan went over to her. 'Everything okay?'

'Um, fine, yes. I just felt like some fresh air.'

Susan put her hand on Hazel's arm. 'Fancy a coffee?'

Hazel looked down. 'You've taken your wedding ring off—'

'It was the right time. Now, are you sure you don't want to come in? It's starting to rain.'

'I don't mind the rain. Actually, there's someone I need to see. Good-night, Susan.' Hazel quickly walked away.

Susan opened the front door and let the dogs in, but knew she had to go back out. She didn't want to. She wanted to stay in here, safe. But she could smell danger, feel it in her bones: she had to follow Hazel.

She left the house again just as she saw Hazel disappearing around the corner and followed, not too close, knowing Hazel wouldn't want her there.

Hazel crossed the road and headed for St Jude's. Susan walked more quickly, her heart racing.

The light over the church porch came on and as Hazel opened the door, Susan started to run. As she did, the adrenaline was surging around her body and thoughts came flashing into her head, bright and clear: rings, coats, pens; they all made sense now.

She was at the church door. Should she go in?

As quietly as she could, she pushed on the door, and it gave way. The church was in darkness. The door leading to the tower was open. She thought she heard a muffled cry from above and then gasped as she felt a hand on her sleeve.

'What are you doing here?' hissed Hazel.

'I was worried—'

'I thought I saw a light up the bell tower and I was scared. I came in, but now I'm too petrified to move.'

'You shouldn't be here; you need to go home.' Susan could feel Hazel trembling. 'Come on, let's get out of here,' she said gently.

As they walked quickly to the door, Susan suddenly heard another muffled cry. There was no mistaking it now. She turned around but couldn't see anyone. Hazel seemed oblivious. Susan knew she had to get her out of here, and pushed her out of the front door.

The security light came on again and Susan watched as Hazel took out her keys. Her hands were shaking and so Susan took the keys from her and locked the door.

They rushed to the gate and then Susan turned to Hazel. 'Go home. There's someone I need to see.'

'Don't go back in there,' said Hazel, crying now.

'I can see Jessie's car. I want to speak to her. I'll see you later.'

Hazel tried to persuade her again, but Susan stood her ground and so, reluctantly, Hazel left her. Susan watched until she'd crossed the road, heading for the close. Clutching the church keys she had taken from Hazel, Susan went back to the church and let herself in.

Inside the church, the cold and dark seemed to envelop her. Her hands shook as she tried to lock the door, but even as she did it, she knew it was no defence against the killer. She knew now that if they wanted to get in, they could. A voice was screaming in her head to get out of there: this was madness. Her breathing was shallow and fast, her head started to spin, and she stumbled over to a small chair beside the door, and sat down quickly before she fainted or threw up. Susan closed her eyes, tried to control her breathing. The carousel in her head ground to a halt. The nausea subsided and slowly she opened her eyes.

Susan got up carefully, still shaking, and realised that in her panic she had dropped the keys. She found her phone and, using the light, she scrambled around on the cold concrete floor, eventually finding the keys.

And then she heard it again, the sound of muffled sobbing coming from the tower.

Turning on her phone flashlight, she made her way to the entrance to the bell tower and listened again. The sobbing was louder now, but she was reluctant to go up. 'Who is up there? What's happened?' she called. There was no reply.

Susan climbed a few steps, called again, but still there was no reply. Suddenly she thought she heard a noise in the church, and she listened: no, it was all quiet down there. The sobbing became louder, more urgent. Susan knew she needed to go up.

She climbed the steps slowly, calling all the time, until finally she was at the doorway. Before she stepped out, she shone her phone around. She could see the whole of the roof, but she couldn't see anyone out there. Only then did she realise what was going on. She started to step back, but a fearsome push from behind propelled her forward onto the roof and she fell flat.

Before she could get up, a heavy rock came crashing down on her head. The pain was agonising, but she was still conscious. Before she could move, she felt her arms being grabbed, her ankles tied tightly together, and then her wrists bound also.

Susan was pulled like a rag doll over to the parapet. She knew that any moment she was going to be flung over the side to her death.

Susan felt herself being propped up against the wall, and was aware of blood trickling down the back of her head. She looked up, seeing her attacker for the first time. Where did someone who appeared so weak and vulnerable only minutes before find that sort of strength and aggression?

And then she looked into the wild, burning eyes that stared down at her, and she saw the rage that was fuelling this attack.

'Surprised?'

Susan blinked the blood out of her eyes and swallowed hard. 'No.'

'Liar,' screamed Hazel. She picked up a mobile phone and pushed it into Susan's face. 'That was your sobbing damsel in distress, my ringtone. It was so easy, and you fell for it.'

'You fooled me there, I admit it. But then you are an accomplished actress. Your sister told me that.'

'It's why I was brilliant at opera. I had the voice, and I could act. I had it all.' Hazel held her head up proudly.

Susan watched her. She looked pathetic, in a way, but still so dangerous. Behind her, Susan could see the vast expanse of the night sky. A million stars this evening were sprinkled like tiny diamonds on granite. Despite her fear and pain, she still saw beauty.

'But why did you start all this? The police had accepted that Lawrence died as a result of an accident,' Susan asked, but she looked up again at Hazel, saw the look of exultation on her face: a prima donna standing in the spotlight. And then she knew. 'You wanted the attention,' she whispered.

Hazel's mouth twisted into a hard, ugly grin. 'I deserved it, but the police weren't interested. Typical. Even when I commit a bloody murder, no one takes any notice. I'd been clever. But of course, I had you, you jumped-up little amateur sleuth. You're a fool.'

'Not so stupid that I didn't solve this crime. You thought you were playing with me, but this wasn't a game.'

'I guessed you were getting close a few times.'

'And so, you tried to frighten me off with messages, whispered voices—'

For a moment the grin faded, and Hazel looked completely confused. 'I never did anything like that, I don't go round with paint sprays like some vandal.'

Her confusion was genuine, and Susan knew she was speaking the truth. 'No, of course not. No, I know who it was.'

'Not that it will do you any good now. You went too far, Susan.'

'And so you lured me up here, presumably to kill me.' Susan couldn't believe how calmly she was speaking but somehow the whole scenario felt unreal.

She saw a flash of steel as Hazel produced a small but lethal scalpel and pressed it to her throat.

'How did I do it, then?'

Susan could feel her heart thumping, her head pounding, but she had to play for time.

'I realised when I was talking to Zoe that you could leave a Zoom meeting unnoticed. That is what you did, that Friday night. Of course, you did use the side door key, and you've had it since the night Lawrence died.'

'The side door key didn't work.'

'That's what you wanted everyone to think. You played along for a while, but you knew that when you were ready you could disprove its use and aim to end my investigation.'

'But they found it and it wouldn't open the door.'

'No. They found a false key, one planted and identified by you. Knowing Ross's lax security, you chose to leave it in his caravan.'

'I did. I went in on that Thursday night I knew he was taking you up the downs. I was pretty sure he would prove somehow that he'd been up the downs, so he had no reason not to tell anyone he'd found it. However, when I saw the mess in his caravan, I did wonder if he would ever discover it. I remembered seeing the whisky and the ashtrays and decided on the fire. It was certainly a way of ensuring that someone official would find it.'

'You could have killed Ross.'

'I suppose so, but he got out, didn't he? I was sure Fiona would spot it.'

Susan was horrified at the casual way she spoke.

'And all the time, somewhere in your house, you have hidden the original side door key. You originally took it before Lawrence and I went to the bell tower. I checked on the dogs and when I returned you were coming out of the house. It was very easy for you to surreptitiously remove it from the drawer and hide it before we left.'

'You got that right. I decided during that meeting I was going to kill Lawrence. Seeing the key in the drawer, a key I knew worked, was essential to my plan. I wasn't going to chance shouting up to Lawrence. And I was prepared: I took a spare pair of shoes, wore them inside so there was no sign of any mud.'

'You did throw them away, didn't you?' asked Susan.

She saw the panic on Hazel's face, and raised an eyebrow.

'I know that before you went inside you put two of those solar lights you'd taken from Jessie's path in the pot, and now I think you put a mobile phone there too. You climbed the tower, chatted to Lawrence, asked to borrow his binoculars, and looked over the wall. Unseen by him, you phoned the mobile. This is where your drama came into play. I can just imagine it: "What is it, what can I hear, what can I see?" I bet he came to the edge, saw the light, heard the noise, maybe a recorded owl sound, I don't know, and he looked more closely through the binoculars. The next thing he knew, he was falling.'

'Hmmm, that does all sound very convincing,' said Hazel. 'You really think you have it all worked out.'

'And, of course, you took the ring, the pen, and the bunch of keys from the rucksack. You let yourself out, put the front door keys in Lawrence's pocket, and took the pen home, ready to plant on someone if you should ever need to.'

'But why would I kill Lawrence? I meant it when I said I wasn't jealous of Cerys.'

'You had no problem with Cerys when you thought she was conceived before you married Lawrence. However, one day Cerys let it slip that her birthday was in December, didn't she? I know you knew. You told me you were planning a birthday trip with her. I knew from the Christmas tree in the photo at the fete. Now that all means one thing. Cerys was conceived in March, after you were married.'

Hazel pushed the scalpel into Susan's neck. 'So what? He had a fling. I don't care.'

'Oh, but you do, because you sacrificed everything for him. And you didn't mind so much if he'd been your prince charming, your one true love, but he wasn't. You had sacrificed everything for a man who cheated on you with the woman he said he'd split from: Blodwen.'

'What sacrifice?'

'You gave up that opportunity to sing in a professional opera. You knew it would never come again. That had been your chance to shine. And you have an incredible voice. I have no doubt you were extraordinary.'

'I was. They said I had the potential to go all the way. You have no idea how hard it was to leave it all. I'd always regretted it deep down, but I kept telling myself I'd done it for Lawrence. But to find then that he had slept with that woman within weeks of us getting married, that was too much.'

Hazel took the scalpel away from Susan's neck and leant against the cold stone wall.

'How could he do that to me? When Cerys told me the date of her birthday and I worked out when she was conceived, it destroyed any love I'd felt for Lawrence. Love turned to hate. I could hardly bear to look at him but, even then, I wasn't sure I would kill him.'

As she talked, Susan realised that the scarf securing her wrists was slack, and by twisting her hands, she managed to squeeze them free. Her feet, though, were more tightly bound. She kept her freed hands hidden behind her back and spoke. 'Lawrence's fate was sealed at that meeting when he said he was terminating Ross's contract. Ross's arrival was some kind of miracle for you. You'd given up on your singing, but he was offering you the chance to finally fulfil your dream. At last, you might get the recognition you deserved. You were going to be the soloist with professional musicians for the fundraiser, a concert that was going to be recorded and featured on the radio. And he was going to ruin it all.'

'You don't understand what it's been like for me, always living under everyone's shadow. My sister, and then Lawrence, but when I sang, I was something, I was special.'

'And because yet again he'd taken away your right to shine, you killed Lawrence. But you made mistakes.'

'Like what?' asked Hazel.

'Lawrence's wedding ring. You took it off his finger after he fell, and placed it on a chain around your neck, but I saw it on his finger that night when he was writing in his journal. The police didn't return his belongings to you until the week of the funeral, yet I saw you wearing it days before that when the police came to check out that side door.'

Hazel shrugged it off. 'I put that ring on his finger the day we married. I was going to be the one to take it off. It was mine.'

'And then there was the pen. You took that pen for insurance, but it also had a deeper meaning for you. Lawrence told you about the pen from the staff in Cardiff. However, when you found out about Cerys, you looked at it again, saw the engraved heart and knew it was a romantic gift and that it must have been from Blodwen. I should have realised when Lawrence showed me the pen and how gently he handled it. That pen meant a lot to him. He kept that with him all the time, as if he had never let her go.'

'As soon as I realised it was from Blodwen, I hated that pen. I took it that night, intended to plant it on someone if I needed to and, eventually, I left it in the vicarage.'

Hazel held the scalpel firmly against Susan's neck. One slip, Susan knew, would be fatal.

'You're not going to be able to convince anyone I died accidentally up here.'

'No, but they'll never suspect me, and that is all that matters. They may have a look at Cerys. This is one of her scarves. Earlier today, I asked Cerys to look after one of my spare main church door keys on her key ring. I told her that would mean she would have a spare if Daniel, Ross or I ever needed it. She is very naïve and took it. I, of course, will deny that conversation ever took place. I also told her I needed to speak to her privately this evening. She's waiting out there in the dark alone, at the far end of the school field where no one ever goes.

'The rock that hit your head is from the vicarage garden. They may trace that. Look at Daniel or Jessie. The thing is, you've wound people up, Susan. Everyone, of course, apart from me.'

An owl screeched above them. Hazel, distracted, looked up. Susan took her chance. She lifted her tied feet and kicked her away with all her might. Hazel fell backwards and the scalpel flew from her hand.

Susan grabbed it, sliced through the scarf tying her feet and staggered up as Hazel was trying to get back on her feet.

Susan ran to the steps and started to head down them, but she was scared she might fall. She remembered the room for the bell-ringers, that pile of chairs by the door. As she went past, she pulled them out and kept going.

She heard Hazel stumbling, swearing. She was awfully close, but Susan ran towards the side door.

Thankfully, Hazel hadn't locked it, so she pulled it open and staggered up the path to the front of St Jude's.

To her amazement, she saw the security lights come on and then she saw someone standing at the church gate. It was Cerys, holding her phone, crying. She ran to Susan, put her arms around her. 'You're okay. You're safe. I've phoned the police. I saw light up there. I heard Hazel shouting.'

'She's in there. She killed Lawrence.'

Susan heard a thin screeching sound above her. Reflected in the security light in front of the church, she saw a single bat. She watched as it flew towards the moon and disappeared out of sight. 'Goodbye, Lawrence,' she whispered. 'You can be at peace now.'

39

At that moment, there was a screaming of police cars and ambulances, and police officers came running towards Susan.

She handed them the keys to St Jude's and one took her to an ambulance. Cerys insisted on going with her to the hospital.

Once they'd checked her head, Susan was taken to a bed on a side ward for observation overnight.

Cerys was still with her. Once they were alone, they were finally able to have the conversation they'd been waiting to have.

'Why were you at St Jude's?' Susan asked.

'I went to the field to meet Hazel, but then I got to thinking. I hadn't believed anyone had killed Lawrence, but I was scared. I had this feeling that I was getting deeper and deeper into something, that the police would suspect me. I decided to go back to the vicarage. That's when I heard all the racket at the top of the bell tower. Sound really travels around there.'

'It does, but Cerys, you've certainly not helped yourself. That crazy excuse of the second accident. It didn't add up. Falling wouldn't have crushed those tiny bones. That was caused by you dropping something very heavy, one of Jessie's weights, on your foot, denting the lino at the same time, wasn't it?'

'I wasn't thinking straight. I was in such a panic.'

'To injure yourself just to create a fake alibi: that was desperate.'

'Do you know the rest? Do you know why I did it?' asked Cerys.

'I do. I think you wanted to talk with Lawrence after that choir committee meeting. You'd only told him the day before that he was your father. You had a lot to say. But then I was going to see the bats with him, so you couldn't speak to him immediately. On your way out of the cottage, you stumbled, which complicated things more, because I drove you home. Ross then met you at the vicarage and when he left you there was the phone call with Fiona. But after that, you still wanted to speak to Lawrence, so you decided to go and see if he was still up the bell tower. You went to the church, walked around to the base of the tower, aiming to shout up, but then you found his body—'

Cerys nodded, tears running down her cheeks. 'It was awful, I felt I'd known him for a day as my dad, and now he was dead. But I was scared: what would happen if someone knew I'd gone to the tower? How would I explain why I'd gone there? The police would be investigating everything.'

'And so you went back and had the idea of making out your first accident had been bad enough to be your alibi.'

'How do you know this? How do you know I didn't kill Lawrence?'

'You didn't make it easy for me! The fact Jessie said your coat was wet worried me. It meant you had been out around the time Lawrence died as it didn't rain at any time earlier that day. However, Fiona said the call you had with her lasted until the rain started, so I knew exactly the time you were at St Jude's, and it was after Lawrence had fallen to his death.'

Cerys sniffed. 'I was so stupid to lie like that. I just panicked.'

'Everyone has lied. Ross told that lie about being with you. It was silly. It was obviously going to get disproved and that would make him appear guiltier than if he'd told the truth in the first place.'

Cerys screwed her eyes up. 'You know why he lied?'

'I do. I remembered that "bird food" his friend Dave gave him at the end of our birdwatching. The whole transaction had seemed staged, somehow. Then I remembered Tracy said he'd bought a packet of tobacco and some cigarette papers, which was odd. Why the papers? He didn't smoke roll-ups. I'd seen that. Then I realised, of course, he needed them for something else.'

Cerys shrugged. 'Ross buys his weed from Dave. I hate it, but that's what he does. The police know what Dave is up to, and Ross thought it better not to draw attention to the fact that he'd been with someone who they knew dealt in weed.'

'He was fortunate his alibi held up.'

Cerys gave a heavy sigh of relief. 'So, what about the other suspects?'

'I know what Daniel was doing. A barman called Kev told me he had been in there the night of the murder. Jessie's online sales history shows she was trading at the time Lawrence died. You are, of course, Fiona's alibi because you were both on the phone until the rain started.'

'Thank God for the rain. I'll leave you to get some rest now.'

As Cerys left, Susan saw another visitor making her way to her bed.

'I had to come and see ye were all right,' said Fiona. 'I've been feeling so guilty.'

'It's okay. I know what you did. I should have realised when I saw you spray-painting that sign at the fete.'

'You've worked it out? I'm so sorry. I was scared. I knew you were getting closer all the time. I wanted to frighten ye.'

'You succeeded in that.'

'Aye, well, it was wrong.'

'You're forgiven. I hope you can get your life sorted out now.'

'I will. I hope you've not been put off the village after everything that has happened.'

'Oh, no. This is my home now, I'm not going anywhere,' said Susan.

40

It was a week later when Susan went to see Alice. She was in her room with piles of photo albums on the bed beside her.

'Susan, how lovely to see you. Come and tell me how everyone is. I've heard bits of gossip from my cleaner and Tracy.'

'As you know, Hazel has been arrested for Lawrence's murder. They found a pair of shoes in a bag at the bottom of her wardrobe. These were the clean ones she changed into to go into the church, but she carried on wearing them after, while she was planting the keys on Lawrence. They have his blood on them, and they have found traces of blood on the coat she wore too. She tried to argue she had found the body, but nothing added up. Despite advice from her solicitor, she has been talking a lot.'

'Maybe she's enjoying the attention,' said Alice. 'After all, I assume that's why she came to you asking you to look into Lawrence's death.'

'You're right. She said she'd been frustrated that the police weren't investigating. I think she spent her life feeling that she's missed out on being noticed. She'd given up her big chance in opera for Lawrence when they left Cardiff, and he was about to thwart her again. All this anger and resentment was stacking up like a heap of fuel for a bonfire. But it was the news that Lawrence was going to, in effect, sack Ross, and destroy her chance at that solo, which finally lit the touchpaper. Hazel's emotions went wild, out of control, and that led to her killing Lawrence.'

'It's frightening, isn't it? When you think how we first thought of her, some shy woman happy to live in the shadow of her high-achieving husband.'

'People are always so much more complicated than we think.'

Alice put her head to one side. 'It's not nice, is it, but, because of you, Hazel will be brought to justice.'

'Don't underplay your hand in all this. You've been there from the word go, encouraging me, pointing me in the right direction over the pendants with Cerys, and Alan Smithee. It can be lonely work searching for a killer in a small community, and at time it feels as if no one is your friend, and yet every time I can come to you.'

Alice smiled. 'You and I have one thing in common. We both care about truth. That means facing the darker side of life, but we have, and the village, the community, will thank us for it. Now, tell me, do you have news of any of the others?'

'I spoke to Jessie. She and Daniel have had a long talk. It sounds as if Daniel is seriously thinking of leaving the priesthood, and I'm afraid she is talking about a time of separation for them both to think again about what they want to do with their lives.'

'Oh dear, that is so sad, but I think they're wise. What about Ross and Cerys?'

'Ross asked for a meeting of all the choir. He told us that he will be leaving. He wants a fresh start somewhere else. I'm afraid the fundraiser is not taking place, and the choir is going to disband, at least for the time being,' said Susan.

'And will Cerys be going, do you think?'

'Oh, no. Ross made it clear he was going alone. He actually said he thought Cerys may set up some kind of school choir in the autumn.'

'And how did she seem to you?'

'We did have a quick word. I think she'd known in her heart that Ross wasn't as keen as her and she doesn't want to leave the island. Despite everything, she feels at home here and touched by how supportive everyone has been.'

'She's been through so much for such a young girl.'

'You're right. I hope it works out for her. I hear Fiona is on sick leave now, I'm not sure what her next move will be.'

Alice smiled. 'And what about you? You have your wonderful grand-daughter, of course, and the dogs.'

'I have my new home. I have plans to decorate. I shall make it light and bright.'

'Will Robert be helping you?'

Susan smiled. 'I want to do this on my own but, of course, he won't be far away. There will be other things to look forward to as well. I will be getting a new neighbour. I wonder who it will be?'

Alice's face lit up. Her eyes twinkled mischievously. 'It all sounds very exciting. And you're not the only one with surprises.'

'What is it?' asked Susan, excited.

'Ah, you'll have to wait until your next visit to find out.'

* * *

MORE FROM MARY GRAND

The next book in The Isle of Wight Killings cozy murder mystery series from Mary Grand, *A Christmas Murder*, is available to order now here:

https://mybook.to/ChristmasMurderBackAd

ACKNOWLEDGEMENTS

Firstly, an enormous thank you to you, my lovely readers, for taking the time to read *A Parish Murder*, and thank you for all the messages of support.

An enormous thank you to my wonderful publisher Boldwood, and the whole team for your outstanding dedication and hard work. A very special thank you to Sarah Ritherdon, for your insight, knowledge and kindness, and yet again taking a very messy first draft and enabling me to craft this story. Thank you also, to all the editors for your exceptional work, the cover designer and everyone involved in bringing this novel to life.

I would like to thank Jon Whitehurst at the Isle of Wight Bat Group for the extremely helpful information about bats, particularly about the grey long-eared bats which feature in the story. Thank you for all the work you and the group do for these remarkable and unique mammals on the island.

There are quite a few dogs in this story, and I'd like to thank all the owners for allowing me to use the names and descriptions of their very special dogs. Thank you, Diane Lister, for allowing me to mention Libby (Libs), Pat Pearson for Rocco, Pauline Trimmings for Gemma (Gem Gem), Fiona McGregor for Dougie and Wendy Coates for Lottie. All these people are members of the fabulous group *Cocker Spaniels* on Facebook.

A huge thank you as always to my gorgeous family, my husband, and children, Thomas and Emily, for their unending support and encouragement.

Thank you to everyone on Facebook, Twitter and Instagram, writers and friends. Your kind words and support mean so much to me. Also thank you to the wonderful group of bloggers who work tirelessly reading and reviewing books and offer so much encouragement to writers.

Thank you so much Karen Cass for again adding a touch of magic with your wonderful narration of the audiobook.

ABOUT THE AUTHOR

Mary Grand is the author of six novels and writes gripping, page-turning suspense, with a dark and often murderous underside. She grew up in Wales, was for many years a teacher of deaf children and now lives on the Isle of Wight.

Sign up to Mary Grand's mailing list here for news, competitions and updates on future books.

Visit Mary's website: www.marygrand.net

Follow Mary on social media:

 x.com/authormaryg

 instagram.com/marygrandwriter

 facebook.com/authormarygrand

 bookbub.com/profile/mary-grand

ALSO BY MARY GRAND

The House Party

The Island

Good Neighbours

The Isle of Wight Killings Series

A Seaside Murder

A Parish Murder

A Christmas Murder

Poison
& Pens

POISON & PENS IS THE HOME OF
COZY MYSTERIES SO POUR YOURSELF
A CUP OF TEA & GET SLEUTHING!

DISCOVER PAGE-TURNING NOVELS FROM
YOUR FAVOURITE AUTHORS &
MEET NEW FRIENDS

JOIN OUR
FACEBOOK GROUP

BIT.LYPOISONANDPENSFB

SIGN UP TO OUR
NEWSLETTER

BIT.LY/POISONANDPENSNEWS

Boldwood

Boldwood Books is an award-winning fiction publishing company seeking out the best stories from around the world.

Find out more at www.boldwoodbooks.com

Join our reader community for brilliant books, competitions and offers!

Follow us
@BoldwoodBooks
@TheBoldBookClub

Sign up to our weekly
deals newsletter

https://bit.ly/BoldwoodBNewsletter